Collide
By Mahogany Jones

Copyright © 2021 Mahogany Jones.

All rights reserved. No part of this publication may be reproduced, distributed, or transmitted in any form or by any means, including photocopying, recording, or other electronic or mechanical methods, without permission from the author.

ISBN: 9798542655963

This book is a work of fiction. Name, characters, places, and incidences are fictitious and a product of the author's imagination.

Front cover image by D.Lacy Photography.
Cover design by Roseville Designz.

Printed in the United States of America.

IG: @author_mahogany_jones

1

STACEY

"I, Stacey Ambria Hill, promise to leave fuckboys alone. I promise to value my time - *and vagina* - enough to limit the access I allow these no good, lying ass muthafuckas to have in my life. I am extraordinary. A melanated queen placed on this earth, destined for greatness and I will demand that others treat me as such."

I rolled my eyes after my little self-proclamation and let out an exasperated, "but a bitch has needs!" through clenched teeth as my best friend Rachel stared at me with folded arms and a head tilt only a Black queen could master.

"Alright, you keep running around here being a hoe if you want to! It won't make up for your mommy and daddy issues and it's only going to hurt you in the long run. Don't say I didn't warn you!" Rachel sneered. "And really all you're doing is buying time with these other men waiting on Savior James to finally express his love after two years!" Rachel exclaimed, while shoving a piece of chicken and waffles into her mouth.

A smirk spread across my face, and I knew she was ultimately right, as usual. I waved my hand for the waitress to come to our table.

"Hi, could I have another mimosa please? With orange juice and a splash of grenadine. Oh! And no more for her!" I said, shifting my gaze towards Rachel.

"Ummm excuse me! Don't try to limit my brunch libations! You're just mad because when I get a little drank in my system, I start telling your ass the truth!" Rachel teased.

"Yeah, yeah, yeah, you sure know how to fuck up a vibe, Rach!" I said, as I rolled my eyes so hard it caused a twinge of pain behind my eye sockets.

"Speaking of mommy and daddy issues, have you spoken to either one of them recently?" Rachel asked hesitantly, as she tipped up her third mimosa.

"Nah, I haven't spoken to my mom in about four months and my dad tried calling last week, but I wasn't trying to hear that shit!" I said, pursing my lips.

"Maybe you should just give him a chance to explain, Stace," Rachel pressured.

Stace was the nickname Rachel gave me; a shortening of my first name, as if just adding the 'y' on the end was too cumbersome for her, but I didn't mind.

"Here you go pushing boundaries! Explain what, Rachel? How he decided to dick down my mom's best friend after thirty-five years of marriage? No thank you! I'll pass," I said as I sipped my mimosa unbothered.

Rachel knew this conversation wouldn't go far, but she decided to push the envelope anyway. I was undeniably hurting and she knew it, so the least she could do was encourage a conversation between my parents and I.

"Well, I get why you aren't talking to your dad," Rachel said, "but what about your mom, what did she do to deserve the silent treatment?"

I rolled my eyes again. "You mean other than the fact that she's moved out of the country with a man half her age, as she enters into this midlife crisis she's on? Like...what the entire fuck!?"

Rachel raised an eyebrow and I knew she was undoubtedly contemplating how to navigate the conversation. "So, let me get this straight. You're mad at your mom for moving on?"

"No, Rachel! I'm mad at her for not even making an attempt to reconcile a thirty-five year marriage. I'm mad at her for leaving the country without asking me how I feel about it. Shit! I'm mad that her little fuck buddy is twenty-nine years old. I'm twenty-nine Rachel, *twenty-nine*! That shit is just nasty! I'm pissed at my dad for his role in this Jerry Springer shit show and for his piss poor efforts at trying to get my mom back! I'm even more irritated that he won't stop calling, trying to repair his relationship with me. I'm not his damn wife! Fix things with her first! Why won't he just allow me time to process this shit? I'm—"

Rachel politely interrupted me. "Sis, stop and listen to me. I'm about to tell you something, and you're not going to like it. It'll probably even piss you off, but it needs to be said, and I wouldn't consider myself your BFF if I didn't say it. You're spoiled, Stacey!"

I reclined my neck to the side, raised both eyebrows and folded my arms across my chest with a bewildered look on my face.

"Ooooooh, am I now?" I asked, disdain coating my words as I made no attempt to camouflage my irritation.

"Yeah Stacey, you're spoiled fucking rotten. I'm talking white kid, throw a tantrum on the middle of the grocery store floor, spoiled. Now I love your spoiled ass, but facts are facts. You see, you've managed to make this entire debacle about you! Yes! It's fucked up what's happening to your parents, but those are two grown muthafuckas doing what grown muthafuckas do, which is make decisions for themselves. Your dad made a mistake, which was his choice and your mom made the choice to *not* forgive his ass and to move on with a *younger man*! Neither of which, have anything to do...with you. Their decisions regarding one another should not affect your personal relationship with them," she said, causing me to shift in my seat.

I unfolded my arms and softened my scrutinizing glare as Rachel continued to go in on me.

"And another thing! You're lucky to have the experience of parents being married for thirty-five years, Little Ms. Princess. You could have struggled in a one-parent household, relying on welfare to make it like I did! You'll never know the struggle of paying off student loans because your parents paid for every penny of your bachelor's and master's degree. *With cash*, Stace. Shit! Some months I have to decide which bills to hold off on to make sure my student loans get paid before those bitches go into default. Even after giving your dad the silent treatment, the nigga is still paying for your penthouse in the heart of downtown Houston! Shit's not cheap, Stacey, and you have the audacity to be upset because their relationship didn't go the way you wanted it to?

Newsflash, sweetheart! Welcome to the real world! All your parents have ever done is take care of you. They put you in amazing schools, purchased that fucking ridiculous penthouse, gifted you a two-seater, drop top BMW for graduation, and if the Houston Princess calls, they come a-running. Your daddy is so good to you, you can't help but to fall helplessly head over heels for any nigga that gives off even an inkling of a 'daddy vibe'. You're constantly on the lookout for a man that's going to take care of you like your dad does. Your parents are good to you and don't deserve what you're putting them through. Leave those grown ass people alone and allow them to live their lives. Fucking with my pseudo parents! Excuse me, waitress, another mimosa please!" She concluded her rant by snatching my mimosa and gulping it down, as she waited impatiently for the waitress to bring her own.

I glanced in Rachel's direction, with a slight smile-frown on my face as I struggled to contain a giggle.

"Well, I guess you told me, bitch!" I said.

"Well, I guess I did!" Rachel giggled.

If there was one thing I valued about Rachel, it was her blunt, oftentimes crass, no bullshit taking personality. She was every bit of Dallas, TX born and raised, and I was overjoyed that this straight shooter was my best friend.

I didn't appreciate "yes men" – or women, in this case – I would always respect a friend that didn't beat around the bush or sugarcoat every little thing, because who had time for that? Rachel was a little rough around the edges, but she was my girl.

"You still dropping by Friday night to watch a movie with me?" I asked.

"Yeah, as long as you're not mad at me for ripping you a new asshole, I'm there," Rachel said, raising an eyebrow.

"Ain't nobody mad at your ass. I know what you're saying is true, even though I despise hearing it. I'll give Mom and Dad a call this week. Oh! And I'm paying for the bill. Don't gimme any shit about it either."

I snatched the check from the table before Rachel could even reach for it.

"You're asking me if I'm sure about Friday as if I have anything else to do. You're the one on a date every other night," Rachel teased as she intertwined her arm with mine as we walked to our cars. I giggled, waving my hand in the air, dismissing her comment.

I embraced Rachel sincerely. "Thank you for being such a great friend to me and always telling me the truth, even when my stubborn ass would much rather not hear it," I said.

Rachel returned a sincere smile and hugged me tighter. "You know you're my girl and I love your spoiled ass."

Monday mornings always came too soon. The fact that I loved my job as a personal trainer and fitness coach made the Monday Blues a bit more tolerable, but nevertheless, a Monday was a Monday. My days were long, strenuous and jam packed with high intensity workouts, but I wasn't complaining. My week started with a personal workout at 5 a.m. I ran a mile, followed by ten sprints as my warmup. I consistently worked my arms, legs, and abs throughout the week to keep my body in formation, which my suitors seemed to truly appreciate. Once my personal fitness was insured, I began taking clients around 9 a.m.

I loved the flexibility of my work. Not to mention the money was outstanding. My dad had purchased me a small space in an old, abandoned building in Third Ward, an urban area of Houston near two of the city's major universities. I poured my heart into renovating the space into a chic, upscale gym that was now home to over one hundred members. Some choose to workout independently, with a vast majority requiring personal training services.

My schedule had gotten so hectic, I had to hire three new personal trainers to help with the one-on-one training sessions. I lived a first-class life, to say the least, and I was thrilled to *actually* utilize my degree in kinesiology because I knew way too many people who had never stepped foot into a job focused in the field they majored in.

My first client Ms. Ann pranced in for her Monday morning HIIT training in a sporty, lime green, spandex one piece. Ms. Ann was the spiciest sixty-year-old woman I had ever met. She walked with her head elevated in the air and spoke with conviction. I was sure Ms. Ann was still turning heads and breaking hearts even as a seasoned woman. She looked good — and she knew it.

"Good morning, darling," Ms. Ann greeted me, as she touched both of her cheeks to mine.

"Good morning, Ms. Ann! How was your weekend? I hope you're ready for this workout I have planned for you."

I gave her a sinister grin.

"Oh darling, I was born ready! You don't get to be sixty years old with a body like this without being *ready*."

I laughed and responded, "I heard that!"

I began guiding Ms. Ann through stretches when she asked, "Any new *eligible* bachelors, darling?"

I twisted my face. "Well...there are plenty of bachelors, but I don't know how eligible they are."

"You know what your problem is, darling?" Ms. Ann murmured through pursed lips.

"Do tell," I responded, shaking my head before whatever off the wall comment Ms. Ann would assuredly make.

"You don't know the power of the pussy!" Ms. Ann stated.

"Wha-what?" My bottom lip dropped. Although I thought I was ready; Ms. Ann had successfully stunned the shit out of me.

"You heard me! You don't know the power of the pussy."

I had become accustomed to Ms. Ann's vulgar tongue but it would always catch me off guard. I let out a laugh and Ms. Ann's intense countenance revealed the seriousness behind her words.

"Oh darling, this is serious. You young girls are just clueless. When I was in my thirties, I had men eating out of my hands — among other places! They would have done anything to marry me. You young girls with your tight bodies and your young snatch can't seem to keep a man around longer than a month!"

I giggled at Ms. Ann because she really was a comical old lady.

"Oh please, wise leader, teach me of this 'pussy power' you speak of! Wise and all-knowing one, teach me your ways!" I playfully groveled towards Ms. Ann causing her to laugh out loud.

"Okay, okay, no need to beg young grasshopper," Ms. Ann responded.

"Alright! Enough joking," I laughed. "Let's get this work in, you want to keep that sixty year old body tight don't you?"

"Mmmhmm," Ms. Ann responded, admiring her physique in the full-length wall mirror. "But we're not done with this conversation, I could teach you a thing or two!"

I giggled and pointed towards the far wall, signaling for her to begin sprinting.

It was finally Wednesday, and hump day was hastily coming to an end. *Only two more days until Friday*, I thought. I wasn't sure why I counted down to Friday. It wasn't like I had the type of job that I didn't work on the weekends. Clients wanted to be fine on weekends, too. However, I was able to create a more flexible schedule on Fridays and Saturdays, scheduling private sessions early to enjoy the weekend.

As the rain tapped at my penthouse window, I stared out at the city lights ruminating over the conversation with Ms. Ann from a few days ago. That was meant to be a joke; however, I couldn't help but wonder if there was any truth to what she'd said.

Was I the reason I was alone? Was there something deeply rooted within me...causing my relationships to falter? Hmmmm... I flippantly shook my head at allowing Ms. Ann to get under my skin. At that moment, I made the decision to push our conversation to the back of my mind; laughing it off. I was feeling exceptionally lonely this Wednesday and could really use a warm body to keep me company.

I could call Xavier.

He was a good fuck, but had absolutely nothing going for himself other than a big penis and a mesmerizing smile. I would occasionally allow the fact that Xavier had a big dick to overshadow the fact that he was twenty-eight, had no car, lived with two roommates, and asked *me* for Uber money when we did see one another.

Then there was DJ. The last time I heard from him – *actually, the last time I heard from his wife* – I was a bitch, a hoe, a slut, a home wrecker, and every other similar word in the English and Spanish dictionary. He tried to reach out and apologize for his wife's actions, which was pretty unbelievable in hindsight because the woman had every reason to be furious with me. In my defense, I hadn't known he was married. One thing I didn't do was frolic with married men. Karma was a bitch, and I'd be damned if I willingly allowed it to come back and bite me in the ass. DJ was no longer an option.

Quinton called less than an hour ago begging to "swing by" and if my memory served me correctly, the last time he *"swung by"* resulted in an hour of fucking, sucking, and licking, but I hadn't minded. I wasn't really in the mood to talk, so I quickly came to the realization that Quinton could give me exactly what I needed tonight. His dick was less satisfying than Xavier's, however, Quinton's tongue could create waterfalls between my thighs. And that was the only reason he was awarded the opportunity to share the same space as me.

I liked to think of myself as a sexually expressive woman. I refused to settle like so many of my counterparts because, to me, a ring was nothing more than being locked in a wrought iron cage without a key. Unless the right one, which I had yet to find, came along? The enjoyment of life was the principal theme I chose to live by. I was free, liberated, and did what the fuck I wanted to do. I phoned down to the front desk to inform Randy, my doorman, that I was expecting company and gave him permission to allow my guest access to the private elevators.

I heard the strong knock but had no intention of getting up to answer the door.

"It's open!" I called from the comfort of my bathtub.

I'd planned on Quinton letting himself in, which would allow him to find me butt ass naked in the tub, exactly how I envisioned the beginning of what I hoped would be an eventful night.

The front door crept open as Quinton called from the threshold, "Stacey, you in here?"

I delayed my response purposely. "I'm in the tub, Q."

Quinton left nothing to the imagination. He was enamored with me, his adoration knowing no limits. He begged for me with no apprehension or regard for his masculinity. Most days his idolization was nothing short of unhealthy and excessive, but tonight his clingy demeanor was precisely what I needed. I never lied to Quinton — never gave him false hope or pretended to possess a glimmer of the feelings he had for me. I communicated clearly that our friendship was purely physical, and he was in full agreement.

The penthouse was dark, except for the incandescent city lights illuminating the living room through the floor to ceiling windows. Various scented candles released a tropical aroma that I knew would invade his nostrils upon closing my front door. I heard him walk in and lock the front door, and from the pace of his hurried steps, I was sure he was fully anticipating what he referred to as my *sweet pussy*. I listened closely and heard him drop his briefcase next to the couch; grinning at his predictability. As a sports attorney, he carried important documents that he rarely left in the car.

Quinton had recently expressed his displeasure with how I *handled* him; his words, not mine.

"I'm not exactly sure why I continue to allow myself to be wholly immersed in you or why, after weeks of unanswered phone calls, I would continue to call, in hopes that you might feel differently," was what Quinton had said, putting us on a three week no call, no answer hiatus. I didn't have time for his emotions...but tonight, I needed him to fulfill the insatiable desire that only a dick could scratch.

I purposely left the sliding bathroom doors parted, allowing him a sneak peek before crossing through the doorway. As he glanced into the master bathroom, his eyes quickly observed my erect nipples through the sparsely spread bubbles in the bathtub. I reached up to begin rotating each nipple between my pointer finger and thumb, making sure to tug on my nipple rings gently for added visual arousal. He stood in the center of the sliding bathroom doors; his bottom lip between his teeth and a worshipful expression on his face.

You possess a spark that sets you miles apart from the women who throw themselves at me on a daily basis. Words Quinton had spoken to me during one of our fucking sessions reverberated in my head. As an attorney and former NFL player, there was never a shortage of women for Quinton, but according to him, I was the one he craved. *You reside on a pedestal in my heart.* Again...his words, not mine.

It was lights, camera, action as he stood there lusting for me. I remembered our last conversation, which helped me put on an unforgettable show for him as he stood in the doorway staring longingly.

"There is an it factor that is undeniable when you enter a room, Stacey, and I find myself with a one-track mind because you occupy my psyche an alarming majority of my days," Quinton said.

"Tell me what you think about, baby," I replied.

"I envision your milk chocolate colored, almond shaped eyes with the longest lashes I have ever seen. Your plump pink lips, the type of lips women pay for, you already possess. Your luscious brownish-black textured curls make me daydream about what a daughter might look like between the two of us," he continued.

He always praised women with natural hair, saying fuck societal norms. Quinton thought that flaunting the crown beautifully flourishing from a woman's scalp was fucking sexy; the versatility of it, the femininity, hell, even the smell. He always said I smelled like the sweetest juices and berries and that my smooth peanut butter complexion was soft to the touch and appeared to glow from within.

I slowly rotated my head towards him, greeting him with a seductive grin, as I slid my right hand from my nipple, down my stomach allowing it to disappear under the bubbles.

"Damn girl, you're the sexiest thing I've seen all day," he said, in response to me purposely teasing him.

I slightly lifted the left corner of my lips, smirking, flashing him a deep set dimple. I closed my eyes as I released my neck and let out a soft moan. When I lifted my gaze to glimpse in Quinton's direction, my eyes lingered on his body before rolling down to his erect dick pressing against his tailor-fit slacks. Quinton was a charmer and an attractive man to look at. He just wasn't a ten on the nasty meter. I'd place him at about a six and on most nights my body just simply required more than he was capable of offering. He didn't do it for me, but tonight was less about a long-term love and more about a short-term fuck. So, on this rainy, lonely, gloomy Wednesday, Quinton's dick would just have to satisfy my highly inappropriate desires because I was out of options.

Quinton wasn't hard to miss with his broad shoulders and muscular frame. He was a tad shorter than I preferred, standing around five feet ten inches tall. He effortlessly towered over my fun-sized frame, but that wasn't a difficult task. He was solid from his professional football days and had taken phenomenal care of himself since then. He wore his hair cut low, with deep waves and small, round diamond studs graced both earlobes. His wide nose, full lips and chocolate skin was picturesque and I had never witnessed him wearing anything other than a tailored, three-piece suit.

It was no surprise that he was often mistaken for *still* being a pro football player because the brother looked good. He was some woman's manifestation, just not *mine*. He and I had met in a crowded nightclub last year and he managed to charm my panties off the first night we met. My very first one night stand, might I add. I was young, beautiful, and fine as hell and deserved a little treat every now and then.

I rose from the tub as water trickled from my petite frame. Pretending as though Quinton was not gawking at me, I released my curls from a low bun, which caused my fluffy tresses to cover the top of my breasts. I noticed Quinton loosening his tie as he strode towards the bathtub, sliding his hand southbound, slowly gripping the firmness of his erect penis with unadulterated lust monopolizing his movements.

"Hey, you," I greeted him coyly.

Quinton slid his eyes over my entire body as if he were preparing for his favorite meal and I was prepared to give him exactly what he needed.

With a raised eyebrow and a slightly tilted head Quinton commanded, "turn around." So I did.

His voice was so confident and demanding, the sound of his words made my nipples tighten as I obeyed his instructions. I slowly pivoted through the water leaving my legs slightly open. Quinton placed a gentle, yet forceful grip around the front of my neck as he leaned in to place passionate kisses down the nape of my neck before transitioning to my earlobe. His hands crept down the dip in my back until he reached my behind and grabbed both of my ass cheeks with such aggression, I couldn't help but to gasp from excitement as I bit my bottom lip. My ass seemed to be my prized possession. My petite frame and large derriere never ceased to amaze men and even caught the attention of women when I passed by.

He dropped down to his knees behind me and I felt a stinging sensation as Quinton smacked my right ass cheek with enough aggression to startle me. I wasn't accustomed to his sudden display of dominance, but I liked it.

About time this nigga grabbed his nuts and actually showed me something worth fantasizing over!

He placed kisses on my ass to soothe the sting after each smack. This was new and left me wondering what had overtaken this man.

"Ahhhhh," I moaned softly as Quinton smacked, kissed and then rubbed both ass cheeks together as if he were kneading dough, before spreading me wide open and placing a wet kiss right between my legs. My eyelids slammed shut as Quinton placed another kiss onto the center of my ass before licking me from top to bottom. Eating the booty like groceries was an understatement in this moment. Quinton was eating the booty like the warden had just served him his last meal on death row.

I looked back at him and smiled because no way was this the same mediocre man I had given my treasure to three weeks ago. Through soft moans Quinton pulled away from my center long enough to ask, "did you miss me, baby?"

Here we go, I thought. *The dick isn't amazing enough for you to start asking me questions! Don't get beside yourself. Just do what you came here to do!*

My thoughts and actions didn't coincide, as I grinned and closed my eyes. "Ahhh yes, I missed you, Q," I moaned, rolling my eyes internally.

He slid his right hand around my thigh until he reached my vagina and began rotating my clit in a circular motion as his mouth continued licking and slurping my juices from the back. I moaned as my body grinded with the motion of his fingers on my pussy. *How had this man transformed in a matter of three weeks?* I thought. If the way he was licking my pussy and ass were any indication of how he was about to fuck me, this negro just might have me sprung tonight! Nah! Who was I kidding? He didn't have a chance.

Quinton moved his fingers faster against my swollen clit, causing my juices to flow down my legs. I could feel my wetness spreading and my pussy began to quake as I squirted all over Quinton's beard. No warning because he was here on my terms, so I did whatever I desired and he just had to deal with it. To my surprise, he didn't stop consuming me when he felt my wetness flowing down his face. He simply moaned and forced his face deeper into my core as he began licking vigorously. I was completely folded in half, hands grasping the side of the tub, ass in the air, squirting my sweet nectar all over Quinton as I screamed, "Fuck! Yes, yes, *yes*, don't stop! Shiiiiit!"

Quinton ascended from his knees after devouring the pussy and ass dinner I had so graciously allowed him to demolish and asked, "Is it safe to assume that you *really* missed me?"

The irksome questions were beginning to flatten the high of my orgasm, but I decided to play nice because he waited patiently, three weeks to be exact, for this pussy, so what the hell! I'd stroke his ego a bit.

"I had no idea how much I missed you until tonight!" I said, my body still trembling from the aftermath of his tongue.

No, I didn't miss Quinton. But his tongue? I wish I could keep that bitch in a box to use leisurely. He smirked as he glided his large hand down his lips and beard wiping my juice from his face.

"Well, lucky for you we're just getting started."

He lowered his stare down to his erect penis, which was now practically bulging through his slacks. Quinton swept me out of the tub as if we were in a damn fairytale and carried me to the bedroom where he tossed me on the bed and got down on his knees *again*. He grabbed me by the thighs and with one strong pull, his nose was buried in my pussy. Quinton could lick a mean punanny, even more, he enjoyed it; he found his home in it. He owned that shit when he put his mouth on my pussy. It was quite a magical experience. Eating pussy was such a turn on for him that he would often text me begging for it.

"Let me see you play with that pussy," Quinton requested.

I placed my pointer and middle fingers into Quinton's mouth and rotated my slippery fingers onto my clit before inserting them inside of myself as I allowed my eyes to drift closed, arching my back and releasing a soft moan. I relished the touch of a dominant man; however this sudden display of dominance was not customary for Quinton. He was unleashing all his hidden gems. He was working to prove a point. Quinton was striving to show me what I had missed during the three weeks I had decided to leave all his text messages on read, which I often did once I had become bored.

I bet she won't ignore any more of my texts was what I imagined Quinton thought as he sucked my clit while moving two fingers in and out of my pussy. He had to put in work to ensure that the next time he wanted this pussy, I would answer. He flattened his tongue and pressed it firmly against my clit before sucking on my swollen bulb causing me to scream, "*Shit*, Q!"

"Turn over." Quinton's deep forceful voice echoed through my bedroom.

Taken aback by his tone, I raised both brows as my mouth fell slightly open in surprise. I quickly flipped my ass over. He grabbed my ass, pushing it further into the air to gain more leverage I suppose, and simultaneously slapped both ass cheeks before pushing my head down into a pillow.

Did this muthafucka just push my head down? Oh I know somebody has taken over this nigga's body, because there is no way!

The sound of a wrapper quickly pulled me from my thoughts as Quinton retrieved a condom from the pocket of his slacks and threw his pants across the room. He inserted his thumb into my ass as he tore the condom wrapper with his teeth and rolled it over his hard dick with one hand. Without saying a word he grabbed my waist, twirled his dick around the outside of my pussy lips and then sank inside of me as deep as he could.

"*Fuck*!" I screamed into the pillow as I gripped the sheets between my fingers.

He pulled out completely and thrust his dick back into me repeatedly. I began throwing my round ass against his wide dick. The sound of skin smacking filled the room.

"Fuck, Stacey! Throw that ass back! Throw it back, baby!"

Quinton was not ordinarily a talker but I loved that shit. The dirtier the talk, the wetter I got. I knew he wouldn't last much longer because he never did. I rose from my elbows and pressed my hands into the bed as I began to wind my hips, causing my ass to move in a circle. I caught his thrust each time and looked back at him while licking my lips. I had gotten what I'd needed from him and it was time for me to take the reins and speed this night along.

"Right there, Q! Fuck me like that! Ahhhhh! Don't stop! Don't stop!"

Now why the fuck did she have to start doing all that screaming? was all I imagined Quinton thinking to himself based on the twisted expression plastered across his face as he tried to hold back his nut.

"Stick your finger in my ass, baby," I moaned. And that did it.

"Shit Stacey, I'm about to cum!" he groaned in an animalistic tone.

"Is this pussy about to make you cum, Quinton? Cum for me, baby," I provoked.

Quinton pulled out of me and grabbed his dick jerking it repeatedly as his seed spewed into the condom.

"Damn, Stacey! You know when you start doing all that talking a nigga can't hold back."

I shrugged innocently and grinned as I responded, "What did I do?"

I bit my bottom lip before licking it as Quinton made his way to the trashcan to dispose of the condom. I wandered to the bathroom and turned on the shower; Quinton's deep voice causing me to jump as he crept up behind me.

"Mind if I join you?"

I closed my eyes, contemplating how to tell Quinton it was time for him to go home.

"Actually, Quinton, I have a few errands to run." Making an attempt to at least *sound* like I was telling the truth.

"But it's pouring down rain outside!" he quickly responded, rubbing his hands over my shoulders as I stood naked in front of the shower door.

"Oh, I'll be fine. I told my dad I would swing by tonight."

My voice sounded confident, truthful. He was visibly disappointed, but sauntered to the corner where he had thrown his slacks. He grabbed his belongings and prepared to exit my home. Before leaving, Quinton gazed at me.

"You're amazing, you know that?" he said before smiling and exiting my bedroom.

I couldn't remember the last time I had sex with a man and allowed him to stay the night and tonight was no exception. Quinton brought his "A" game tonight, there was no denying that, but he would have to show some consistency with the dick before I extended the invitation to spend the night. He would never, *could* never possess what it would take to stake his claim with me. I required a certain type of man. Although Quinton was charming, he didn't give me butterflies. I didn't stare at the phone anticipating his call. He just didn't do it for me.

I showered, stuffed my hair into an oversized satin bonnet, applied a clay mask and plopped onto my white down comforter. I grabbed the remote for the adjustable bed and tilted the bed frame, placing me in an upright position. As I flipped through Netflix aimlessly, *The Best Man* flashed across the screen. What better way to end the night than with a classic?

2
STACEY

I sighed when I approached the keypad of the gated, five acre, seven bedroom home in Sugarland, TX where I grew up. The house was no longer occupied by my mother, since she had chosen to skedaddle her ass out of the country with Marco, Markel, Mack, whatever the fuck his name was. I drove down the half mile stretch of paved concrete before pulling into the circular driveway and parked in front of the oversized double doors.

Lord, please allow this conversation to go better than I'm expecting.

I swung my car door open and stepped from my two seater BMW. Before I could approach the threshold of the entryway, George – our family butler – opened the door, greeting me with a smile.

"Ms. Hill, how nice of you to stop by. We've missed you!"

George was genuinely excited to see me. He'd been a part of my family for over fifteen years and I couldn't help but to return an elated, toothy smile.

"Hi, Georgey! I've missed you, too!"

I flung my arms around the old man as he returned the embrace. George was basically family and he had helped care for me since I was a teenager. I loved the old grump.

"I've got it, George, thank you." I heard my father's voice from behind George as he moved aside and my six foot three father appeared in the doorway.

"Hey, Baby Girl. This is a pleasant surprise."

"Hey, Daddy. I was hoping we could talk," I muttered in a childlike tone, which I often found myself using when speaking to my father.

I followed him through the massive, marble paved foyer, passing walls filled with family portraits and rare paintings. I'd always admired the stunning artwork featured in our family home. Collecting art was a hobby my mother and father acquired through their world travels. Upon entering my father's study, I realized everything was just as I had remembered. Books lined the four walls of the room from floor to ceiling. My father's extensive book collection was compliments of my mother, whom he frequently awarded credit for exposing him to literature, which resulted in him becoming an avid reader.

"Take a seat, Baby Girl." My father gestured toward the brown, ostrich leather office chair, also compliments of my mother. God knows he wouldn't know where to begin to find such an elegant piece.

As I sat in the oversized chair, crossing my legs, I grabbed the arms of the chair and braced for impact, preparing for the uncomfortable conversation to begin. With a furrowed brow my father began, "Baby Girl, first let me say—"

"No, Daddy, let me go first...please."

Daddy was a sucker for me. Let him tell it, the day they brought me home from the hospital he knew that I – a six pound, five ounce baby girl – would change the trajectory of his life forever. Patrick Hill vowed to protect me as long as he had breath in his lungs. This was proven true during a series of countless, unfortunate moments I'd found myself involved in during my high school years. He traveled through life with blinders on in regards to me. I'd be lying if I said I'd never taken advantage of the knowledge that if I were ever in a bind, he would bend over backwards to clear my name. To see me visibly upset tore his heart to shreds, and I knew it.

"The situation between you and Mom has been devastating," I finally mustered up the courage to say. I'd never had a conversation like this with my father and feeling the need to confront him was just flat out uncomfortable. I took in a deep breath, holding it for a second before releasing it and blurting out, "Daddy, how could you do this to Mom? How could you do this to our family?"

I lifted my tear filled eyes to my father who sat helplessly watching the pain he alone was responsible for. As he opened his mouth to speak, he couldn't seem to find his words all of a sudden.

"Baby Girl...I...I...I'm so sorry. I know this may be hard for you to understand."

"That's bullshit, Daddy, I'm twenty-nine years old. Nothing about this is beyond my comprehension."

I realized how inappropriate my tone and words were as quickly as they'd escaped my lips. Disrespecting the one man whose love for me had proven to be unconditional wasn't an option. I immediately regretted my sassiness and the fact that I had purposefully used profanity in the presence of my father.

"Now wait one minute, young lady. Pissed off or not, I am your father and you will show me some respect! Do we understand one another? I worked my ass off building Hill Architecture to leave a legacy for my family and I'll be damned if the child I reared will ever speak to me in such a disrespectful tone. And the next time you decide you want to curse in my presence...don't, because you're not too old to get your ass whooped!"

I cleared my eyes of the lingering tears as I focused my melancholic gaze on my father. "Yes, sir. I apologize."

"Now are you prepared to discuss this situation like an adult or are you still in spoiled brat mode?" my father asked facetiously.

I chuckled because he was the second person this week to label me as spoiled.

"There must be some truth to the statement," I mumbled.

"What was that?" my father asked.

"Oh nothing, you're just the second person this week to identify me as a spoiled brat, so I figure there must be some truth to the statement."

We both laughed, which helped ease the tension in the room and I was relieved my father had forgiven me so quickly.

"Daddy, not that it's my business, but I was really hoping you would help me understand what happened with you and Mom."

My father shifted guilty eyes to the ground for a moment before speaking.

"Baby Girl, I love your mother very much. How could I not? She gave me you and Patrick Jr.," he sighed, "but the honest to God truth is, your mother and I had not been happy for a very long time. We initially stayed together for you and your brother. We made the decision to go our separate ways after you graduated college. Your brother was already an adult living his life and we didn't want to disrupt the normalcy in your life, so we made the decision to stay together for you, despite our plan to separate."

I gasped at the realization that I had been living in a fucking bubble.

"What?" I couldn't believe what I was hearing. "How long, Daddy? How long had you two been miserable?"

"Stacey..." my father started, "there is more to it than that."

"How long, Daddy?"

"Upward of fifteen years, Stacey," my father responded.

How had I been so blind? Was I that self-absorbed that I had not noticed? I was upset with myself for being oblivious to what was happening with my parents.

"I'm confused, Daddy. Why Ms. Linda? Why Mom's best friend? You could have chosen anyone else, why would you choose Mom's best friend? She was family, practically an aunt to me and PJ. We loved her, Daddy! Did you neglect to consider what would happen to our relationship with her?"

My father cleared the lump in his throat and paused for a moment.

"I thought I loved her," he lowered his gaze and closed his eyes before emphasizing, "I did love her, but I took it too far. She had been around the family for so many years. She made me feel special, Stacey. She made me feel like a man."

I gripped my forehead with the palm of my hand in disbelief.

"Baby, cheating on your mom was the worst decision I have ever made."

I regained my composure long enough to ask, "Why didn't you try to fix it? Why didn't you try to get Mom back if you regret the decision so badly?"

"It wasn't until she moved on with Marcus that I realized I made a terrible mistake. We had fallen into a sorrowful place in our marriage, but now I realize I should have fought harder. I tried to get her back but you have to realize, your mother and I were teenagers when we started dating. I'm all she has ever known. I tried my damndest to get her back but I guess the excitement of something new kind of...took hold. I would do anything to get your mother back, baby, but I made an unforgivable mistake, and I don't blame her for wanting nothing to do with me."

Observing the hurt, tears, and remorse from my father immediately softened my heart. All feelings of contempt and anger were now obsolete. He had redeemed himself. He was a man, a flawed man, and he made a mistake. I had fucked up on more than one occasion in my twenty-nine year life span, and in this moment, I found it impossible to continue to be angry with him.

"So have you spoken to your mother?" my father asked, genuinely concerned.

"It's been a few months," I replied nonchalantly.

"A few months!" my father stated in an alarmed tone. "But why, Stacey?"

"I was upset with her, Daddy. How could she leave you? Why wouldn't she try to make it work? Then she moved on with this asshole who's the same age as I am!"

My father raised an eyebrow.

"Sorry, Daddy, I didn't mean to curse, but really! The guy is only twenty-nine years old. Am I the only one who sees the problem with this?"

"Well actually, little sister, you are!" PJ's voice rang out from behind me causing me to whip my neck around.

"PJ!" I squealed before running to my brother and flinging myself into him. He wrapped his arms around my waist and gave me a full circle spin before putting me down.

"Let me look at you, you little squirt!" PJ was six foot six, quite taller than our father.

I chuckled and punched my brother in the chest. He had moved to New York ten years ago.

"What are you doing here?" I smiled and stood back to get a better look at my big brother.

"Oh, I just stopped in to check in on you and the old man. I was planning on surprising you later on tonight, but George called and informed me that you stopped by the house, so I decided to make my way over here from the hotel."

"Hotel?" I stated in confusion. "Why would you be in a hotel when this house has more than enough rooms? There is an entire guest wing with literally no one there."

"Well, little nosey girl. If you must know, I brought my lady friend with me from New York." I was surprised and a tad bit annoyed that I didn't know about this "little lady friend" my brother spoke of.

"A lady friend! Oh heck no, when do I get to meet her?" I pushed PJ in the chest and folded my arms across my body.

"You don't, hence the reason we are staying in a hotel and not here at the house. I'm not ready to introduce her to this dysfunction just yet."

My father, Patrick Sr. sat silently in his chair watching the two of us bicker back and forth as he shook his head.

"Dysfunction?" I was visibly annoyed by my brother at this point.

"Absolutely, Stacey! When I walked in you were just grilling Dad about Mom and why she chose to run off with a twenty-nine year old. As if Dad isn't the root cause of all of this. Sorry Dad, no offense intended," PJ said with a shrug as he looked in our father's direction.

"None taken, son. The truth is the truth and I don't hide from it. Call a spade a spade."

I knew exactly what Patrick must have been thinking. He had finally found someone he could actually see a future with and he wouldn't allow his spoiled sister, his cheating father, or his *How Stella Got Her Groove Back* mother to ruin this for him.

"You will meet her in due time, little sis. I promise."

"Well, can I at least know her name?" I scoffed.

"Her name is Pilar. Now stop being a brat, leave Daddy alone, and call Mom. She misses you," Patrick Jr. stated in a stern, big brother tone.

"If you two are done bickering like school aged children, I'm starving. Having the two of you under the same roof is a rare occurrence, so I figure I better take full advantage. You two care to have lunch with your old man?"

My father shifted his eyes from me to PJ waiting for our response.

"I don't have any more clients for the day," I responded.

"I'll let Pilar know that I'll be gone a little longer than expected," PJ stated.

My eyes narrowed to slits at the fact that my brother had such high regard for a woman I hadn't even known existed before today.

"Perfect!" my father responded.

"I'll have George reserve our usual table at Grace's. Glad you two could make time for your old man."

I finally felt at ease now that my father and I were back on speaking terms. Whoever this Pilar chick had to have had my brother's nose wide open and his mind completely occupied because his weekly phone calls had stopped. He still texted me often, but the calls were becoming more infrequent. I didn't mention my frustration with PJ during lunch because I was enjoying time with my two favorite guys and didn't want to spoil the mood. My thoughts fixated on my mother, how much I missed her as well as my brother and father's words, and that damn PJ was now the third person to call me spoiled. I smiled and let out a breath. *They can all kiss my ass!* Instead of continuing to give her the silent treatment, I decided to reach out and text my mom.

Hey Mom, I know it's been a while. I'm really sorry for shutting you out. I miss you. I'd love to catch up when you have time. Hugs and Kisses.

3
STACEY

"Bitch! You're not special just because you have multiple niggas sniffing up your ass all day long! You ain't worth two damn pennies!" Rachel exclaimed.

"Yo mama!" I responded as Rachel and I burst into laughter falling all over one another.

There was never a shortage of shit talking coupled with laughter when we were together.

"You know, Rachel, I really don't know. I guess it's a blessing and a curse...I mean, it's not like I want it to be this way, hell, it's just how the cards fell for me," I sighed, brushing my shoulder arrogantly.

"Well, enough about your overactive pussy! Pour me another glass of wine and let's start this damn movie you've been raving about," Rachel teased. "And it better be good too! Got me out on a Friday night watching a movie when I could be out scouting some dick!"

"Girl! Shut up! You're over here every Friday, you ain't got shit to do!" I laughed as I walked toward the kitchen.

I was intentional about being present in my friendship with Rachel because she mattered to me, but tonight, I couldn't remain in the present due to my mind drifting to a dinner date later tonight. No one special, just some guy I bumped into after an afternoon run two weeks prior. He was fine and I was pretty sure he knew that, running through the trail with no shirt on looking lickable. I was already juggling way too much and wasn't particularly excited about adding anymore male testosterone to the mix. However, a girl had to eat, so I figured, why not?

"Don't forget the hot sauce!" Rachel yelled from the living room sofa.

I returned from the kitchen with a bottle of Louisiana Hot Sauce and two small bowls of popcorn. I grimaced as

Rachel shook the hot sauce bottle until the top layer of her popcorn was doused in red.

"What the hell are you looking at, Stacey?" Rachel inclined her neck and smacked her lips at me.

"That shit looks like a stomachache." I quivered in disgust as I poured two glasses of Stella Rosa Blueberry Wine.

"Aht! Aht! Mind your business. You eat your plain ass popcorn and leave me alone. I don't say anything when you eat raw ass red meat!" Rachel said, pointing her index finger at me.

"For your information, I order my steaks cooked medium, not raw, and you could learn a thing or two from me with your overcooked, well done steak, hot sauce on popcorn, pickle juice drinking ass!" I said.

"But you luh me though!" Rachel replied with a smirk on her face.

I threw my arms around Rachel's neck and began kissing her cheeks repeatedly. "You know I love you, girl! Don't know what I would do without you. That's why I'm going to find you a nigga to knock the cobwebs off this pussy so your ass will stop being so mean!" I said through a giggle as I hunched Rachel's leg playfully. "That's all you need! A little dick and you'll be a new woman!"

"Get your hot twat off my leg and start the movie!" Rachel laughed and pinched my boob until I finally left her alone.

We sat side by side, watching the classic, *Boomerang*, because to my dismay, Rachel had never seen the movie. She claimed that her family was too poor to watch movies when she was growing up. So on Friday nights, I made it my mission to introduce her to all the classic movies she'd missed growing up. Even though *Boomerang* wasn't necessarily a movie I should have been allowed to watch as a kid, having an older brother had its perks.

"Okay girl, that movie was definitely an A-plus!" Rachel admitted. "I know you have a date tonight, so I'm going to run. Text me the nigga's name, phone number, license plate number, where y'all are going and the time you plan on meeting with him! Oh! And keep your damn location on!"

"Yes, mother dear!" I responded sarcastically.

"Yeah! It's all fun and games until a muthafucka tries to snatch your ass!" Rachel scoffed.

"Okay, okay! Location on, license plate number, name, phone number, I got it!" I kissed Rachel on the cheek and shut the door behind her.

With two hours before my nine p.m. date, I decided to take a bath instead of a shower. The R&B station on Spotify set the mood perfectly as I pineappled my fluffy curls onto the top of my head and stepped into the lavender infused bubble bath slowly. I nestled my head onto the hanging bathtub pillow and began bobbing my head to Mary J. Blige's "Real Love" as I drifted into relaxation.

I opened my eyes, what seemed like ten minutes later to cold bathwater and five missed phone calls.

What the hell? What time is it?

The clock on my phone read ten p.m. I gasped and hurriedly exited the tub, wrapping the Egyptian cotton towel around my dripping wet body. I was an hour late to my date!

How had I let this happen?

Just as I slathered my body with shea butter and misted Yves Saint Laurent Mon Paris perfume over my body, my doorbell rang.

Now who in the entire hell could this be?

My doorman Randy was adamant about informing me before allowing visitors to enter through the lobby. Confusion set in because I hadn't received a call notifying me that anyone was on the way up. The short silk robe I'd placed over my naked body clung to my narrow waist. My wide hips slightly shortened the length of the robe, causing it to stop right above the bottom of my ass cheeks. I rose onto my tiptoes to peek out of the peep hole and my heart skipped a beat.

What was he doing here? He was supposed to be traveling for preseason.

I sprinted to the bathroom to check my appearance in the mirror, snatching my hair out of the pineapple ponytail, and giving it a vigorous shake releasing my bouncy curls that fell past my shoulders. I quickly rubbed the pads of my fingers over my moist vagina and gave them a quick sniff check before bolting back to the door, as I inhaled deeply, slowly gliding the front door to my penthouse apartment open.

There stood Savior muthafuckin' James. All six feet seven inches of him. To describe him as a walking orgasm would be an understatement. His rich chocolate brown skin in addition to his incredible height made him a spectacle in any room. Savior's perfectly straight white teeth and deep set dimples only made him more enticing to me. His eyes penetrated my damn soul. Brown was the eye color inscribed on his driver's license, only because sienna wasn't an option, but I'd had the pleasure of witnessing those sienna eyes transition to green as the vein in his forehead would protrude after he ejaculated. He rocked a low cut taper fade that he allowed to grow into gorgeous curls in the winter. His full beard was always tamed, with a perfectly crisp edge-up and just happened to be my favorite place to sit. His thick, sensual lips and chiseled abs made my knees buckle, but I couldn't care less because anytime Savior was around, I was bound to be on my knees anyway.

As I held the door open, my eyes lingering on this sensational man, I could feel the wetness slipping around my thighs. Savior's stamina was comparable to an energizer bunny and his fine ass was standing right in front of my face. He was more than a walking orgasm, like his name referenced, he was a god. Savior James was the small forward for the Los Angeles Legends and my once-a-month dick appointment when he visited Houston. However, he hadn't called this time and we didn't do…pop ups.

I was now more than an hour and a half late for my date and realizing there was no way I would make it. I conceded defeat and surrendered to whatever the night had in store for me. The intensity of Savior's stare made it abundantly clear that even if I tried to leave, he'd terminate the notion with no regrets. He was preparing to pounce and I was the prey.

"You happy to see me, baby?" Savior's low growl caused me to shift my weight anxiously as he licked his full lips, slightly biting his bottom lip while staring at me with those mesmerizing sienna eyes.

"As a matter of fact...I am," I gushed as I grabbed Savior's belt loop giving it a slight tug, causing him to slowly stride through the doorway.

It wasn't a lie. I fucking missed him. Missing him was the only reason I entertained other men every once in a while. I know it was ass backward to fuck someone different because you missed the one you wished you could have, but I'd never claimed to have it all together. Although I hadn't anticipated Savior popping up, this man could give me the love, money, power, status, and dick I always dreamed of. I would be damned if a little "pop up" was going to ruin this for me. Savior peered down at my five foot two frame in adoration as he slid his pointer finger down the opening of my silk robe exposing my picture perfect breasts. He grabbed my chin between his pointer finger and thumb to lift my head and bent down to kiss my lips as he placed his free hand on my ass.

I was extremely proud of my butt. I worked hard in the gym to keep my body fit and my ass fat. Savior's acknowledgement of my full, round behind caused me to smile a seductive grin as I pushed my tongue into his mouth. He slid his hands down to the back of my thighs and effortlessly lifted my tiny frame as my legs straddled his rock hard abdomen. I was short in stature but pretty solid and the bottom half of my body was definitely all muscle. However, the way Savior lifted me, hell, you'd think I was weightless. He carried me to the kitchen island and placed me on the countertop. He watched me for a moment, absent of words. He just studied me before twirling one of my curls around his finger and pulling the robe from my shoulders freeing my breasts. Leaving me exposed.

Savior backpedaled slowly, as if he were admiring a rare piece of artwork.

"Go put your hair in a ponytail," Savior commanded, his eyes glued to mine, his stance firm and assuring.

This nigga! I know this muthafucka didn't just pop up to my spot expecting to get his dick sucked. That was the only reason he wanted my hair in a ponytail. Fucking asshole! Hopping off the island, I made my way to the bathroom, rummaging through my drawer until I found a ponytail holder to lightly hold my hair back. I placed my hands on the bathroom vanity and stared at my reflection in the mirror.

I coached myself in the bathroom mirror. *It's okay Stacey, he wouldn't have popped up here if he didn't like you. He could have gone to any other woman, but he came to you! You have to keep him happy if you want a future with him. Just do whatever nasty shit he wants you to do.*

And it's not that I didn't enjoy the "nasty shit" I would just prefer to have more from him. I wanted to be more to Savior than just a monthly fuck. He was the exception to all of my rules. Savior could pop up, spend the night, force me to clear my schedule, and give me the desire to do freaky shit I had never thought of with anyone else.

"And put on those Louboutins I bought you," Savior shouted from the kitchen, interrupting my train of thought.

I rolled my eyes and replied, "Which ones? You buy me a new pair every time you come to town."

"The red ones!" Savior shot back.

I strutted into the living room to discover Savior sitting on the couch and he was butt ass naked, dick in hand. He slowly stroked himself as he eyed me. Any hesitation I was feeling had completely gone out of the window when I saw this god of a man in front of me. I was frozen. Dickmatized. I felt a tingling sensation in my clitoris. How the fuck? He hadn't even touched me yet. How was my body already yearning for him?

"Come here," Savior called.

I slowly made my way over to the couch, carefully placing my steps on the wood floor in the six inch stilettos.

"I've been thinking about you," Savior admitted, staring at my naked body, still stroking himself slowly as I stopped in front of him.

"Have you? What exactly have you been thinking?" I inquired.

"How remarkably tight your pussy is," Savior growled.

His response caught me off guard as I raised an eyebrow and began to blush.

Thank God for weighted kegel exercises.

"Also been missing that fire ass head," Savior disclosed as he bit his bottom lip.

And there it was. The reason he'd asked me to put my hair in a ponytail.

"Ohhhh, so let me guess. Is my fire ass head, as you call it, the reason you asked me to tie my hair back?" I asked, unable to suppress the sass in my tone as I stood with my legs parted and folded my arms across my chest.

"Come closer baby; don't misunderstand," Savior responded. "When you get down on your knees and you wrap those pretty ass lips around my dick, I want to see your face. That face, that body, you as a whole, you belong to me. I want to see my baby when she puts in work. That's the reason I ask you to pull your hair back."

Savior Muthafuckin James was in the building and there was nothing ordinary about this man. He wasn't like any of the other men I entertained from time to time. This man was a boss and nothing about him was mediocre. He delivered every single time. I never had to wonder what I would get with him because he was the master of his craft on and off the court. How could I say no to this man? Why would I say no?

"Come kiss on it for me, baby," Savior said, his baritone voice causing a chill to travel up my spine as goosebumps randomly began to envelop my arms.

I stepped closer and bent down to his face, allowing his soothing gaze to wash away my irritated disposition. He gently grabbed the back of my neck and kissed my lips, slipping his tongue into my mouth. He let go of his dick and reached for my pussy, cupping it with his massive hands, trapping my warmth in his grasp as his tongue circled around inside of my mouth. Savior traced my lips with his tongue and I was frozen, at his mercy as he massaged my vagina with the palm of his hand. I could feel my own wetness slipping around my thighs.

He kissed my lips again before slowly guiding my head to his lap and without hesitation I gently gripped his dick with both hands and guided my mouth up and down while rotating my hands in opposite directions. I paid particular attention to the tip as I sucked, licked, spit, gagged, and deepthroated Savior's dick until I felt an involuntary tear descend from the corner of my eye. He held my ponytail tightly in one hand as he rotated my left nipple with the other hand. My head bobbed up and down as Savior threw his head back and allowed his mouth to fall open as he experienced pure ecstasy.

"Just like that, baby. That's my girl. Shit, Stacey!"

When Savior began to talk to me, I lost my damn mind. I tried my damndest to swallow his dick, which wasn't an easy task. I wanted all of him. I wanted to prove that I was the only woman he ever needed. He grabbed my head forcefully, which I didn't mind and began to thrust himself into my mouth. His thrust was so strong that with each push, the lower part of his body elevated from the couch. With every gag another involuntary tear fell until Savior pulled me off of him.

"Shit Stacey, what the fuck are you doing to me?" he moaned, wrapping his hand around himself and rubbing gently.

I smiled as I used my pointer finger to seductively wipe away the evidence of what I had been doing.

"It's okay, Savior," I moaned while caressing his solid thighs, "You can cum if you want to. You don't have to hold back."

I fondled my nipple rings and licked my lips while watching his sienna brown eyes transition like a mood ring. This wasn't like me, to not care about getting mine. However, at this point I was so wrapped up in Savior, my needs were secondary.

"Nah, you know it doesn't work like that, baby." Savior stood up from the couch and stared down at me. "I love you," he said, wiping the leftover tears from my cheeks. Tears that were proof of how hard I went for him. I couldn't speak. I was literally speechless.

"Wha— I. I mean...Savior. What are you saying?" I couldn't believe what I was hearing.

Was this man bullshitting? Because saying "I love you" had never been a prerequisite for what we did. Savior picked me up and I straddled him. We were now face to face.

"Stacey Ambria Hill, I love you," Savior stated sincerely, unflinchingly as he reached the depths of my soul through his gaze.

It was as if the room launched into a full spin. It was common knowledge that I loved Savior. Love and commitment, however, were two very different things and I was intentional about not blurring the lines. By no means had I been committed to Savior, but I definitely loved the man.

"I...I love you too, Savior," I stammered, my voice shaking, and feeling confused. Before I could get another word in; his tongue was in my mouth again. He carried me to the nearest wall, and as if I were featherlight, Savior suspended my body into the air. My back pressed against the cool wall and my legs draped over his shoulders. Savior placed a death grip on my waist as he kissed the outside of my vagina before parting my lips with his tongue. This man made love to my pussy with his entire face. Nose, lips, tongue, he was the master.

I didn't have to teach Savior what to do, he just knew. As he sucked my clit like a damn vacuum, he released one hand from my waist to insert two fingers into me. My legs began to tremble as I grasped Savior's head tightly.

"Mmmmm, Savior," I moaned through the intoxicating vibrations simmering at my core, threatening to create an explosion.

Savior sucked my clit firmly holding my engorged pearl between his soft lips, interchanging his firm sucks with skillful licks when it appeared as if my body could no longer withstand his wrath. He moved the two fingers he had inside of me in and out steadily. I was tight and wet and visibly about to cum and when he removed his fingers from my pussy and reached up to rotate my nipple I lost control. My body erupted from the inside out. Immense pleasure... absolute satisfaction seized my body and I was no longer in control of my words.

"I love you Savior, I fucking love you! Don't stop! I'm cumming, *fuck*, fucking shit, damn, shit, oh fuck, damn-fuck!"

I shuddered as Savior removed me from the wall and carried me to the bedroom. I knew it may not have been the smartest idea, but Savior and I never used condoms. We made a mindless promise to one another two years prior that we would always use protection with anyone else we slept with, but when we were together, no one else mattered. I had to admit, it was absolutely ridiculous, irresponsible, and downright fucking dumb that I had unprotected sex with Savior but for some unexplainable, preposterous reason; I trusted him. Savior placed me on the bed and kissed my lips gently before positioning his back against the seven foot tall, crushed velvet headboard.

"Come sit on it for me, baby," Savior commanded as I crawled over to him, straddling his lap and reaching between my legs to guide his penis inside of me. He embraced me tightly and laid his head on my chest as I began to bounce up and down. As my speed increased, Savior pressed down on my ass signaling for me to stop. Puzzlement plagued my stare.

"You okay?" I whispered, searching his eyes for an explanation.

"I'm better than okay, baby, but I'm not going anywhere, you can slow down," he said, pressing kisses to my breasts.

My ears were playing tricks on me. My mind was trying to convince me that he wanted me to "slow down", which translated to "let's make love" in my brain. I wasn't sure what the hell was happening, but I was going to enjoy every moment with Savior James.

4
STACEY

I woke up the next morning feeling pretty confident that I had dreamed of Savior James. He had popped up, proclaimed his love after two years, and made love to me. I fixed my eyes on the ceiling fan as I pulled the comforter under my chin and blushed. My body was practically tingling just thinking about him.

I was startled when I heard a noise in the kitchen. I popped up in the bed clutching my comforter before reaching into the nightstand to grab the .380 pistol my father insisted I keep inside of my penthouse at all times. I hated that damn gun. I'd end up accidentally causing more harm to myself than an intruder. I didn't even bother putting clothes on before tiptoeing into the kitchen with the gun drawn.

"Whoa, baby! What the fuck!" Savior yelled in an octave I'd never witnessed his voice reach as he spilled coffee onto the hardwood floor.

"Oh my God, Savior! I'm so sorry!" I screamed, still aiming the gun in his direction.

"Baby, put the damn gun down!" he shouted, both hands elevated in surrender.

I placed the loaded gun on the kitchen countertop and cupped my breasts with one hand while attempting to cover my vagina with the other.

"Savior, what are you doing here?" I asked.

He stared at me as he slid towards me slowly, eyeing the loaded gun.

"What do you mean? Please don't tell me I was that unmemorable last night."

It hadn't been a dream. I hadn't concocted any of it in my mind. Savior had actually been there with me and the nigga spent the night, something I'd given up on asking him to do over a year ago.

What the fuck was happening?

"Savior—I...I'm so sorry, you know that's not what I meant. Nothing about you is unmemorable," I responded, raising a brow and slightly tilting my head in the direction of his penis.

Savior placed a hand on each side of my face before leaning in for a kiss, which I quickly rejected by turning my head.

"I haven't brushed my teeth, Savior," I said through clenched teeth, trying to avoid blowing my dragon breath in his face.

He forced my head back in his direction. "You think I give a fuck about your morning breath? I just sucked your soul through your pussy last night, now give me a kiss," he demanded aggressively.

He leaned in again, placing a wet kiss to my lips and slid his hands from my cheeks down to my ass. I could feel his dick hardening against my stomach and figured I better interrupt him now before he decided to suspend me in the air again.

"Savior, don't you think we need to talk?" I said, folding my arms over my chest.

Savior raised an eyebrow. "About?"

With pursed lips and an exasperated sigh I said, "Well, you caught me by surprise last night. You popped up, told me you love me, fucked the shit out of me, and spent the night. Seems like we have quite a few talking points if you ask me."

The sound of my phone ringing disrupted our conversation.

"Give me one second," I said.

As I turned to retrieve my phone from the bedroom, Savior slapped me on the ass and winked at me. I smiled and felt my coochie jump. I looked down at my vagina. *Down girl!* I whispered as my clit tightened. I snatched my phone from the nightstand. Nine missed phone calls, nine missed text messages. My face scrunched as my heart raced with alarm, was someone hurt? Five of the missed calls came from

Quinton, two from the date I stood up the previous night, and two from Rachel. Seven of the text messages were from Quinton, one from my ditched date, and one from Rachel.

What the entire fuck could Quinton possibly want?

```
    Quinton: Stacey, give me a call when
you get this message.
    Quinton: Stacey, I've called you a
few times, give me a call when you get
this message.

    Quinton: Stacey, I've been calling
you! Where are you?
    Quinton: Stacey! So you're just gonna
ignore me like this? What about the other
night, it didn't mean anything to you?

    Quinton: Fuck you! I'm tired of this
shit. You think you can just treat me
anyway you want and just call me when you
get lonely or want to fuck and then you
ghost me whenever you feel like it??? I'm
not doing this shit with you anymore.

    Quinton: Stacey Baby, I'm so sorry
for my previous text. I let my attitude
get the best of me.
    Quinton: You know I rock with you
Stacey. Please call me back.

    Ditched Date: Hey pretty lady, I hope
you're okay. I assume something came up.
I'd like to reschedule when you're free.
```

Rachel: BITCH!! I know you see I called you. Don't make me put out an APB on your ass! Call me back!

When Savior stepped into the bedroom he immediately noticed a change in my disposition. A mixture of concern and resentment spread across my face.

"Uhhh...you okay, baby? What's going on?" Savior asked, his voice full of apprehension.

"Oh nothing, just Rachel's crazy ass. You know how she can be!"

There was absolutely no way I would disclose my dirty deeds when Savior and I seemed to finally be moving towards something. Although one night didn't count for much, it was something. To share Quinton's disturbing text messages meant I would also have to share that I had slept with him recently. Savior and I had never agreed to be monogamous but I also didn't want him to know I had been with another man that same week. My gut was telling me not to ignore Quinton's insolent text messages, or the fact that he had blown my phone up as if he had papers on me or a damn ring on my left hand. However, Savior and I had more pressing business to attend to.

I slid a crop top over my fluffy bed head hair and rolled a thong over my butt before dragging Savior and his hard penis back to the living room. I lifted myself onto the kitchen counter with a little hop as I focused my gaze on him.

"I'm just trying to figure out what's going on, Savior. Don't get me wrong, seeing you has been the highlight of my week, but...what are you really doing here? You've never popped up before, you've damn sure never told me you love me or spent the night, so I'm just trying to figure out what's up."

Savior grazed his hand over his face tracing his long fingers through his thick beard.

"Shit...I don't know, Stacey. I guess I've just been thinking about what really matters to me. I know since I was an asshole last year and told you I didn't want a relationship you've kind of been letting me do my own thing. You haven't really hounded me about it since then and I just couldn't help but to see how consistent you've been. You've been holding a nigga ten toes down. And I mean, I know last year I wasn't really trying to hear that relationship shit, but I kinda want to see where this can go," Savior answered, raising his eyes from the ground to meet mine as he slid a hand onto my thigh.

My heart skipped a beat. Was this really happening? Was I actually about to snag Savior muthafuckin James? I felt my cheeks heat up and my palms began to sweat.

"So are you saying you want to..." I waited for Savior to respond.

"I'm saying, let's see where this goes," he finished.

Although inconsequential after a two year wait, Savior's words sang a beautiful medley in my ears and his words held weight in my heart.

"*Bitch*, I got something to tell you!" I gushed to Rachel over the phone as I sank into my plush couch placing my hand over my heart.

"You better be getting ready to tell me why your triflin' ass didn't let me know you made it home last night," Rachel scolded.

"Well, that would be because I never left home," I said through a wide smile.

"I know the fuck you didn't invite that nigga to your penthouse on a first date! I just know you didn't!" Rachel yelled. I could practically feel her breath as she fussed at me.

"What! Nooooooo, you know me better than that!" I responded frowning, inclining my neck at Rachel's assumption that I would allow a complete stranger to enter into my home.

"Oh! Okay. Girl, you had me nervous for a minute. So wait…if you never left the house…" Rachel said, confusion plaguing her tone.

"Savior popped up last night, bitch! He just popped up out of the blue, screwed the shit out of me, told me he loves me, spent the fucking night, and told me he wants me to be his girl. Well he *kinda* told me he wants me to be his girl, but you get my point!" I was speaking so fast I had to stop and inhale a deep breath after speeding through my words.

Rachel sat silently on the phone.

If looks could kill, I would be a dead bitch because by Rachel's silence, it was evident that she was not pleased with me.

"Ummmm……hello? Best Friend! Did you hear what I just said?" I asked, irritated at her silence.

"Yeah, Stacey, I heard you but I'm not quite sure how you would like for me to respond." Rachel's dry tone didn't go unnoticed.

"I— I mean… aren't you even a tad bit happy for me?" I stammered; my face twisted in disbelief.

"You want me to tell the truth, or you want me to tell a lie? It's your choice." Rachel was unable to hide her frustration at this point.

"*Damn*, Rachel, for real?" I scoffed, pulling my ear away to stare at the phone.

"You don't want to do this right now, Stacey. I promise you don't. Let's just stop while we still can," Rachel warned.

"You know what, Rachel? I actually *do* want to do this. I can't believe your jealous ass has the audacity to pull this shit when I tell you some good news. I should have known you wouldn't be excited for me. How could you? When was the last time *you* were actually happy yourself? It's my fault for thinking you could set yourself aside to feel at least a hint of elation for your best friend."

I was wounded by Rachel's demeanor but attempted to conceal the brutal sting with my own malicious words. Rachel let out a laugh and without words, I knew exactly what she was thinking. Her tone screamed *I know this bitch didn't.*

"Fuck it! Let's do it then! You obviously want me to lie and feed you bullshit, so here you go. Yeah, girl! I'm happy for you. I'm happy about all the times that muthafucka made you cry. I'm happy about all the times he fucked you, left you with high hopes, and then didn't call again until timing was convenient for him. Oh! You know what!? I'm happy about all the other bitches you've seen him flaunt around LA on Bossip, TMZ, and The Shade Room, all while never taking you on as much as a single date in public, can't forget that one. You want me to be happy about an *ain't shit nigga,* Stacey, but I can't because you deserve better. So what! The nigga has money! So do you! Remember what you said Stacey because I remember it clear as day! I, Stacey Ambria Hill, promise to leave fuck boys alone. I promise to value my time and my vagina enough to limit the access I allow these no good, lying ass muthafuckas to have in my life. You know why I remember that Stacey? Because I'm the one who has to help you pick up the pieces when the shit hits the fan. Savior is going to hurt you again and you're just too blind to see it."

A few moments of complete silence passed.

"I'm not really sure how to respond to that, Rachel," I admitted, my eyes pooling with tears as I disguised my sniffles by covering the bottom of my cell phone.

"Then don't respond," Rachel shot back. "Look, I have to go. I'll catch up with you later, good luck with Savior. I really hope things are different this time." Those were the last words Rachel spoke before hanging up the phone.

ANTHONY

I waited up for Stacey to call…but she never did. I even tried calling, just to make sure everything was okay – no answer. Shit kinda puzzled me, I wasn't exactly a *get stood up type of guy*. I had seen Stacey around the way, knew of her and was pretty interested in getting to know her on a personal level. As an affluent businessman in the city, I'd hired architects from her father's firm to remodel a few buildings for my company, but I'd never had the pleasure of actually meeting Stacey…until I ran into her on the trail. That damn girl was –shall I say – blessed…in all the right places. But it was more than that because I'd fucked plenty of modelesque women , the percks of being young, rich and quite handsome in a bustling city like Houston. It was the fact that Stacey seemed unfazed by me. My lingering gazes went unnoticed when I'd spot her running on the trail, it was as if she were immune to – me.

    She was a refreshing alternate to the women who served their pussy up on a platter, begging for my attention. That shit got old fast, everyone wanted what I could provide them, and didn't give a damn about who I really was. Stacey….she didn't seem to give a damn about either. She piqued my interest, a hard task when awarded limitless leisurely experiences that could easily fill my idle mind.

    My pride wanted me to say *fuck it, her loss*, but another part of me, a part of me that I didn't allow to make executive decisions frequently…my heart, was telling me to give it one more shot. I chuckled at how fucking ridiculous I felt, actually planning a follow-up date – for a no call, no show date – with a woman…who clearly wanted nothing to do with me. I rested my chin between my thumb and pointer finger as I thought about this damn woman. *What the hell is wrong with me?* "Aye yo Boss, you ready to roll?"

    I looked up to see my bodyguard towering over me, realizing quickly that I had zoned out. Whatever witchcraft this woman had blown my way was going to have to cease because being distracted – in the middle of the day, with my workload wasn't going to work for me. The sooner I actually saw her again, the better because if this shit was just some sort of *'you rejected me, so now I've gotta get a piece to show you I'm the man,*' I was way too old for that shit, and needed to get over if promptly.

I followed my bodyguard to my SUV and slid my cellphone from the breast pocket of my suit, "Charles Renee, I need a favor."

5
STACEY

I haven't spoken to Rachel in a week. A long, grueling week, particularly because Rachel and I hardly went a few hours without calling one another about something, no matter how minute or random the moment might be. It wasn't unusual for us to share unpleasant words, but not speaking for multiple days was uncharacteristic of our relationship and was, quite honestly, driving me crazy. However, as miserable as I felt, I was unwilling to be the first person to cave.

As I prepared for an afternoon jog I realized I hadn't grabbed my earbuds and there was no way I could complete my three mile run without music. I backtracked and entered the gym, making my way to my office.

"Hey, boss!" Shannon greeted me with a smile.

"Some guy keeps calling for you, but he won't leave a name. He just calls, asks for you, and when I tell him you're not here he hangs up," Shannon said.

It didn't take a rocket scientist to figure out Quinton was behind the phone calls. He was the only person blowing my phone up on a daily basis. I was beginning to wonder if I should tell someone about his irrational behavior, but what was there to tell? I figured his feelings were bruised and he'd eventually move past our situation.

"Hey Shannon, I'm headed on my run. Be back shortly!" I said as I exited the rear door of my gym which fed into a neighborhood and directly to the trail I visited weekly. I enjoyed running this particular route due to its location and the number of people utilizing the trail. There were usually numerous runners and I rarely had to worry about anyone harassing me. Although I was in the middle of Third Ward, I felt safe. I typically ran with my stun gun tucked inside my running waist belt, along with pepper spray. I was grateful I hadn't been forced to use any of the protection measures I carried around for precaution. I adjusted my wireless earbuds as I began a slow jog.

DJ Screw's "June 27th" blared in my ears as I followed my normal running route. I passed familiar faces and extended a wave accompanied by a smile. Half a mile into my run my heart rate quickened as an eerie feeling told me I was being followed. I turned my head slightly, peering over my shoulder to find a man walking behind me swiftly with a baseball cap tilted down over his face.

Of all days, I was surprisingly alone on this particular part of the trail which never happened. I thought I was being paranoid until I realized the man's speed was increasing as mine did. Before I realized it, I was in a full sprint and terror had taken over. I could hear the footsteps of the man behind me approaching closer as I reached for my taser and shrieked, "Help! Someone help me!"

Before I could remove the taser from my waist belt I heard a familiar voice yell, "Stacey! Don't run from me!"

I bolted along the trail as fast as my legs would allow before feeling a force slam into my back, sending me crashing to the ground and my head bouncing on the concrete. Blood poured from my forehead as a man forcefully flipped my body over. My vision was blurred, prohibiting me from clearly identifying who had assaulted me.

I cried out in a weak, barely audible voice, "Please, please stop. Please don't hurt me."

"Look at what you made me do! Why couldn't you just talk to me!" the man cried out, shaking me by the shoulders aggressively.

"Quinton?" I responded in a fading voice. I recognized his voice but before I could muster up the strength to speak another word my surroundings turned black and my eyes closed.

"Hey! Hey! What are you doing? Get the fuck off of her!"

A voice yelling from a distance caused Quinton to run full speed into the wooded area of the trail, disappearing into the foliage.

"Someone help! Get some help! She's hurt! We need an ambulance!

ANTHONY

"Hey! We need a doctor! She's waking up!"
It was obvious that she was groggy from the nonverbal mumbles she managed to let escape her lips. She tried lifting her eyelids but couldn't manage to keep them open.

"It's okay beautiful, just relax," I tried to sound comforting, hoping my voice wouldn't startle her as her eyelids continued to flutter.

A female nurse rushed into the room. When she reached Stacey's bedside she opened one of her eyes and shone a bright light before opening the other eye and repeating the process.

"What's happening?" she asked, groggily, reaching towards the stitches in her forehead as she grimaced.

"You've been in an accident, ma'am," the female nurse responded.

"You're lucky this nice man found you, any more blood loss and you may not be here," the nurse admitted.

She finally managed to keep her eyes open, and shifted them around the room, landing on me at her bedside.

"Hi, pretty lady," I greeted with a hesitant smile. I'm sure she hadn't expected to see me – especially after she stood me up for our first date.

"Hi, Anthony," she responded, with a hint of embarrassment etched across her face. "Anthony, I'm …I'm really sorry—"

I interrupted her. "Hey, don't worry about it. I'm just glad you're okay. No need for apologies."

She let out a sigh of relief and smiled at me. "Thank you for being so understanding." The expression on her face changed as she *unsuccessfully* tried to sit up.

"How long have I been here? My parents are probably worried sick! Where is my cell phone?"

There was a spike in the heart rate monitor as she tried to raise herself from the hospital bed.

"Whoa, whoa, whoa, I've got everything under control," I assured her, gently guiding her back into the hospital bed.

"I was able to find you on Facebook. I contacted someone I assumed was your best friend due to the number of shared pictures between the two of you. I believe her name is—*Rachel?* She confirmed she is indeed your best friend and that she would reach out to your parents. They're on their way here now."

She must have started to calm down because the heart rate monitor showed signs of stabilization.

"Where the hell did you come from?" she asked, as a weak smile spread across her lips. Just as my returned lingering gaze began to make our interaction increasingly uncomfortable, my attention was snatched to the doorway of the hospital room to see who I assumed was her mother and father bursting in with Rachel following in their footsteps. Her father raced to her bedside and leaned over to gently kiss her cheek.

"Oh Baby Girl, who did this to you?" her father was visibly pissed.

"I'm not sure, Daddy, I'm having a hard time remembering what happened," she admitted.

"Sweet Girl!" her mother tearfully stepped to her bedside and ran her hands over her curly hair.

"Hi Mom," she responded with a smile at the sight of her mother, "What are you doing here?" Her eyes swept over her, and she stared at her as if she hadn't seen her in a while.

"After receiving your text last week, I booked a flight home to surprise you. When I received a phone call from your father I rushed to meet him as soon as I could," her mother admitted.

"You two rode here...together?" she asked, her tone full of confusion, which caused my nose to wrinkle as I attempted to put the pieces together.

"Yes baby, nothing was more important than making it to you," her mother stated.

"Young man, you saved my daughter's life and I don't know how I can ever repay you." Her father approached me with an extended hand. "Are you a friend of my daughter's?" he asked, shaking my hand firmly.

Stacey's eyes widened as I responded, "Not exactly, but I hope to be one day."

I shifted my eyes towards Stacey, catching her gaze momentarily before she quickly averted her eyes to a blank wall. I could see her cheeks turning red beneath her peanut butter skin. I didn't want to make our encounter anymore awkward than it already was, so I figured I'd excuse myself.

"I think I'll head out. It was nice to meet you all, however I wish it could have been under better circumstances," I stated sincerely before glancing back at Stacey, with a quick wink, "Get well soon, beautiful."

STACEY

Anthony excused himself from the room as Rachel shuffled towards me with tear-filled eyes.

"Hey, Stace." Rachel shifted her eyes from me to the floor as she fidgeted with her hot pink fingernails. "I'm really happy you're okay. I don't know what I would do if you weren't," Rachel admitted as the tears pooling in the corner of her eyes finally fell. She wasn't a crier, so I knew she meant every word.

I reached for Rachel and when our hands connected, I squeezed her fingers reassuringly.

"I love you," I said before shutting my eyes and drifting off to sleep.

I slept peacefully through the night with pain medication being administered regularly, keeping me extremely comfortable as my father, mother, and Rachel stayed with me overnight, refusing to leave my side.

"She suffered a mild concussion and may have trouble remembering specific details from the incident," Dr. Crane informed the room.

My parents and Rachel stood silently listening attentively to the doctor.

"She will need to take it easy for a few weeks, but she should make a full recovery," Dr. Crane said as he read the nurse's notes on my chart.

Sighs of relief echoed throughout the room.

"Stacey, sweetie, I think it would be a good idea if you moved a few things to the house for a week or two, and allowed your father and I to care for you," my mother said as she gently rubbed her fingers through my hair like she did when I was a little girl.

"I agree with your mother, Baby Girl. I don't want you out of my sight, not until they've caught the animal who did this to you."

"Mom, Dad, I understand your concern but I'm ready to go home. I'm safe in the penthouse, no one can get past the doorman without consent," I reminded my parents.

"I don't know, Stace," Rachel sighed, an unsettled expression plaguing her face.

"Are you guys kidding me? What am I supposed to do, live my life in fear because some coward decided to randomly attack me?" I questioned.

My family sighed because they knew this was a battle they wouldn't win.

"Fine, if you want to go home, I'm coming with you," Rachel decided. "There is plenty of room in the penthouse. I'll set up in the guest bedroom for a week."

"Rachel! You have to work, the drive from my place is simply too far."

"I have plenty of PTO. I'm taking a week off and there is nothing you can do about it," Rachel said, crossing her arms and pursing her lips.

I rolled my eyes but eventually agreed to allow Rachel to invade my space for a week. It would keep everyone off my back and truth be told, I could really use the company, especially since Savior was back in LA.

6
STACEY

Houston Police detectives questioned me several times regarding my attack but I couldn't remember anything. The last thing I recalled was being pushed to the ground and waking up in the hospital. No matter how many times they asked, my story never changed because I honestly didn't remember.

"You hungry?" Rachel asked, as she scrolled through Netflix.

"I could eat," I responded, swiping through social media with my body tucked under a throw blanket on the couch.

"Stacey, I was wondering, did the detectives mention anything about recovering your cell phone?" Rachel inquired.

"Not yet," I responded with a raised brow because why in the hell hadn't I thought of that? I turned to face Rachel. "Why do you ask?"

"Well, I was thinking, maybe you could request a copy of your call and text log from the cell phone company. That might give us a clue about what happened," Rachel said, her tone hopeful and sincere.

"Oh, okay, Inspector Gadget! Let me find out you're working for the CIA!" I chuckled.

"I know right! I surprise myself sometimes!" Rachel brushed off each of her shoulders congratulating herself as she walked past me into the guest bedroom.

I honestly hadn't thought about pulling my phone records and the detectives hadn't mentioned pinging the device to find out where it might be. My train of thought was interrupted when the doorbell rang.

"Are you expecting anyone, Stace?" Rachel yelled from the guest bedroom.

"No..." I spoke softly because I seemed to get a piercing headache anytime my voice elevated above a normal talking range. Rachel answered the door, but didn't say a word. I strolled slowly to the door and when I raised my eyes to see who was there, I smiled; relieved to see Savior.

However, Rachel stood guard in the doorway blocking him from entering with a blank stare on her face. I knew she wasn't going to allow him in until I gave her the okay.

"How the hell do you keep getting past the doorman?" Rachel asked with a Doberman stance and a Pitbull attitude.

"It's okay, Rachel, you can let him in," I said, my voice barely above a whisper.

Rachel rolled her eyes hard and stepped aside, allowing Savior to pass through the door. He gave her a side eye as he sauntered past her and approached me, scanning me from head to toe.

"What the fuck! What happened to you? Who did this? I've been calling you." Savior's diarrhea of the mouth gave me very little time to answer.

"I'm fine, Savior. I just had… a little accident." I managed to slip in a few words before he snatched the reins, giving me limited opportunity to speak.

"You couldn't pick up the phone to tell me that?" Savior's tone was vicious.

"Her phone was stolen by the nigga who attacked her!" Rachel blurted out purposely trying to get a rise out of Savior.

Mission accomplished. Savior's body visibly tensed and his eyes narrowed in on me as his head cranked slightly to one side.

"Stacey, can we talk in your room please? In private?" he said, directing his loathsome tone in Rachel's direction.

She folded her arms and fixed her gaze on me.

"You good?" Rachel asked, rolling her eyes at Savior, showing very little effort to hide her aggravation.

"Yeah, girl, I'm okay. I'm in good hands with Savior," I said.

Rachel rolled her eyes one more time for good measure and turned on her heel. "Asshole," she muttered ambling into the guest bedroom slamming the door behind her.

"Let's go to my room," I whispered to Savior, in an attempt to keep our conversation from Rachel.

"Stacey, you're going to have to help me understand what's going on because I'm confused as hell right now." Savior's voice was unnerving and caused me to take a step away from him.

"There's really not that much to tell. I was on my weekly run and got attacked from behind on a desolate part of the trail. Another runner found me in the midst of the attack and scared the guy away. I couldn't call because apparently the attacker stole my phone. I've been meaning to go get another one, but I've been too tired to leave the house."

I was defeated. I had told the same story over and over again and was tired of reliving and rehashing the moment.

"Is there something I can do for you? Anything you need?" Savior seemed genuinely concerned as he grabbed me by my elbow closing the gap I had created between us moments earlier, as he pulled me down to the bed.

"Honestly, Savior, Rachel has been extremely helpful, so I don't really need anything," I admitted, shrugging my shoulders and staring at him.

"Speaking of Rachel, what the fuck is her problem?" Savior asked, his eyes shooting daggers at me as if I was responsible for her discontent towards him.

I laughed because I knew my best friend was one of those people you either loved or loved to hate.

"She's just extremely overprotective, that's all," I said.

"You haven't been telling her our business, have you?" Savior asked, placing a firm grip on my thigh.

I scrunched my face in annoyance. "Savior, you're hurting me!" I pushed his hand away from my thigh aggressively as I stood from the bed.

"I mean...she is my best friend, Savior, and you did tell me you wanted to see where our relationship is headed. That's definitely something you share with your closest friend. Is there a problem?"

I was extremely pissed. Who the hell did he think he was? I wasn't sure what peeved me more, the intonation of his harsh words against Rachel or the fact that he gripped the hell out of my leg like a damn fool.

Savior ran his hand over his beard. "Nah, ain't no problem. I'm just not real big on having my business circulate in the streets."

"Savior, you're in the NBA. When is your business ever *not* circulating in the streets? I mean…what's really going on?" I asked with raised shoulders and upturned hands.

Savior shook his head and blew out a disgruntled breath before brushing past me belligerently, almost knocking me down in the process. "I knew you weren't ready for this! I don't have time for fucking games."

My eyes widened in disbelief.

"Savior, what's wrong? I'm all the way confused right now."

I had no idea what had gotten into him or what had caused this sudden schizophrenic episode, but I should have told his ass to leave. Instead, my silly love-struck ass allowed him to explain.

"Confused about what, Stacey? The fact that I don't want my fucking business in the streets? If we're going to do this, I need you to be a grown woman about the shit and shut the fuck up to your little friends about us."

I was paralyzed. Savior had never raised his voice at me, and he had certainly never told me to *shut the fuck up*.

A series of lock knocks interrupted before I could respond.

"Stace! Are you okay in there?" Rachel called through the door.

She must've heard Savior yelling and she was not going to stop banging on the door until I answered.

"Where the fuck are you going?" Savior asked as he balled his hands into tight fists.

"I'm just letting Rachel know that I'm okay. She worries about me, that's all." I tried to deescalate the situation but Savior seemed to be purposely unleashing the most lethal version of himself with no regard for how I felt.

"Yeah, well make sure you let her know that I'm here now and I got this!" Savior growled.

I slowly made my way over to the locked bedroom door. I hadn't realized how badly I was hurting until now. I was past due for my pain medicine and the pointless argument that had ensued with Savior was only contributing to the pain surging through my body, making my head feel as if it might pop off my shoulder at any moment. Rachel was mid-knock when I gently pulled the door open.

"Bitch, are you okay? I heard that nigga raise his voice. You better calm your bitch ass down because if you don't, I'll do it for you!" Rachel blurted out deliberately looking around me to make eye contact with Savior.

"This nigga has a fucking name and I got your bitch, bitch!" Savior snarled at Rachel charging towards the door aggressively.

Tension gripped my body as fear flooded my core from the ferocity of the words being flung between my best friend and my boyfriend — or my soon to be boyfriend — or hell, I didn't know what Savior was to me, but I knew that I loved him and I wanted this brutal exchange to stop.

"I wonder if your fans know how much of an asshole you are!" Rachel snapped, placing her cellphone in Savior's face. "Hey, world! This is Savior James, attempting to fight a woman! Is this who you want endorsing you, Nike? Huh? Is this your golden boy?" Rachel mocked as she captured Savior on video.

I tried to wedge myself between the two of them, but with Savior's formidable size and Rachel's unrelenting persistence, along with feeling like thousands of microneedles were being plunged into my skull, my efforts were insignificant and did little to separate the two active volcanoes erupting in front of me.

"Rachel, please, it's okay. I've got it, I promise." I tried to comfort Rachel in a gentle whisper because it was the only amount of energy my body could render. It wasn't until Savior attempted to slap Rachel's phone from her hand, which resulted in her springing into the air swinging wildly, her tiny fists connecting with his jaw that I felt my body internally fail me.

My legs buckled and before I could catch myself, I was slumped awkwardly on my bedroom floor, the walls closing in on me as total darkness engulfed the brightly lit room.

"You muthafucka!" Rachel cried, delivering a running start punch to Savior's midsection as she sprinted past him, falling to her knees at my side. I felt a stiff hand against my cheek followed by a stinging sensation as I blinked heavily.

"Bitch! Did you just slap me?" I grumbled, my words slurred and slow and as my vision cleared, I slowly raised my hand to caress my cheek.

Rachel let out a half giggle, half cry as she wrapped her arms around me. "Oh my God! I'm so glad you're okay! I'm sorry I slapped you, it was the only thing I could think of to wake you up." Rachel shrugged slowly, an apologetic look adorning her face.

A sluggish smile pulled at the corner of my lip and I shook my head slightly, still sprawled across the floor. My eyes widened. "Savior! Where is Savior?"

Rachel rolled her eyes as she gradually helped me from the floor and onto the bed.

"Stacey, you really have to stop this shit! He's gone! As soon as he thought I was going to post that damn video, he hauled ass out of here! And it probably didn't help that I threatened to call my brother to come whoop his ass if he didn't leave!" Rachel said deviously, as she gloated, shrugging her shoulders nonchalantly.

Typical Savior, always running. Asshole.

7
STACEY

My feelings were crushed. Seven days had passed since Savior left my penthouse and I hadn't heard a damn peep from him, not a single word. I could be dead for all he knew. Damn jerk. I loathed that I allowed myself to crumble at the mere thought of this man. It made me feel weak, vulnerable, involuntarily exposed and I needed to get him out of my system.

I needed those seven days of rest. My body was exhausted and thanked me for the relaxation. I was beginning to feel like myself again and had finally weaned myself off of my pain medicine. I had just stepped out of the shower when my landline rang. And yes, I knew landlines were predominantly nonexistent, but my father was unwilling to compromise. He always said, "Those damn cell phones are the devil! If you have a home, you need a landline!" I guess it was just the "old-school" in him.

Ms. Ann's name flashed across my caller ID and I snickered in preparation for her foolishness.

"Hi, Ms. Ann! How are you?" I said sheepishly, confident she was unhappy with me for missing a week's worth of our personal training sessions, and aside from that, she was used to checking in on me. So, not hearing from me at all, was unusual for her.

"Oh no, darling! Don't hey Ms. Ann me! Just where in the hell have you been? Aht! And before you say anything, unless you're preparing to tell me you've missed all of our sessions this week because you're on a remote island getting your back blown out by some young, handsome, eligible bachelor, then I don't wanna hear it!"

I stared at the cordless phone with my mouth wide open because I wished I was getting my back blown out, but no! I had been at home resting with too much down time, which inevitably left my brain idle enough to think about Savior every moment I sat home forlorn by his disappearance.

"So listen! I think I may have someone for you. He's pretty well off, owns his own business, and has a beautiful penis!" Ms. Ann gushed.

I gasped, "Ms. Ann! You're terrible! Absolutely terrible." I chuckled at her for being...well...Ms. Ann. I tilted my head as something she said set off a light bulb in my brain and triggered me to ask, "Ms. Ann...how do you know his penis is beautiful?"

"Oh, darling! I've slept with him, but I don't mind passing him along," she said.

"Ew, Ms. Ann!" I placed the palm of my hand over my forehead in disbelief.

"Oh, honey please! All dick is community dick until it's married dick, and even then sometimes...it's still community dick!" she howled in laughter.

"Bye, Ms. Ann! I'll be back in the gym next week," I said as I laughed and hung up the phone.

No sooner than I hung up the phone, I heard my doorbell ringing. Randy was on the verge of getting fired. I neglected to look out the peephole as I swung the door open, agitated due to my peace being disturbed and almost dropped the damn cordless phone when I opened the door to see Savior staring back at me.

He peered around my body into the kitchen and quickly shifted his eyes to the living room. "Is your crazy ass friend here?" he asked cautiously.

"N-no. She uh...she went home to grab a few things and to run some errands," I managed to stammer.

"Look Stacey, I know you're probably pissed at me. I wouldn't blame you, but your girl has some bullshit on her phone that could really fuck up my life, and she threatened to post it if I didn't leave."

I knew he was telling the truth. Rachel despised Savior and would utilize extreme measures to get rid of his ass. I wasn't upset with her because she genuinely believed she was helping me, but with Savior standing there, staring me down with those damn sienna brown, puppy dog eyes begging for my forgiveness, Rachel's stunt felt less like help and more like meddling. Savior invited himself in, invading my personal space, the spice and warm aroma of his cologne assaulted my nostrils as he walked towards me, backing me against a wall.

"I'm sorry, baby. I need you to forgive me. This past week has been miserable for me and I was a coward for leaving you," he admitted, brushing the curls from my face. My chest rose and fell as I allowed my eyes to close, willing myself to make him leave.

Just tell him to get the fuck out! Tell him now! Just go and don't come back!

I slowly moved my eyes up Savior's massive frame until our eyes met. Against my better judgement, I placed my hands on his toned triceps, barely making it even a third of the way around his muscular arms.

"Tell me what you need, baby," Savior said in a tone that made my head spin, as the butterflies in my stomach aided in eliminating every transgression Savior had ever committed against me.

"What do you want, Stacey?" he asked again. This time his voice was giftwrapped in passion, lust, and yearning.

"Something I probably shouldn't have," I responded as I tilted my head and bit the corner of my bottom lip.

"But what about your head?" he asked as he bent down to kiss my stitches.

"I'll be okay…as long as you're gentle," I replied, closing my eyes beneath the touch of his tender kisses on my forehead.

I needed to feel him inside of me, but I was also keenly aware of how fragile my body was. I wouldn't be able to handle Savior if he went animal on me, and I'd potentially end up back in the hospital with a broken vagina and another concussion.

He slid his hand in the front of my boy shorts as he searched my eyes for a sign of doubt. There was none there. He went deeper into my shorts until he found my treasure. My body shuddered as my eyes closed and my head fell back. Our argument, and how Savior had treated Rachel, was now forgiven. My heart and my pussy were exonerating him of all his wrong doings and I was his damn fool again. Shit. No point in me lying. I never stopped being his fool.

His eyes were glued to me.

"You want me to stop?" he whispered.

My chest continued to rise and fall as I sucked in air.

"No," I moaned.

Savior rotated my pearl with two long, thick fingers until he finally slid them inside of me. His presence was intoxicating and I was anticipating feeling his dick penetrate my damn soul! I needed him. After the week I was having, I just needed to feel good. He bent down and snaked his left arm around my lower back picking me up with little effort. I wrapped my legs around his waist and with one arm he carried me to my bedroom, walking to my dresser and swiping everything to the floor with his free arm.

"Tell me what you need," Savior demanded for the third time, this time with more aggression in his voice, intensifying my desire to have him inside of me.

He just wanted to hear me say it. He wanted to know that I needed him.

"You, Savior. I need you," I moaned.

"You need me to what?" Savior said, raising an eyebrow.

I sighed at his senseless torture, never averting my eyes as I narrowed my gaze on him.

"I need you to eat my pussy and make me cum all over your face. I need you to fuck me...gently. I want it so deep inside of me that I have to say the safe word. I want you to — "

Before I could finish my words Savior's lips were in the crevice of my neck. He licked from the side of my neck, up the side of my cheek, and when he reached my lips, he licked those, too. He was nasty and I needed it. He pulled my legs up until I was in a narrow v-position on the dresser. I pushed myself up, allowing Savior to roll my boy shorts up my legs that were resting on his chest. When he rolled my panties past my ankles, he gathered them in his hands and placed them to his nose. He took in a deep breath and licked his lips before staring back at me and sliding my panties into his pocket. *Shit…I really liked those panties.*

He grabbed both of my ankles that were resting over his shoulders and spread them apart. With my legs now in a wide V floating in the air Savior stated, "Hold your legs up. I'll tell you when you can put them down."

I was in a fucking yoga position, holding myself up on the dresser with my legs wide open. *Shit! I guess those Bikram yoga classes actually did pay off!*

He examined my body, peering between my legs and back up to my face. Without blinking he placed two fingers into his mouth and skillfully penetrated my middle, causing my legs to fall limp as I placed them onto the dresser.

"Did I tell you to put your legs down?" he asked boldly.

I shook my head no.

"Well then you've got three seconds to get them back up."

Savior's fingers were still inside of my pussy, moving in and out relentlessly. I engaged my core muscles and lifted my legs back into the air as I moaned, "*Shit*, Savior!"

Still working me with his fingers, he leaned closer and whispered into my ear, "Whose pussy is this?"

I hesitated and stared blankly at Savior because although I had forgiven him for leaving me days prior, I hadn't forgotten. I wasn't going to answer him; and he couldn't make me.

He immediately recognized my defiance as he inclined his neck in response to my silence, a sinister grin pulling at one corner of his mouth.

"Oh, okay." Savior chuckled.

He plunged his fingers deeper inside of me, rotating my clit with his thumb and pinching my nipple with his free hand. And not a gentle pinch, either. He intended to cause me pain, but it wasn't unbearable and it awarded him the satisfaction he was searching for.

"Yours, baby! It's your pussy!" The words escaped my lips quickly as my legs trembled in the air.

"What the fuck! Who is yours?" Savior frowned as he slid his fingers deeper into my pussy moving them in a come here motion, hitting my g-spot.

"I'm going to ask you one more time. Whose pussy is this?" he asked with a straight face.

"Savior's! Savior's pussy!" I screamed because I was about to cum all over his fingers and he knew it, but before I reached my climax he pulled his fingers out of me and backed away.

"Legs. Down." Savior demanded as he turned his back and walked towards the bed. My legs dropped from exhaustion and I craved him.

"Baby, why did you stop? What's wrong?" I asked, confusion plaguing my thoughts.

"You said you wanted to cum all over my face, didn't you? Well, come on."

I hopped my happy ass off that dresser so fast, you would have thought I was running from something as I made my way over to him. He positioned himself upright with his back leaning against the headboard. I straddled him as he welcomed me, whispering, "Come sit that pussy on my face."

I felt my temperature rise as my pussy began to pulse. Imagining Savior's warm tongue and perfectly soft lips made my nipples harden. I propped my right leg on a mound of large decorative pillows positioned on my bed, looking down as I placed one hand on top of his head, and my other hand on the headboard for balance.

He placed his arms between my legs, grabbing me from the back, pushing my middle towards his face, as he placed a warm gentle kiss onto my smooth lips before slowly parting them with his tongue causing my legs to quiver.

"Ahhhhh," I moaned as my head fell back, my pelvis grinding against his tongue.

He flattened his tongue, making deep, firm circles around my clit. As he inserted one finger into my pussy, simultaneously he sucked my pearl causing me to squirm blissfully. The pressure building in my core coupled with the constant electrical current pulsing through my vagina caused me to push away from Savior as I unsuccessfully attempted to escape his grasp.

"What are you doing to me, Savior?" I moaned, convinced he was on the verge of stealing my vagina. He slid down positioning himself flat on the bed and I was now completely on top of his face as he slapped my ass. Hard. I rode his face sliding back and forth, bouncing up and down, and rotating in circles. I gripped his head with both hands, grinding so hard I was sure he couldn't breathe, but the intensity building inside of my body wouldn't allow me to stop.

"I'm... I'm... I'm cumming," I moaned as Savior placed a death grip on my thighs preventing me from evading his clutch. Fireworks exploded behind my closed eyelids. The dark room illuminated as screams of pleasure escaped my lips and Savior kept a steady pace with his tongue until my body had nothing more to give.

I rolled over on my back staring at the ceiling at what seemed to be clouds, sunshine and fucking rainbows.

"Now what was that other thing you said?" Savior brushed one hand down his face and over his thick beard. "You want it so deep inside you that you have to use the safe word?"

Savior reminded me of my own words, forcing me to regret my overly ambitious sentiments.

What the hell had I gotten myself into?

I nodded hesitantly because I wasn't one to back down from a challenge. He spread my legs, pushing them back until my toes met the bed. Everything my body had to offer was on full display, as he bent down, giving my pussy an extra slippery, sloppy kiss before asking, "you remember what to say, right?"

He was referring to our safe word that had proven beneficial over the course of our two year situationship. Grabbing his penis and rubbing the tip around my wetness, he entered me slowly. I flexed my walls compressing his dick, causing him to groan and drive deeper into my depths. He long stroked me, sinking further into me with each thrust. My legs still pinned to the bed by his enormous hands on the back of my thighs, I gasped when he plunged into me over and over again.

"Ohhhh shit!" Savior growled as he mercilessly stroked me.

"Ahhhh, Savior! Savior!" I screamed in a painful, yet gratified tone, causing him to pump harder and deeper, grinning as he looked down at me.

My eyes were glued to the action as I watched us in wonderment. He finally unpinned my legs to free his hands, grabbing one of my breasts with one hand and rotating my clit with the other hand.

"You know this is my pussy, don't you?" he asked while still stroking me.

"Yes! Ahhhhh yes! It's yours," I moaned in agreement.

"So it's time to leave these other peasant ass niggas alone," he said, his face more serious than I could ever recall seeing.

I wasn't sure what to do. I was spread eagle, being dicked down and this was the moment Savior decided to take my pussy captive?

He flipped me over aggressively and whispered in my ear, "I'm not stopping until you say it."

He dove into me tirelessly, grabbing my waist and thrusting himself into me as his dick disappeared and reappeared over and over again. I could feel my body tensing and knew that I was about to cum *again*. He penetrated me so deeply I tried to inch forward for a moment of relief but he wrapped both hands around my hair making a ponytail of my curls.

The sound of my ass slamming onto his dick as he released one hand from my ponytail to wrap around my neck aggressively. I felt myself letting go. I was squirting, making a mess of my bedsheets, the euphoric feeling overwhelming me. When Savior felt the wetness seeping from my pussy he knew I was depleted but he didn't stop. He fucked me doggystyle until I came *again*!

"Savior! Baby, I can't take it, fuck! What are you doing to me?" I moaned.

He ignored my pleas because he only stopped for one word when he was in this mode. He flipped me onto my back without ever pulling out, placing both hands on my throat as he stroked me unyieldingly, causing my breasts to move in a circular motion from the force. I was lost in Savior's wrath, indulging delightfully in every inch he awarded me, but after cumming multiple times, I had expended all of my energy. His hands on my throat were making the reality of my concussion set in as I felt lightheaded.

"Fuck!" Savior growled.

"Cinnamon!" I shrieked as loudly as my vocal cords would allow with the pressure of Savior's hands around my throat.

He immediately released my neck and grabbed his dick as it jumped in his hand, covering my stomach with his warm semen. I watched Savior hovering over me, eyes closed, dick in hand moving up and down his shaft, lightly quivering as he finally collapsed on top of my body.

8
STACEY

"You alright?" Savior's deep voice murmured into my neck as he lay on top of my body.

It had been a while since he'd heard me scream our safe word. Although I'd been the one to request it, rough sex was really something Savior enjoyed and I didn't want to disappoint him. His demeanor had become increasingly aggressive the last few times I'd seen him, especially during sex, hence my confusion when he wanted to make love to me a few weeks prior. I had every reason to believe he would have allowed me to pass out if not for our safe word. He was a stickler for the rules when he was in his dominant mode. I knew what Savior and I shared was unhealthy, every aspect of our situationship would be considered toxic by any clinical standpoint. It wasn't the sex. I enjoyed sex in any form, even if it was a tad bit rough, it was everything else. The way he gripped my leg a little too aggressively, leaving bruises from his forceful touch. His aggressive tone that seemed to be becoming increasingly belligerent each time he visited me.

If I didn't know any better, I'd think Savior was releasing his frustrations on me, but I couldn't figure out why. I hadn't mentioned the slight shoves, the violent wrist snatches, or his crass tone to anyone, especially Rachel. Oh God! She would definitely try to kill him. And the thing was, I knew better. I wasn't some dumb, naïve girl. I wasn't oblivious to the fact that I needed to tell Savior to get the fuck out of my life and never come back! But what if I could get him to change? What if he was willing to change for me?

"Hello, are you okay?" he asked again, yanking me from my daydream.

"You took all of my damn energy, Savior, I was about to pass the hell out," I said, rubbing my neck gently where his hands had been.

He smiled. "I told you I wouldn't stop until I heard you say it." He reached down, playfully groping at my vagina.

"Boy! You are on punishment! Hands off!" I grinned.

"Yeah right, if I wanted to put my mouth on it right now, you wouldn't say no and you know it," Savior teased.

"Wait...are you offering?" I raised an eyebrow and spread my legs.

"See what I mean," he chuckled.

I giggled as I reached for my cell phone that I typically kept on the nightstand. *Shit! I don't have my damn phone*, I thought. I rolled over gazing at Savior with pleading eyes.

"Savie-pooh, do you think we can go grab me a new cell phone? I'm kind of going crazy without one. Rachel was planning on taking me when she gets back, but since you're here, why not?"

"Uhhh, you know Stacey, I try to stay low key when I'm in the city. Paparazzi and shit be following me. I just don't know if that's the best idea," Savior responded.

I twisted my damn face and shot him a grimace that read *what the fuck*?

"So...let me get this straight. You can pop up here whenever the fuck you want to, fuck me damn near unconscious but you can't be seen with me in public?" I was visibly pissed!

"Stacey! Don't start this shit, that's not what the fuck I said," Savior growled.

"I'm not a fucking fool, that's exactly what you're saying, Savior. Just last week you wanted to 'see where this could go'. What the fuck do you think that means? Because I can assure you never leaving the walls of my penthouse ain't what I had in mind!"

Savior turned away from me and laughed. I inclined my neck as my nostrils flared and pure rage filled me from head to toe.

"Really, Savior?" I scoffed in disbelief.

"I didn't come here for this bullshit, Stacey. You're stressing me the fuck out and I've got other shit I can be doing rather than listening to you complain," Savior said in an unperturbed tone that made it unequivocally clear that he didn't give a damn about what I was saying.

"Get out! Now!" I shouted without actually processing the words flying from my mouth.

Savior snapped his neck towards me as he raised both eyebrows, shocked by my tone and my words. I had never raised my voice to Savior. I just didn't, even when he did, but I was tired of his bullshit. He had to go and I didn't give a damn where he went, as long as it wasn't my house. I stood unmoving; arms folded across my chest staring daggers into his eyes.

"Hold up, hold up! Stop!" he tried to deescalate the brewing argument.

"No, Savior! I'm tired of this shit! It's been two — " before I could finish my sentence his lips were against mine in a passionate plea of silence.

"Stacey Ambria Hill. Stop! We can go get you a phone, baby. Damn!"

I threw on a pair of black tights and an oversized long sleeved shirt. I scrunched the sleeves of my shirt up to my elbows after lacing up a pair of black and pink Jordan 1s. I strapped my Louis Vuitton crossbody bag across my chest and fluffed my curls.

"Ready to go?" I asked in a chipper tone.

Shit, who was I kidding, this was our first time leaving the house together in public. I was fucking ecstatic. I wasn't even sure why. I knew this was just another instance providing me with a false sense of security because no matter the angle I chose to look at our situation from, Savior was bad news and I knew it. That didn't stop my desire to have him. If I was honest with myself, I had never met a man that I couldn't have. Never. Until Savior James came along. When I was introduced to Savior two years ago, by his cousin who I happened to attend college with, there was an instant, undeniable magnetic connection. I hadn't been able to shake his toxic ass since then, even though I really, really wanted to. But it seemed no matter the amount of effort I exert toward my goal of snagging Savior, nothing worked. Even worse, it made me want him more. Shit! Was I the toxic one? Persistently chasing an emotionally unavailable man!

Savior and I made our way to the parking garage to my BMW. I hopped in the driver's side and Savior sat on the passenger side flipping his hoodie over his head. I glanced in his direction and rolled my eyes. At least I got him to leave the penthouse with me, so I decided not to fuss about him making an attempt to hide himself. Before backing out of my parking spot I glared at the car parked next to me. I had the strangest feeling that someone was staring at me behind the dark tint, but it was impossible to be certain.

"You okay?" Savior asked, snapping me out of my daze.

"Yeah, I'm fine. Just trippin', I guess. I haven't driven since the accident. I think I'm just a little jittery," I admitted.

"Here, switch places with me," Savior offered.

I stepped out of the car and passed the suspicious vehicle deliberately with unhurried steps, attempting to peer into the car without appearing obvious. Savior drove, but flashes of the suspicious car bombarded my mind. I had never seen it before and I was pretty familiar with most of the cars because tenants had assigned parking spots. Before I could voice my concern to Savior, we arrived at the cellphone store and I quickly pushed my concerns to the back of my mind.

"When we get you all set up, your new phone will have all the text messages and phone calls from your old phone since you backed everything up in the cloud. Once you sign in with your email, everything will be as good as new," Rick, the cellphone sales associate assured me.

Savior was adamant about paying for my new phone, even though I didn't need him to.

"Don't think that because you purchased this phone that you get any special privileges. Don't let me find you trying to go through my shit!" I playfully nudged Savior on the way out of the cell phone store.

"I told you to let those other muthafuckas know that it's a wrap anyway. So me going through anything you own shouldn't be a problem," Savior stated boldly. Even though he prefaced the statement with a smile, I knew deep down that he meant every single word.

Flashing lights caught me by surprise as we exited the cell phone store. Paparazzi swarmed me and Savior.

"Excuse me! Mr. James, is this your new girlfriend?"

"Mr. James! Over here! Could we have an official statement, is this your girlfriend?"

"Savior! What are you doing here in Houston?"

"Excuse me, ma'am, are you Savior James' new love interest? Can you tell us how long you two have been together?"

I was stunned. I couldn't move or speak. The flashing lights, dozens of cameras, and questions flying from every direction confused me.

"She's just a friend. I'm still very much single," Savior admitted to the paparazzi with a smile.

His words stole my breath and almost knocked me to the ground. My head spun as the sour taste of bile filled my throat.

I've got to get out of here.

I ducked and dodged my way through the paparazzi until I was able to sprint to my car leaving Savior, who seemed to be enjoying the shit show transpiring with the paparazzi, behind. I, on the other hand, felt devastated as my heart punched against my chest. When I finally spotted my car, I fumbled with my purse looking for my keys until I remembered that Savior had drove. *Damnit*! I leaned against my car, closing my eyes as I whispered to myself, "don't cry, don't cry, do not cry." I whispered over and over until I opened my eyes to find Quinton standing in front of me.

"Oh my God! Quinton! What are you doing here?" I shrieked in shock.

"Just doing some shopping. I saw you over here and you looked a little upset, so I just wanted to check on you." Quinton's voice sounded sincere, but my intuition triggered a silent alarm in my brain, causing me to believe bumping into him *here* was no accident.

"Oh, that was sweet of you," I smiled, searching my purse for the pepper spray I carried with me. I couldn't remember anything from my accident, but when my intuition raised red flags, I listened…*sometimes*. Savior being the exception. My subtle search was interrupted by Quinton.

"Say, what happened to your head?" he motioned towards my stitches with furrowed brows.

"You know, I'm not really sure. I was attacked by someone when I was running but I don't remember much," I admitted truthfully in a sly tone as my eyes narrowed on Quinton. I purposely made my suspicion known once my fingers located the full bottle of pepper spray inside my bag and my finger settled on the trigger.

"I'm so sorry. You know I'm always here for you if you need me. You know that, right?" Quinton questioned.

"Yeah Quinton, I know," I replied, my eyes glued to his and my finger still pressed to the pepper spray trigger conccaled in my bag.

Quinton was a nice guy, but he wasn't my guy and he was much too clingy for my liking. I probably shouldn't have slept with him the last time because he never seemed to understand that I only called on him when I was bored or had an itch that Savior couldn't scratch because he was back home in LA. But this sneaking suspicion that he could have been the one behind my attack had me on edge. I needed him to get the fuck away from me.

"Quinton, you should probably go. I'm here with someone and I wouldn't want this to get awkward," I said, shifting my eyes momentarily to the corner I knew Savior would round at any moment.

I couldn't believe I was still trying to make Savior feel comfortable after the bullshit he had just pulled. Just as I finished my sentence Savior turned the corner, walking in sync with the paparazzi, answering questions, smiling, and putting on a show like the celebrity he was. He stopped mid-stride when he saw Quinton standing in front of me.

"Stacey, who the fuck is this nigga?" Savior's chest puffed out as his hands balled into fists with no regard for the paparazzi filming him. Quinton grinned and placed his hand on his belt slightly revealing the pistol he kept on his hip. He was licensed to carry in the state of Texas, which immediately caused me to grab Savior by the arm and pull him back for fear of his safety.

Savior returned Quinton's menacing grin at the touch of my hands on his arm. "I'll catch up with you soon," he said to Quinton, trying not to make a scene.

"Looking forward to it," Quinton shot back with a chuckle as he turned to walk away.

"Savior! Unlock the doors!" I yelled, pulling at the car door handle.

Just as I prepared to step into the car Quinton yelled, "Stacey! Don't run from me! I'm here when you need me!" My eyes widened and I began to hyperventilate. My chest rose and fell as tears pricked my eyes. There was no way this could be a coincidence. I didn't remember much from my attack but his words rang clear in my memory.

"Don't run from me, Stacey."

I could hear the voice of my attacker clearly.

"Yo, who the fuck was that, Stacey?" Savior screamed as if he had the right to say anything to me at all. I cut my eyes at him without saying a word.

"You sleeping with him?" he asked.

I didn't respond.

"Stacey! Are you fucking that nigga?"

I closed my eyes and ignored Savior. I blocked out every word as if he wasn't speaking at all. When he pulled into my parking spot, I held my hand out.

"My car key, please!" was all I said, refusing to make eye contact with him.

"Not until you talk to me," Savior responded in a smug tone.

"Fine, Savior, keep the damn key. I have a spare!"

He jumped out of the car and caught me by the elbow. "I don't know who the fuck you think you're talking to, but please don't make me remind you! You're going to talk to me! I'm not taking no for an answer!" Savior responded.

He was hurting me. His firm grip around my arm was paralyzing and when he dug his nails into my skin like the bitch I knew he was deep down, I screamed.

"Ouch! Savior, please! That hurts!" I yelled, looking into his eyes, and when I saw no signs of remorse I became frightened.

I snatched away from the giant of a man with such aggression that I stumbled backwards and hit the ground. When I lifted my arm to inspect where he was holding me, the visible drag marks where my skin had been torn began to drip blood.

"Baby, you're acting crazy! Get off the ground. You have a concussion, you're going to hurt yourself again," Savior scoffed, as if I was the damn problem.

I was wailing on the parking garage floor. A surge of emotions invaded my body and I had finally reached my breaking point at the realization that Savior was stringing me along. Although I wasn't sure, Quinton was most likely the man who had attacked me and I had no fucking idea what to do about it. The man was an attorney, how was I supposed to compete with that? When Savior bent down to help me stand up, I slapped his hands.

"Get the hell off of me, Savior! Just leave!"

"I'm not leaving you, Stacey. You're trippin'! What is all this for?" Savior asked with the audacity to actually seem confused.

Just as I pushed his outstretched hands away from me for a second time, Rachel pulled into the parking garage and parked her car in my second assigned parking spot. The way she flew from the parked car, you would have sworn this bitch had superpowers!

"Get the fuck away from her, Savior! Now!" Rachel screamed running towards me.

Savior scowled. "Bitch! Didn't I tell you to watch how the fuck you talk to me!" He charged towards Rachel but before he entered her personal space, she grabbed the 9mm Glock she kept concealed in a belly waistband under her shirt. Savior stopped in his tracks and held his hands up in surrender.

"Wait, wait, wait!" Savior repeated rapidly, visibly shaking.

"No, go ahead! What was that shit you were talking?" Rachel said calmly, inching closer to Savior.

"Stacey, get this crazy bitch before she does something stupid!" Savior said, trying to keep a calm demeanor.

Rachel pointed the Glock at his kneecap. "Something stupid like this?" She grinned watching Savior squirm.

"That's my fucking livelihood! Are you crazy!?" Savior screeched, no longer making an attempt to stay calm.

I stood to my feet, inching my way over to Rachel.

"Rachel, sis…best friend, put the gun down, please," I pleaded in the sweetest, most sincere tone I could muster up. "Savior, call your bodyguard and have him pick you up." I looked over to Savior as I slowly pointed the gun to the ground with Rachel's hand still on the trigger.

"So you choosing this crazy bitch over me?" Savior's voice was low and irritated as he pointed at Rachel, his eyes narrowing in on me.

"Savior, now is not the time for a fucking power struggle or for your damn ego to get in the way! Leave!" I said through clenched teeth.

"Fuck this! This makes two people that have pulled a gun on me over your little ass today. You're not even worth the trouble. Lose my fucking number."

Savior walked through the parking garage into the building and Rachel wore a look of satisfaction.

"Fuck that nigga, Stacey!" she stated without remorse.

"Rachel! What the hell? Are you serious?" I couldn't believe what just happened.

"Look, I pulled up, saw you crying on the ground fighting this nigga. What did you expect? I wasn't even going to draw on him until his humongous ass charged at me! I wasn't about to let that big handed muthafucka hit me and knock all my fucking fronts out!" Rachel stared at me and we both burst into laughter.

"This shit isn't funny, Rachel! You threatened to shoot the nigga's kneecap!" I said, stunned.

"Ahhhhh hush! The damn gun wasn't even loaded. I took the clip out before I jumped out of the car. Just needed to scare his big ass! That's all. Now start talking! You have a lot of explaining to do!" Rachel giggled.

I wrapped my arm around Rachel's and leaned my head on her shoulder. "Girl, we're going to need wine because you're not going to believe this shit."

9
STACEY

A week passed and I hadn't spoken to Savior. I wasn't purposely avoiding him; he just hadn't called and neither had I. Not to mention, Rachel refused to go back to her apartment after learning about my suspicions towards Quinton. She didn't feel comfortable leaving me alone.

"When do you think you'll be ready to go back to work?" Rachel asked me as she whipped up an egg white omelet.

"You know, I'm not sure. I planned on going back this week, but after running into Quinton, I just didn't feel ready."

For now, all of my clients were placed with the other trainers, so I wasn't in a hurry to get back. Even though Ms. Ann's crazy ass called me every day bugging the mess out of me, I honestly didn't mind. She always managed to make me laugh. I giggled thinking about Ms. Ann's words from our earlier conversation. *You know, darling, new dick fixes old problems!* She was a walking mess!

"You know Rachel, I keep thinking Quinton is going to pop up again," I admitted somberly.

"Wait, Stacey, I thought you *kinda* suspected him, are you absolutely sure now?" Rachel questioned. "Because I want whoever did this behind bars too, but I would hate for you to accidentally accuse an innocent Black man of something he *may* not have done."

I understood where Rachel was coming from. I could potentially ruin Quinton's career, all over a suspicion that might not have been accurate.

"I don't know, I mean... I feel pretty sure. I keep thinking back to the day when I was running. I could feel someone behind me and when I glanced over my shoulder, although his head was down and covered with a hat, the body structure seemed identical to Quinton's. Not to mention what he said to me in the parking lot, 'Don't run from me, Stacey!' Those are the exact words my attacker said to me," I admitted.

"Well girl, if you're sure you need to call Detective Williams and tell him what you remember!" Rachel turned off the gas stove and pushed my new cellphone into my face. I paused.

"What's wrong with you? Why are you hesitating?" Rachel questioned.

"Because I'm not one hundred percent sure and I would hate to ruin his life for nothing," I lowered my head.

"Bitch! At this point, that is not your concern! It's the detectives' job to gather all the evidence and determine if he's a valid suspect or not!" Rachel was adamant.

I remembered what Detective Williams told me. He said if I remembered anything I could call or text him anytime of the day. I was so damn tired of talking about, thinking about, reliving my attack that I opted to text Detective Williams instead of calling him.

`Hi Detective Williams. It's Stacey Hill. I remember something from the night of my attack and just wanted to inform you. I believe I know who attacked me. His name is Quinton Smith.`

A text message popped up on my phone.

"That better not be Savior's sorry ass!" Rachel protested.

I giggled. "It's not Savior, but just so we're clear, I never said I was done with him. Just because your crazy ass pulled a gun on him, that ain't got shit to do with me!" I shamelessly admitted.

"You're pathetic! All a nigga gotta have is a big dick!" Rachel said, shaking her head.

"Sometimes I don't even know how I managed to stay your friend after all these years," Rachel muttered while walking back to the stove to finish her omelet. "So who is it?"

I smiled. "Well if you *must* know, it's Anthony."

"That fine ass man that saved your life?" Rachel raised both eyebrows and grinned involuntarily.

"Uh...yea," I replied hesitantly, "And I hadn't really noticed that he was all that fine." I shrugged.

Okay...I lied. The nigga was fine-fine.

"That's because you've always got your head in Savior's damn lap and you're too blind to see what's right in front of you!" Rachel never spoke with a filter. Raw, truthful and straight to the point.

"Well, what did he say?" she asked impatiently.

```
Anthony: Hey beautiful. How you
feeling over there?
Me: Hi Anthony, I'm okay, not
perfect, but okay. I never got to say it
but I'm really sorry for standing you up a
few weeks ago. Something unexpected came
up. I should have, at the very least,
communicated that to you.
Anthony: I'm sure you could tell that
I'm not pressed about it. I would expect a
woman of your caliber to have a busy
schedule. When you're feeling better I'd
still very much like to take you out.
Me: Well...since you saved my life, I
might be able to make that happen (winking
emoji)
```

I smiled.

"What the hell are you smiling at?" Rachel blurted out, interrupting my blissful moment.

"He wants to take me on a date," I admitted.

"Still!? Even after you stood him up? Girl! You better go!" Rachel insisted.

"Don't try to pawn me off on him just because you despise Savior!" I laughed and rolled my eyes.

"I don't despise that nigga, he's just no good for you and if you would close your legs long enough, you'd see that shit crystal clear!"

I threw a pillow at her. "I'm not here for your shit today Rachel! Is my omelet ready?"

I pulled into the circle driveway of my parents' estate and was greeted by George. I hugged his neck and gave him a kiss on the cheek as I walked through the foyer. I entered my father's study to find my mother sitting on his lap giggling, as my father playfully kissed her neck with his hand up her skirt. I dropped the bag of lunch I'd brought for my father and my mouth practically hit the floor. My mother was startled as she swiftly stood from my father's lap. Their divorce was nowhere near finalized, so technically they were still married.

"Honey! What are you doing here?" my mother asked in a high pitched voice.

I stood silent for a moment with bulging eyes.

"I—I came to have lunch with Daddy, but now I'm more concerned with what the heck is going on here!"

I invited myself into the study and sat in the chair opposite my mother and father.

"Baby, we can explain…" my father interjected.

"Oh, please do, Daddy! Please explain why you and mom are in here fooling around like teenagers! Your hand was up her skirt! Ew! You're definitely paying for my therapy!" I responded, pressing my fingertips against my forehead.

My parents looked at one another and intertwined their fingers.

"Your mother and I have been thinking and we've decided that our relationship, our history, our children and everything we've built is more important than any of the mistakes we've made," my father responded, looking my mother in the eyes and then kissing her lips.

I shifted my eyes from my mother to my father. "So what about Linda and Marcus?" I asked without hesitation.

"They're in the past," my mother responded, rubbing my father's salt and pepper curls.

"And you're just okay with this, Mom?" I couldn't help myself.

"Stacey, your father made a mistake and I can't blame Aunt Linda for wanting this fine, successful man. I mean look at him, who wouldn't want to jump his bones?" my mother said, reaching into the chair, grabbing my father's butt.

"Okay! Too much for me! This is getting disgusting!" I covered my eyes with my hands.

"Oh cut it out! Don't think we don't know about your little love life! You've grabbed your fair share of asses I'm sure!" my mother responded as she chuckled and wrapped her arms around my father's neck.

I definitely got it from my Mama.

"And on that note, I'm going to leave! I would kiss you both goodbye but God knows where those lips have been. Blah!" I headed towards the door, stopping to turn back to my parents who were snuggling and whispering into one another's ear.

"I love you guys," I said with a wide smile.

"We love you too, Baby Girl!" my father responded without looking up.

"Love you too, Honey Bun!" My mother looked up and flashed me a smile.

I sauntered to the kitchen and plopped on a barstool at the kitchen counter as I picked up my cellphone to call my brother.

"Yo! What's up, sis?" PJ greeted me, causing a grin to spread across my face.

"Did you know that your mom and dad are fooling around?" I asked in a disgusted tone.

"What! Shut the hell up! How do you know?" PJ asked in disbelief.

"Oh, I just walked in on them and his hand was up her skirt!" I responded and then covered my mouth with my hand from embarrassment.

"Now *that* shit is nasty!" PJ made a fake vomiting noise.

"I know! Freaking disgusting! But I'm kinda happy about it, I'd rather see them happy together than happy with someone else," I admitted. "So where's *Pilar*?" I said in a drawn out, condescending tone.

"Will you ever grow up, you jerk?" PJ laughed.

"There is a very high probability that I won't," I giggled.

"She's right here," PJ responded.

"Put me on speakerphone!" I requested.

"Oh hell no!" PJ responded

He was not having it.

"Oh come on, PJ! Trust me!" I petitioned.

"Fine! But you better behave or you'll never get to meet her. You're on speaker!" PJ informed me.

"Hi Pilar! How are you?" My voice was genuine.

"Hi Stacey, I'm doing well, thank you so much for asking, and what about you?"

Pilar's voice was sweet, almost motherly.

"I'm doing really well. I'm definitely looking forward to finally meeting you, my brother has said some really nice things about you," I said truthfully. "And don't listen to any of the bad things my brother has told you about us! We're not as crazy of a family as he likes to make us seem!" I laughed.

"Alright! Enough of that!" PJ interjected, taking the phone off speaker.

"You're such a hater, PJ. You're just mad because she likes me already," I giggled. "I was just calling to tell you about your nasty ass mama and daddy!" I said.

"I love you, lil big head girl," PJ said.

"I love you too, PJ. Don't stay gone too long." I hung up the phone and realized I had missed three text messages while talking to PJ, from Rachel, Savior, and Quinton.

```
Rachel: Hey! I'm ordering pizza,
Canadian bacon with pineapples, right?
    Me: Thanks Boo! You know what I like!
(Smiling emoji)

    Savior: I purchased you a flight to
LA this weekend, don't miss it. My driver
will pick you up from the airport when you
land and here is the address just in case.
I'm in Baldwin Hills, 1848 Don Diablo Dr.
Oh! Here is the driver's number in case
you can't find him for whatever reason
213-555-6289. If you don't respond, I'll
assume you rejected my offer.
    Me: I haven't spoken to you in a
week. Didn't you tell me and I quote, "I
wasn't worth the trouble and that I should
lose your number??" Kiss my ass Savior
James!

    Quinton: We need to talk.
    Me: I don't think that's a good idea
Quinton. I know what you did and I've been
in contact with the authorities.
    Quinton: If you would just allow me
to explain.
```

I decided that the best option was to block Quinton until Detective Williams finished his investigation. On the drive home I decided to stop at my favorite local lingerie store. I needed to grab a few pieces for my LA trip. I hadn't planned on giving Savior the satisfaction of informing him that I was actually planning on coming to LA.

"Excuse me, would you happen to have this in a medium?" I asked the associate in the lingerie store.

"A medium! Girl! With that tiny waist, you're going to need a small!"

I turned around allowing the store associate to see my butt.

"Ohhhh, yeah *that* ass is definitely going to need a medium!" She laughed. "Who's your surgeon girl? I need to make an appointment!" the associate asked seriously.

"I got it from my mama, girl! If you think this is something, you should see her! Honey, she's the reason they made the song 'Brick House'!" I joked.

The sales associate found the set I wanted in a medium and handed it to me.

"Is there anything else you can recommend while I'm here? I've got a pretty crazy weekend planned with my man," I admitted, rolling my hips.

Yeah, I knew my ass was in denial, but what business was that of hers?

The sales associate beamed excitedly. "Oh girl! Say less! We've got throat numbing cream, handcuffs, whips, anal beads, oh! We have this toy that you can insert while he's inside you and it vibrates on your clit too!"

"Damn!" I said, clutching my imaginary pearls. "Let me get a pair of handcuffs, throw in a blindfold, and that toy that I can put in while he's inside." I left the store with a smile on my face hoping Savior would be as excited to see me as I was to be visiting him in his hometown for the first time.

10
STACEY

When I arrived home the smell of pizza seized my nostrils.

"Dang, girl! Is it somebody's birthday? What are all these bags for?" Rachel inquired.

"For my weekend trip to LA to see Savior," I smiled.

"Fuck that nigga!" Rachel wrinkled her face in disgust.

"Oh! I plan to!" I teased.

"I got you something, too!" I divulged.

I tossed Rachel a package and she ripped into it, stalling when she realized what it was.

Rachel inspected the package's details. "Soft touch vibrating dildo."

I laughed as she read out loud. "I figured this might come in handy," I said with a raised eyebrow and pursed lips.

"You know what, heffa? I'm getting tired of you making fun of my nonexistent love life. But because I haven't had a real dick in over a year, I'm going to take this silicone ding-a-ling and put it to good use, on your amazingly soft, guest bedroom sheets!" Rachel laughed as she waved the dildo in my face. "Who's got the last laugh now!" She giggled as she headed to the guest bedroom.

I sat curled up on my couch eating the last of my half of the pizza when my phone buzzed with a text message.

Anthony: Hey pretty lady. I was thinking about you. Wondering if you'd be free to grab a bite to eat this weekend?

Me: Hey Anthony. I'll actually be out of town this weekend. Catch you when I get back?

Anthony: I'm going to hold you to it.

I strolled down the long hallway to the guest bedroom and just as I prepared to knock, I heard the unmistakable sound of soft moans creeping from the opposite side of the door. I quickly covered my mouth with both hands and giggled before beating on the door.

"What are you doing in there, nasty?!" I teased.

"Shit!" Rachel whispered.

I could hear her fumbling trying to turn her vibrator off.

"Stacey, you're an asshole!" Rachel called through the closed door. When she finally opened the door her hair was disheveled and one bra strap was hanging off her shoulder.

"I guess you and Mr. Dildo are having a good time!" I laughed, folding my arms over my chest.

"Shut up, Stacey! You bought the damn thing, now you wanna bother me when I decide to use it. What the hell do you want?" Rachel asked.

"Can you take me to the airport Friday morning?" I asked.

"Bitch! You could have texted me that!" Rachel said, slamming the door.

I stood at the closed door with my mouth on the floor. *I know this bitch didn't!* As I prepared to knock again, Rachel quickly snatched the door back open.

"You know I'll take you to the airport. I love you! Now goodnight!" she closed the door again.

I spent the entire next day cleaning, washing, folding and putting clothes away, my least favorite task. I hated coming home to a messy house after a nice vacation. My phone rang and I was taken aback to see Anthony's name flash across my screen. He was actually calling. I contemplated whether or not I should answer. My suitcase was packed and everything was ready to go, so I didn't really have anything to do before my flight the next morning. I mean, this man did save my life.

"This is Stacey," I answered in an overly seductive voice, because why not?

"Hey gorgeous, I hope I didn't catch you at a bad time." Anthony's voice floated through the phone like a beautiful melody to my ears.

Why hadn't I remembered him sounding so…good?

"No, it's not a bad time at all, you actually have perfect timing," I flirted.

"What are your plans for this evening? I know your flight leaves tomorrow, but right now, what do you have planned?" he asked, invasively.

"Uh…I…" I was caught off guard by the question because he spoke so confidently, as if he were already expecting my schedule to be free.

"By the hesitation in your voice I'm going to assume you're available," Anthony insinuated.

"Uh…okay." I raised my eyebrows unsure of what the hell was happening. I didn't have control of my words. My brain was telling my one thing, but my lips were saying another.

"I'll have a car pick you up at seven p.m.," Anthony informed me.

"Um, you'd need my address for that, wouldn't you?" I questioned in a confused tone.

"Ms. Hill, one thing you'll learn about me – and yes, I'm confident you will be around long enough to learn everything about me – is I'm a persistent man, a man that gets what he wants. Nothing happens in this city that doesn't get approved by me first. My driver will be there at seven, oh and you'll have a delivery at your front door momentarily. Hasta pronto, Amor," Anthony said before hanging up the phone.

I looked at the phone in complete shock. "He spoke Spanish. He spoke fucking *Spanish*?!" I yelled in disbelief. Before I could gather my thoughts I heard the sound of my doorbell.

"What the hell?" I said, making my way to the penthouse front door. I wasn't sure what was happening, but the one thing I was sure of was that Randy, my doorman, was on his way to being jobless. I didn't even look out the peephole before swinging the door open when three individuals I had never seen before, dressed in all black brushed past me.

"Oh, *honey*! We have our work cut out for us!" an overly flamboyant man with a full face of makeup and six inch Tom Ford stilettos stated in a flustered voice. I recognized those Tom Fords because my father had gifted me a pair for Christmas.

"Well, at least her skin is pretty, that'll make makeup application a breeze," a beautiful woman standing around five feet tall with a blonde buzz cut and a hoop nose ring said through a wide smile.

"Yas curls! All we have to do is freshen those bad boys with a little water and oil to get those curls poppin' like bubblicious!" a thick woman with a beautiful gravity defying crown of her own said with a grin.

"Uh…hi. You all seem really nice, but I think you have the wrong person." I was certain they had knocked on the wrong door.

"The boss said you might say that!" the thick, natural haired woman informed me.

"*Stacey, right*?" the flamboyant man asked.

"Yes…I'm Stacey, but—"

"Well then chop chop, girlfriend! El jefe is a stickler for being on time! Oh! And my name is Charles Renee!" the handsome, yet beautiful man informed me with a tight lipped smile that surprisingly made me feel warm and fuzzy inside.

"And I'm the face slayer, but you can call me Shay," the petite makeup artist informed me.

"Hey girl, hey! I'm Nicole, I'll be sprucing up those curls!"

I stood still unable to comprehend what was happening and where these people had come from. Charles Renee made a beeline back to me and stood behind me scooting my body, as Shay and Nicole grabbed either hand to give me a pull.

"Ms. Stacey, honey we've got to start moving if you're going to make it to dinner on time!" Charles Renee grunted as he pushed me down the hall.

"But you guys! I really don't know what's going on!" I admitted.

"Look girl! When Anthony DeLeon invites you *anywhere*, you go!" Nicole stated as Shay and Charles Renee cosigned her sentiments.

"At least let me take a quick shower!" I protested.

I started toward the bathroom and heard the doorbell ring *again*. Where the hell was Randy and how did everyone manage to get past him?

"I'll get the door Ms. Stacey, it's just the wardrobe arriving. Mr. DeLeon took the liberty of asking me to pull a few items for you. He assumed you're around a size six. Chop! Chop! Wash that thang and hop on out honey!" Charles Renee clapped his hands in an attempt to rush me as he pranced towards the front door.

This was not happening right now! Was this nigga really summoning me? I mean, yes, he saved my life, so I guess the least I could do was entertain him for a little while, right? He went through the trouble of hiring a wardrobe stylist, makeup artist, hairstylist and was sending a private car to pick me up were my last thoughts before Charles Renee reached into the shower and turned the water off.

"Here! Dry off and come with me," he said, handing me an oversized purple bath towel.

I dried my body and tiptoed to my living room where two clothing racks stood in the middle of the floor with a hefty number of items on each rack. Dresses, jumpsuits, rompers, sequins, blazers, jeans, there was practically a mall sitting in my living room. Accompanying the breathtaking clothes were shoulder bags, clutches, jewelry, and various designer shoes. A few prolonged blinks helped me realize that I was in fact, *not* dreaming. I was no novice in the realm of luxury but the experience in which it was being presented now was undoubtedly a first.

Acknowledging the astonishment on my face, Charles Renee spoke softly, "Take it all in, honey. You must be a very special lady for Mr. DeLeon to pull out all the stops for you. We're his personal team and he doesn't deploy us unless it's for someone important."

The warmth and sincerity being extended to me was felt and very much appreciated. I decided to stop fighting and just go with the flow because although I didn't know what to expect from the night, what I did know was that in two years, Savior James had *never* done anything remotely as romantic as this.

ANTHONY

I hadn't had a clear thought since running into Stacey weeks prior. She occupied my brain in a way I hadn't experienced before. Love at first sight sounded corny, and I'd never admit it out loud, or to anyone else for that matter, but something about this woman captured my damn soul. When I noticed her jogging on the trail I ignored the urge pressuring me to interrupt her, but eventually lost the struggle when she paused near a bench for a mid-run stretch. Her beauty was mind-boggling and I could hardly string a sentence together in her presence, which was uncharacteristic of me.

When she stood me up for our initial date, I knew she was different. I'd become so accustomed to the procurement of any woman I desired, that this particular woman left me fucking puzzled. Had me second guessing the type of pull I possessed as a man because I didn't get stood up, not now, not ever. After performing an extensive background check on Ms. Hill, I understood her better. She wasn't one of these thirsty women I had acquainted myself with more times than I'd cared to admit. She lived an upper class life and had never *needed* anything. Every woman I had ever been involved with viewed me as a meal ticket, and with a limitless budget, I couldn't say that I allowed it to make a difference.

I was persistent and eagerly chased what I considered to be mine, and she was without a doubt *mine*; she just didn't know it yet. I dispensed every imaginable luxury I deemed acceptable for a first date to ensure she didn't blow me off again. Even if, for some outlandish reason she declined my offer, she'd memorize the efforts and compare them to every man after me. Every plan made for the night was calculated. I wasn't ashamed to admit that, but upon learning that she's been connected to some pretty influential individuals, it was blatantly obvious that it was going to be a go hard or go home type of night.

I was sitting at my desk when I received a text message from Charles Renee informing me that Stacey looked fucking fabulous—his words, not mine. I loved my cousin, and even though he wasn't particularly a family favorite, his lifestyle held no bearing on my love for him. I kept him employed with my company and ensured he never missed a meal. His little glam squad managed to book quite a few events throughout the city and made themselves available to me anytime I needed them. Family meant everything to me and in my line of work, loyalty and dependability ranked high on my list of non-negotiables.

STACEY

When Rachel entered through the double sliding doors of my master bathroom, my legs were being greased down with shea butter by Charles Renee, Shay had beaten my face to oblivion and was applying my lashes as Nicole finger coiled individual curls on my head, giving my hair the life only a professional could give.

Rachel smiled immediately when she caught a glimpse of me.

"Rachel!" I screamed with excitement. "These are my new friends, Charles Renee, Shay, and Nicole! Everyone, this is my best friend Rachel!"

After greeting everyone Rachel was still smiling from ear to ear.

"What's going on, Stace?" she asked with an amazed smile.

"Here, read this!" I unlocked my phone, flipped to Anthony's text messages and handed the phone to her.

"So wait! This is the delivery he mentioned in the text message?" Rachel inquired.

I nodded. "Yep! It's crazy, right?"

"Now *this* is how you treat a woman!" Rachel said.

I could not believe she looked genuinely happy for me. She seemed to think I had horrible taste in men, and no one I picked was ever good enough for me, according to her.

"I knew there was something special about that nigga the day I met him at the hospital!" Rachel admitted.

I had never seen my best friend in such a good mood about a guy I was going on a date with. It had to have been because Anthony saved my life. I received a text while my glam squad worked their magic.

```
Dad: Hey Baby Girl, dinner tonight
with your mother and I before your trip in
the morning?
    Me: Hey Daddy! I actually already
have dinner plans tonight
    Dad: With?
    Me: Nosy! (Laughing emoji) Anthony.
    Dad: The nice young man that saved
you? Be nice, that boy might be my future
son in law.
    Me: Daddy! What in the world?!
    Dad: Have fun Baby Girl. Let me know
when you touch down in LA tomorrow.
```

I stood in front of my full length mirror with Charles Renee standing behind me adjusting my undergarments. Nicole and Shay stood back smiling admiring their hard work and Rachel was just happy to know I was occupying my time with someone other than Savior.

"Girl! If Anthony is willing to do it *this* big for a first date, imagine what he will do for a damn wedding!" Rachel teased.

I rolled my eyes. "Bitch! You always have to go from zero to one hundred," I laughed.

Charles Renee helped me slide the red, one-shouldered bodycon dress over my curves. I slid my freshly pedicured toes into a nude pair of Jimmy Choo stilettos, pairing it with a gold sequin clutch. I looked *good*.

"I feel like a proud mother hen! Sweetie, you are going to knock his fucking Gucci loafers off!" Charles Renee gushed.

I shifted my eyes around the room. "Thanks, guys," I responded before peering at the ground.

"Why the long face, sugar?" Nicole asked.

I hesitated. "It's just that I don't know this man. He seems amazing and all, but all of this..." I rotated my hands around the room referring to my glam squad and the racks of clothing sent to my penthouse. "All of this, it's just too much."

"Ah, shit! Here you go bitch!" Rachel blurted out in her usual uncouth tone.

Charles Renee laughed. "Oh Ms. Rachel, honey, I like you! A woman after my own heart!" Charles Renee pranced over giving Rachel a high five.

"Stacey, dear, I know we just met today but let mut ha give you a word of advice. When Mr. DeLeon calls......you go and without hesitation. Bitches jump city and state lines groveling for his affection and he doesn't extend it easily, trust me, I know!" Charles Renee said sincerely.

I locked eyes with him and smiled.

"Mr. DeLeon can afford you everything you ever wanted in life. This little penthouse is cute honey, but you ain't seen shit yet," Charles Renee said.

"Oh! Charles Renee!" Shay shouted, "Don't forget the gift!"

"Oh my goodness! How could I forget?!" Charles Renee dug into a ruby red Cartier gift bag and pulled out a small red box. He unclasped the gold snap on the front of the box to reveal the most exquisite pair of brilliant cut, diamond earrings I had ever seen. My mouth fell open and Rachel nearly fell out.

"Wha— are—I don't— " I fumbled my words until Rachel yelped, "Those have to be at least three fucking carats! Who the fuck is this man, Jeff Bezos?!"

"Actually, they're five carats. Perfect color, cut and clarity. You like?" Charles Renee asked.

I was at a loss for words. "Like them? I love them!" I jumped up and down like a child who had just received everything they asked for from Santa. "Can I wear them tonight?" I asked, peering at my glam squad.

"Honey! You can wear them whenever you choose. They're not loaners, they're yours, along with all the shoes, clothes, and accessories."

"Get the hell outta here!" I responded in disbelief.

"No bullshit! Now come on here, it's time for you to get out of here!" Charles Renee nudged me towards the front door.

Rachel grabbed me by the shoulders before kissing me on the cheeks and wrapping me in a bear hug. "I love you girl! Please have fun, just go with the flow, and do what feels right!" she said sincerely before leaning in to whisper, "and fuck Savior! Nigga ain't never shown out like this for you!"

I giggled and nodded my head in agreement.

"I'll help the team get packed up and see them out," Rachel assured me.

11
STACEY

When I opened the door to the penthouse I let out an abrupt screech, sending my friends into a momentary panic. A gargantuan, positively lethal looking man was standing at my front door. He had to be at least seven feet tall, teetering the scale at over three hundred pounds of semi lean muscle, and although he wore a suit, the tattoos covering his neck and hands were completely visible.

"Hey, Tank!" Charles Renee greeted from the kitchen where he made himself at home digging through the refrigerator.

"You know him?" My bulging eyes and shaky voice proved just how terrified I was.

"Oh yeah, girl! That's just Tank, one of Mr. DeLeon's bodyguards," Shay laughed.

"You *really* have no idea who you're meeting up with tonight!" Nicole giggled.

"Mr. DeLeon doesn't travel anywhere without his bodyguards and if you're with him, neither will you!" Charles Renee informed me.

I looked at Rachel who shrugged her shoulders with raised eyebrows.

"I mean, at least you'll be safe," Rachel teased.

Tank held out his hand for me, I took one last look at Rachel and my new friends before hesitantly grabbing Tank's massive hand. He led me through the lobby of the building, which I rarely saw because I almost always utilized the side entrance parking garage and rarely had a need to travel through the front of the building. When I laid eyes on Randy I burned holes through him with my death stare.

"You and I need to talk when I get back!" I said to Randy in a nice but nasty tone.

His face flushed with red patches and he knew that a good ass kicking was coming his way or at least a stern talking to. Tank opened the door to the black Denali and helped me step inside. He sat in the passenger side seat next to the driver.

"Hello, I'm Stacey Hill," I greeted the driver, an older looking, but handsome Black man with a full head of gray hair.

"Nice to meet your acquaintance, Ms. Hill. I am Roman Salazar and I'll be your driver this evening."

What kind of name was Salazar for a brother? I wondered and his accent was definitely not American. I thought back to Anthony speaking Spanish but before I could complete my thought, Tank's gruff voice startled me, "You have champagne and chocolate covered strawberries sitting on the bar."

"Thank you," I responded with a smile. Just as I reached for a strawberry, the partition slowly crept up, separating me from Mr. Salazar and Tank. What kind of tricked out SUV was this? A partition and a built in bar? Not to mention the back seats had been transformed into limo seating. I captured a plump strawberry from the Godiva container between my fingertips and closed my eyes as the chocolate melted on my tongue and the fresh strawberry juice dispersed throughout my mouth. I noticed a card addressed to me peeking out of the box. I opened the card and read the note.

Ms. Hill,

I hope you will find these accommodations to your liking. Looking forward to seeing you.

-Anthony

I pressed the card against my chest, exhaling a deep sigh as an involuntary ear to ear smile crept across my face. I didn't know much about this man, but the difference between Anthony and *you know who* was that Anthony was a damn gentleman.

The partition rolled down and Tank informed me, "We're here, Ms. Hill," in that gruff voice that still managed to catch me off guard when he spoke.

Ava's of Houston. I had heard great things about the restaurant, but hadn't dined here yet. I expected to walk into a crowd of people but the restaurant was surprisingly empty, with the exception of two bartenders, a waitress, and a live band. Tank held his hand out and I grabbed it in confusion.

"Where is everyone, Tank?" I whispered, gazing up the length of the tower of a man holding me steady.

"The boss rented it out, *for you*," he responded.

He escorted me to the back of the restaurant where another mammoth of a man stood with his legs slightly gapped and his hands clasped together in front of his body.

"There's two of you?" I gasped in astonishment.

"That's my twin brother, Bear," Tank responded. I could only imagine the hell their mother experienced birthing these two big ass giants. As I eyeballed the two Goliaths now in front of me, I hadn't noticed Anthony step from the table behind Bear until I heard his voice which caused Bear to step aside.

"Ms. Hill, I see you've met the head of my security detail, Tank, and his twin brother, Bear," Anthony said.

His voice possessed an assertive, yet quiet certainty. He was indeed The Boss, as everyone deemed necessary to remind me prior to my arrival in his presence. I forgot all about the twins when Anthony appeared. Six feet three inches tall, a low taper cut with deep waves. Mmmmmmm. Those waves had the hallmark of beautiful curls suppressed by a durag, but could be unleashed under a stream of water, just like Savior's.

Damnit, Stacey! Stop thinking about Savior!

Anthony's skin was a deep, velvety, chestnut brown and smooth, like *really smooth*. His beard was neatly trimmed close to his face and connected perfectly to his mustache, which I found extremely sexy. There was nothing I hated more than a raggedy ass beard. I shifted uncomfortably when I found myself ogling him in those tailored black slacks and black button down shirt with the sleeves slightly rolled at the wrist and pushed up to his forearms. I tried to look away, but my eyes rolled back to this man with the bottom of his slim fit shirt tucked snugly into his slacks. Anthony's arm and chest muscles were visible through the tailored shirt and I was almost certain I caught a glimpse of a dick print through his slacks. I determined that I must have been mistaken because if that was indeed a dick print, Mr. DeLeon was packing an abnormally large penis.

Get your mind out of the gutter, Stacey!

The leather on his belt was noticeably expensive but brandished no visible brand on the buckle. He wore a diamond earring in both ears and a simple chain inside of his shirt that was only visible due to the top button being undone, which exposed ink across his chest. I was stunned when I noticed the gun holster draped over his shoulder blades, with a pistol resting under each arm. The man had two giants protecting him. What use could he possibly have for keeping two pistols that close to him? I wasn't sure if it was the bad boy demeanor or just the fact that Anthony DeLeon was fine as hell, but my yoni was definitely doing a dance and managed to soak through the thin g-string panties I was wearing.

"Amor, you look ravishing," Anthony said before reaching for my hand.

Ravishing? Well damn. I didn't know how to respond to that! I delicately placed my fingers into the palm of his hand as he slowly pulled me towards him indubitably admiring my curves. When we were finally face to face, I responded, "Thank you, Mr. DeLeon."

Shit! My knees were wobbly. The scent of Dior Sauvage invaded my senses, heightened my arousal, and had me standing there with slightly parted lips, staring longingly at a man I didn't even know. He returned my gaze intensely, without blinking as he ran his tongue over his bottom lip.

"Call me Anthony, the only people required to call me Mr. DeLeon are the ones on my payroll."

He kissed my hand softly and escorted me to our table. Anthony pulled my chair out and allowed me to settle in comfortably before sitting across from me.

"Didn't want to sit next to me, huh?" I teased, smiling as I briefly shifted my eyes down, straightening the white napkin over my lap.

The corner of Anthony's mouth raised into a smirk. "You know, I believe everything has beauty, but not everyone sees it, however on the rare occasion when that beauty is undeniably remarkable, you should be in a position to admire it. Me sitting across from you puts me in the prime position to see God's creation right before my eyes."

Beauty? Undeniably remarkable? God's creation?! Sweet Jesus! This has got to be a dream! The ten person table seemed a bit excessive for just the two of us, but I didn't ask any questions. I sat quietly sipping a glass of water, unsure of how to strike up a conversation with this man.

Say something, Stacey! Don't just sit here like a damn idiot! I admonished myself.

"Ummm...thank you for the beautiful wardrobe and earrings, I truly appreciate it, but it wasn't necessary," I finally managed to speak.

"It was no trouble, Ms. Hill," Anthony said.

"Please, call me Stacey, Ms. Hill sounds so formal," I informed Anthony.

"You know, it's not every day I get stood up on a first date, so I figured I better pull out all the stops to get your attention." Anthony smirked, settling his eyes on me.

I felt embarrassed and averted my gaze to a painting of Bourbon Street on a nearby wall.

"I'm really, really sorry about that," I murmured.

"I'm just teasing you, Amor, don't mind me," he assured me. "So tell me about yourself Ms. Stacey Hill."

"Well, there isn't really much to tell," I admitted, with a sigh, "I don't really do much."

"I'm interested in everything about you, so even if you find it boring, I promise you…I'll find it intriguing," he said.

"Well, I own a gym in Third Ward, which is how you met me on the trail. I come from a great family. My parents were married for years, got separated for a few months, and now they're back together," I giggled. "I have an older brother PJ. He lives in New York. My best friend is Rachel, who you met in the hospital. I'm pretty passionate about physical health, so many people in the Black community are unhealthy and dying prematurely due to health related issues. That's why I opened my gym in Third Ward. I wanted to have a place where our people could stay healthy and nourish their temples. We have healthy eating seminars and offer resources to the community to empower them to take control of their personal health. It's kinda a passion project of mine. I mean, that doesn't mean I won't eat a slice of pizza every now and then. I also love to travel, although I rarely get to because I'm always overseeing the day to day activities at the gym. I've been off for the first time in years and the only reason that happened is because of the attack. What else, what else? Oh! And I kind of consider myself to be free-spirited," I explained.

Anthony's eyes were glued to me, as if I were the most important person in the room. Well hell, maybe I was since I was the only one in the room.

"And what about you Mr. De—I mean, Anthony. What do you do?" I asked.

He smiled, taking his time as he swirled the *Blk Royalty* cognac around in his glass.

"I'm…an entrepreneur," Anthony replied.

I laughed and gave Anthony a slight smirk before responding,

"Hmmmm……well, as a fellow entrepreneur, I've never had to have two bodyguards and two pistols on my person, so I must ask Anthony, what type of entrepreneur are you?" I questioned.

He grinned. "A very important one."

The jazz band played in the background as Anthony and I indulged in everything on the menu. Literally, everything.

"Anthony! Why did you order so much food? I'm pretty sure I'll be twenty pounds heavier when we leave here," I joked.

"I wanted to give you a taste of everything," he admitted. "And even if you were twenty pounds heavier, you'd still be bonita."

"Beautiful," I translated his words out loud.

"Very," he responded.

"Anthony, I've noticed you slip Spanish into our conversations casually, and I hope I don't offend you with what I'm about to say, but when I look at you, you look like a Black man." I shrugged my shoulders innocently, trying not to look or sound insulting. "Your driver Mr. Salazar also looks very Black but his last name is Salazar. I'm intrigued. What's the story behind that?" I rested my chin in the palm of my hands and stared into Anthony's eyes hoping he would clear some of my curiosity. We had gotten extremely comfortable throughout the course of dinner and Anthony had removed my Jimmy Choo stilettos and commenced to rubbing my feet.

"Well, I'm very much Black, probably as Black as they come, but my mother is Latina," Anthony disclosed.

"So you're Afro-Latino?" I questioned.

Anthony chuckled. "No, I'm just Black, but I happen to be fluent in Spanish."

"And Roman is my cousin, he's also Black but he grew up in Mexico," Anthony explained.

"Which explains his strong accent," I said.

"Exactamente," Anthony said with a smile.

"Anthony…" I paused. "Am I safe here with you?" My eyes bored into his and my voice trembled a bit. He stopped rubbing my feet and his demeanor shifted, as he tilted his head to the side.

"With me is the safest place you can be. I did save your life, didn't I?" he grinned.

"That you did," I admitted.

"You know, I was thinking about something. Your team told me you don't go anywhere without your bodyguards, but where were they when you were on the trail or when you came to visit me in the hospital? I don't remember seeing them." My face mirrored my confusion as I tried to remember the day I met Anthony.

"They're always there. I try not to bring too much attention to myself, so they're usually a few paces behind me, but rest assured, they're there. When I visited you in the hospital, they stayed posted at the end of your hallway, making sure no one entered behind me, with the exception of your people," Anthony admitted.

"Well damn!" I was shocked, they really did follow him everywhere.

"Anthony…" I called.

"Sí, Amor?" he responded.

"How did you know where I live? I've been thinking about it and just for my own peace of mind, I would really like to know. Did you look at my driver's license the day you found me on the trail? Did you look at my hospital records?" I asked in confusion.

He laughed and released my foot, rubbing his hand over his thick waves before speaking. "I own the building," Anthony stated, with a raised eyebrow.

My eyes shot up to him. "Wha—what? The entire building?" I was completely shocked.

"The entire building," Anthony said, "along with countless others around the city."

"Oh wow!" I was awestruck because I knew just how expensive my penthouse was, so if he owned the entire building, he had to be a millionaire from that one building alone. God knows how many other buildings he owned. I wasn't moved by money but I definitely appreciated a man who could hold his own. My gym pulled in well over three hundred thousand dollars per year, and at twenty-nine years old, no children and my father insisting on covering my large bills although I tried to get him to stop, I was doing well for myself.

"Do you own any other buildings I may know of?" I inquired. He smiled and gazed around the room we were sitting in.

"Shut up! Anthony, no way!"

He smiled. "Yeah, I don't broadcast it, but I own this place too. Do you like to dance?" he asked.

"Uh…yeah! I'm like a young J-Lo in her Fly Girl days!"

Anthony laughed as he stood from the table, dropping what looked to be around thirty-five hundred dollars in hundreds on the table.

"Excuse me," Anthony called one of the waitresses, "This should cover the meal, drinks, and a pretty sizable tip for you, the other waitress and bartender." He turned back to me, and grabbed my hand while staring at me mysteriously. "Let's go."

12
STACEY

"But where are we going? I need to put my shoes on!" I giggled like a schoolgirl, quickly grabbing my Jimmy Choos from the restaurant floor.

With Bear in front of us and Tank behind us, Anthony bent down, sweeping me from my feet before flashing his perfect pearly whites; our faces only inches apart. Traces of cognac on his breath intermingling with the sweet scent of mint drifted to my nose and in that moment, I marveled at the man before me. How hadn't I noticed how undeniably beautiful this man was during our first encounter? With a slight grin tugging at the corner of his full lips, his heavy-lashed bedroom eyes were low, but focused intently on me. Not to mention, he held me effortlessly against his chest, legs draped over his arms, sending an unusual tightness through my belly that quickly traveled southbound. Where the hell had this man come from?

"Ready?" he asked through that grin of his, pulling me from my Anthony induced trance. With a bashful smile, I nodded my head yes; never removing my eyes from his. Anthony's long strides were confident, his foot placement strong each time he took a step forward. Hell, he moved as if my weight weren't a factor. I knew with all this ass I was dragging, it was no easy task getting me to the SUV; but he made it look, *and feel*, uncomplicated.

"Anthony! Where are we going?" I smiled, slipping my feet back into the stilettos as Roman pulled away from the restaurant with Tank in the front seat and Bear following along in a car behind us. Anthony leaned back into his seat, adjusting himself.

"Just ride, Amor," he said and I couldn't help but to smile.

We crept into a dimly lit alley with no visible cars...or people. I silently questioned where the hell we were, but oddly enough I felt safe, even though the current situation seemed anything but safe. Tank opened the backdoor and Anthony stepped out, adjusting his slacks and sliding his arms into his black blazer, conveniently covering the pistols he kept concealed on him at all times.

When he reached down to grab his penis and adjusted it in his pants I stared on accident, but chose not to avert my eyes when he caught me. He exhaled a short, audible breath through his nose as a cunning smirk crawled across his face. I hadn't been mistaken earlier at dinner; his dick was actually laying on his thigh. I felt a sudden surge of embarrassment flood my core as I broke my gaze to stare at the concrete.

"I'm so sorry, that was rude of me," I said, my voice overflowing with shame.

"Amor, don't be sorry."

He extended his hand, placing his pointer finger under my chin, as he lifted my head and winked at me. I playfully rolled my eyes because, shit, how many more times was this man going to cause my entire top and bottom row of teeth to show? I placed my hand into his palm and stepped out of the SUV, inching my dress down a bit and smoothing the palm of my hands over the front as Bear approached us. There was an unmarked door in the alley that could have easily been overlooked in the dimness of the night. As we approached, Tank knocked three times before I heard his thunderous voice call, "DeLeon." That was all he said, and the door swung open, as a wide, heavy set man, dressed in all black stepped out and bumped fists with Tank.

Tank stepped aside and the large man directed his conversation to Anthony. "Good to see you, boss man," he stated, giving Anthony a personalized handshake, different from the one he gave Tank. After he fist bumped Bear, we wandered into the building as I wrapped my arm around Anthony's and pulled myself closer to him. He glanced down at me.

"Do you trust me?" he asked, raising an eyebrow and gliding his tongue over his bottom lip.

I locked eyes with him, still gripping his arm tightly. "Surprisingly...yes, I do," I said as we exchanged grins and paced until we approached a set of white double doors. Tank punched a four digit code into a keypad located on the wall and the doors slid open. I gasped silently at the secret elevator.

What kind of Top Flight Security, James Bond shit is this, I thought to myself. We stepped onto the elevator and Bear pressed a single button, causing the elevator to descend when I heard my phone ring. I retrieved it from my clutch to see Ms. Ann's name flash across the screen. I giggled because whatever preposterous, nonsensical mess she was calling to spew would have to wait until tomorrow. Ms. Ann and I had become friends over the years and I actually enjoyed our little chats, but at the current moment someone other than Savior James had captured my full, undivided attention, which no man had been able to do in the past two years. So yeah, Ms. Ann would have to wait.

"You okay?" Anthony asked, peering down at me.

"Absolutely," I replied, flashing him a grin.

When the elevator doors slid open, music blared through strategically placed speakers and flashing strobe lights occupied every square inch of the room. My feet were cemented to the ground as my eyes widened and my fingers fidgeted around Anthony's arm.

"What the hell?" I accidentally said out loud.

I had never seen a party on this level in my hometown ever! How did I not know about this place? Stunning people I had never seen danced around the room—grinding, rubbing, and swaying their bodies to the tempo of the music. Alluring women in lingerie rolled their bodies in cages wearing nothing but tasseled pasties, thongs, fishnet pantyhose, and agonizingly high heels. Several women performed aerial acrobatics while hanging from the ceiling—slipping, sliding and twirling their bodies through fabric tethered to the ceiling. The men were just as breathtaking as the women, dressed in tailored fitted suits in an assortment of patterns and colors.

The DJ's voice blasted through the speakers. "Alright Houston, y'all ready to party tonight!? Get a drink from the bar! Don't forget to tip the gorgeous bartenders! And there's only one rule tonight in The Dungeon! Turn the fuck up!"

Waka Flocka's "No Hands" blasted through every speaker, seemingly shaking the ground, and every girl in the club managed to drop their asses to the ground. I stood still, amazed at what was transpiring before my eyes. *Dirty Dancing* popped into my memory, as I remembered the steamy, unsanctioned dance parties in that movie; only this party was full of beautifully melanated bodies and my hips began to sway from the excitement of it all. I leaned in to Anthony's ear attempting to converse over the deafening music. "Is there a beauty prerequisite for entering this place?"

I knew my question probably sounded ridiculous, but I needed to know, because how the hell did so many attractive people end up in the same place? Anthony threw his head back, releasing a deep, throaty chuckle.

"Not necessarily, but it is a private club, so we don't get a lot of riff raff in here," he said, leaning in so close that I felt his lips brush against my ear, sending an involuntary shiver down my spine.

A woman dressed in a lace bra, matching boy shorts, and thigh high boots stepped in our direction.

"Mr. DeLeon, right this way."

I inclined my neck to glance at Anthony and then back in the direction of the woman and then back to Anthony. *Who was this man?* We followed the woman to a balcony overlooking the club and when I realized the entire section was reserved for Anthony, I couldn't hide the stupefied expression on my face. I noticed Roman enter with an assortment of stunning women, along with two men trailing behind them. The balcony was almost as large as the main floor of the club. Anthony placed his fingers around mine and gently guided me to the glass rail and we peered down.

"So let me guess, you own this place too?" I inquired, focusing my gaze on him with raised eyebrows as I gripped the railing.

"Guilty," he replied before someone caught his attention, causing his eyes to shift from me to the entry of our section.

A man equally handsome as Anthony came into view as he ascended the final step leading to the private balcony and I could feel Anthony's energy shift as he released my fingers, using one hand to unbutton his blazer and coolly sliding the other into his pocket. It wasn't meant for me to notice, but Tank and Bear gradually relocated from the outskirts of the sizable private area and moved closer to Anthony as if they were preparing to protect him. Anthony removed his hand from his pocket, placing it in a position that undoubtedly meant stop, which caused Tank and Bear to stand still. As the man drew closer, he bore a striking resemblance to Anthony, but was completely of Hispanic descent.

"Adrian, this is Stacey. Stacey, Adrian, my cousin," Anthony introduced.

"Damn primo, is this you?" Adrian asked, glowering in my direction as he licked his lips, undressing me with his eyes while inching uncomfortably close to me, invading my personal space. It made me feel dirty.

Anthony's powerful arm stretched across my body as he gently nudged me to scoot behind him with one swift arm sweep.

"Back the fuck up!" Aggravation plagued Anthony's voice, but he hadn't allowed his frustration to disrupt his demeanor.

His words felt lethal, but from a distance the interaction would have been mistaken for casual conversation. His cousin was able to feel the energy behind Anthony's murderous tone because he took a step away from me. Adrian was handsome with a low taper fade haircut, just like Anthony's, minus the waves. Tattoos covered his neck and knuckles and the tailored, houndstooth patterned suit he wore was almost identical to the fit of Anthony's suit. The two teardrop tattoos under his eye made me nervous as hell.

"Okay, okay! My bad, bro! Y'all have fun. Nice to meet you Stacey." Adrian bit his bottom lip before chuckling and then shifted his attention back to Anthony. "I'll see you soon, primo." Adrian stared at Anthony before walking away.

"I'm sorry about that; he's a clown sometimes. He's part owner of the club," Anthony clarified before leaning down to whisper directly into my ear, "So how long will you be gone and when can I expect to see you again?"

His lips brushed against my ear for the second time tonight. He had one more time to make that mistake and I was going to fuck him in the car on the ride back to my place. The small gesture of an ear graze had completely eliminated the awkward encounter with his cousin from my mind. I'd smelled Anthony when he'd greeted me in the restaurant, which made him practically irresistible then, but now…being this close to him was tantalizing and all of my damn hormones were sending SOS signals because my body needed to be saved by this man. He smelled…grown, refined, shit, the nigga smelled like wealth. I felt my nipples pebble under the skintight dress as he continued to speak into my ear, his hand finding its place on my waist.

"I would very much like to see you again...sooner than later," Anthony informed me before pulling away to stare at me.

I returned his gaze because I was completely wrapped in the presence of this man. I felt him glide a finger down my bare arm.

"Eres hermosa, sabes eso?"

I smiled a silly smile, gritting my teeth in confusion and responded, "English, please."

He returned my smile and repeated his phrase in English. "You're beautiful, you know that?"

I blushed and averted my eyes from his seductive stare, finding the silver leg of a chair to focus my attention on instead. He lifted my head with his finger and just as he was preparing to move in for a kiss, a tall, skinny, extremely fucking attractive woman put her hand on his shoulder, which prompted Anthony to halt and give her his attention. The woman was exquisite and, due to her comfort level in approaching him, it was obvious that she was definitely not a stranger.

"Hola papi, donde has estado?" the flawless woman asked.

My brain was working overtime, attempting to tap into the three years of Spanish I'd taken in high school to decipher what the woman was asking him. I was pretty sure she was questioning where he had been. I could feel the tension between the two of them and decided to excuse myself. Anthony tried holding onto my finger before I walked away, but I slid from his grasp and made my way to the restroom. I braced myself on the restroom counter before checking my appearance in the mirror.

Bitch! Get it together! You don't even know this nigga. Get out of your fucking feelings! You've got a man waiting on you in LA. Tonight you're just here to have fun! I reminded myself while observing my reflection in the mirror. I reapplied the MAC Ruby Woo lipstick Charles Renee had given me, made sure my lashes were still attached in the corners, and swung the restroom door open to find Tank standing in front of the door waiting on me.

"Oh! Tank! You scared me!" I yelped, placing my hand over my chest as I closed my eyes momentarily to catch my breath.

"Sorry, Ms. Hill, the boss doesn't want you moving around alone."

I smiled at Tank because although he resembled a killer on the outside, he was nothing more than a plush, huggable teddy bear; a deadly one, I was sure, but plush and huggable, nonetheless. I returned to the balcony to find Anthony still standing at the glass rail waiting on me, but he was alone. When I joined him, I glanced down to see Bear escorting the beautiful woman out of the club by one arm. She was kicking and screaming until Bear physically picked her up and removed her from the premises. I raised both eyebrows and released a loud audible smack from my lips.

"Well, that was interesting," I said before turning on my heels to face Anthony.

"Look, Amor, I'm really—"

I placed a finger over his lips.

"No need to explain, truth be told, there are a few men right now that might try that same stunt if they saw me here with you, so don't worry about it. You brought me here to dance, now let's dance."

Anthony walked over to our table and pressed a button which signaled the DJ across the room and he nodded at him. He held his finger up and pointed down towards the ground, signaling for the DJ to take it down a notch. When I heard Bando Jones "Sex You" begin to blast through the speakers, I closed my eyes, grabbing hold to the glass rail and began winding my hips slowly to the words. Anthony stepped behind me, allowing me to work. I twirled my hips, winding and rocking, as he grabbed the rail pinning me in. I felt the urge to turn and face him, so I did. I danced to the melodic tune, sliding my body down into a squat as I bounced in front of his crotch before placing my hands on his hips and sliding back up. I stared at him for a moment before turning back around to place my hands on the rail, leaning over to poke my ass out and rotate against his dick.

When I felt him harden against me, I smiled and grabbed his belt to pull him closer to me as I threw it back harder. Anthony ran both hands down his waves before backing up and falling into his chair. He placed one hand over his hard dick and leaned an elbow against the arm of the chair, resting his pointer finger and thumb on his temple as he watched me in astonishment. I let go of the rails, placing both hands behind my head, lifting my bouncy curls from my neck and rotating my ass down and back up again. I looked over my shoulder to see Anthony watching my every move. I just winked at him and continued to put on a show.

I danced until my feet hurt and then I danced some more. I jumped when I felt Anthony's hands on my waist. He pulled me down onto his lap and wrapped his arms around me before whispering into my ear, "Did you have a good time tonight?"

I pressed my back into his chest, allowing my curls to graze his face because whatever Nicole had put in my hair to define my curls had me smelling edible!

"I had a phenomenal time."

"What time does your flight leave?" he asked.

"Five in the morning," I sighed, poking my lips out.

"Come on, let's get you home," he said, rubbing my thigh softly, signaling for me to stand up.

We walked through the crowded club hand in hand, following behind Tank, with Bear trailing us. On the ride home Anthony held my feet in his lap, rubbing them gently.

"You must be a foot man?" I inquired.

"What makes you say that?" he asked, with a slight grin on his face.

"Well, you've rubbed my feet twice in one night. I don't know many men that really fool with feet like that," I admitted.

"Ha! You must be fucking with little boys," Anthony laughed. "I'm an everything man. Feet, titties, ass, pussy, lips, fingers, toes, thighs, if it's on a woman…I'm into it. Especially if it's on you."

My bottom lip dropped in response to his boldness and I just sat there, eyes wide, mouth agape as an unbothered Anthony grinned and continued to rub my feet. Soon we pulled up to my place. He opened the entry door to the apartment building with Tank and Bear following.

"Mr. DeLeon! It's good to see you!" Randy rushed towards Anthony with his hand extended.

Tank stiff armed Randy causing him to stumble backwards.

"It's okay, Tank, he's good," Anthony responded.

"Nice to see you as well Randy, everything running smoothly in the building?" Anthony asked.

"Ye—yes sir! Everything is perfectly fine!" Randy stammered.

I frowned and turned up the corner of my lips because everything was certainly *not* okay. Randy's ass was letting muthafuckas into the building left and right! I noticed Randy's eyes silently pleading with me not to tell Anthony he had allowed an uninvited guest into the building, so I didn't. I could handle Randy all on my own, but I didn't want him to be fired, so now wasn't the time.

"Well, if you'll excuse us, we're going to escort Ms. Hill home," Anthony said.

After stepping off the elevator and walking down the long hallway to the corner penthouse, Anthony intertwined his fingers with mine as he lifted my hand to his face and kissed the back of it gently.

"I'll have Tank and Roman escort you to the airport in the morning."

He was not asking for my input; he was telling me what would happen.

"Anthony," I whined, dropping my shoulders and preparing to put up a fight, but he shook his head.

"I'm not taking no for an answer and I'll pick you up Sunday night when you get back into town."

How was I going to tell this man no? He wasn't asking. He was handing out commands and I was ready to obey. Anthony took one step closer to me and cupped my face with his hands as he gazed down into my eyes. I held my breath for a moment in an attempt to calm my nerves as he pushed my curls from my face and gently kissed the scar on my forehead before kissing my cheek.

"Sleep tight, Amor," was all he said as he turned away.

13
STACEY

When I opened the door to my penthouse, I was surprised to see Rachel, Charles Renee, Shay, and Nicole sitting on the couch cackling like they had known each other for years. The empty wine bottles and half empty bottle of *Blk Royalty* cognac gave me further insight as to how their night had gone.

"Stacey!" they yelled harmoniously.

"Bitch! Was his dick big? Can he kiss? Did he let you ride his face?" Rachel was visibly inebriated as she giggled and stumbled towards me.

"Did you have fun?" Charles Renee asked before taking a shot of cognac.

I grinned at my drunk best friend and my very drunk new friends as I caught Rachel before she tripped and sat her on the couch.

"It looks like y'all were cutting up while I was gone!" I laughed.

"Bitch, start talking!"

"Yes, he has a big dick, at least he seems to, based on the imprint I saw in his slacks! We didn't kiss, he was a gentleman and kissed me on the forehead, and yes I had an amazing time," I gushed.

"Oh! And you don't have to take me to the airport in the morning, Rachel. Anthony is going to have his *driver* take me." I smiled and gave Rachel a side eye expecting her to talk shit, but she didn't.

I looked down at my phone to see that it was two in the morning. I wouldn't even have time to close my eyes before heading to the airport. *I guess I'll have to sleep during the three hour flight,* I thought to myself. I told everyone goodnight and retreated my room. By the time I stepped out of the shower, I heard my phone buzzing on the nightstand. I glanced at the phone to see Anthony's name flash across the screen.

I smiled as I answered. "Hi."

"Hey," Anthony responded in a deep, bedroom voice.

"Missing me already, huh?" I teased.

"Is it that obvious?" he questioned, causing me to smile from ear to ear.

"I mean, not really. You didn't kiss me goodnight, so I wouldn't assume you'd miss me too much," I admitted.

"Amor, just because I didn't...doesn't mean I didn't want to. I told you I'm a man that gets what I want, so I'll give you time to wrap up your little LA situation before I start making major moves."

He spoke confidently but I felt terrible. Did he know I was going to see another man? Had I accidentally slipped up at some point in the night and divulged the details of my trip? He did claim that nothing happened in the city that didn't get approved by him first. My mind shifted through dozens of thoughts in my moment of silence.

"Ummm—" I couldn't find the words to properly respond.

"Do I seem worried?" he interrupted.

I was confused by the question. "What do you mean?" I asked.

I heard a slight chuckle as he said, "Handle whatever you need to handle in LA and I'll see you when you return, and for the record, whatever you're handling in LA...I'm not worried."

This was a grown ass man and he had just made it very clear to me that I was accustomed to immature boys. *Damn.*

"You mentioned wanting to travel, where would you go? If you could pack up right now and just go, what would your destination be?" Anthony inquired.

"Oh I don't know! Mexico maybe? Somewhere with beautiful scenery, overwater bungalows maybe. Oh! Or the Maldives? It's located—"

Before I could finish, Anthony interrupted. "Right between India and Sri Lanka in the Indian Ocean —might have to take you one of these days."

Un-be-fucking-lievable.

I had never met a man who knew the exact location of the Maldives . I was a tad bit overwhelmed with excitement and more than a little aroused. He was cultured. I met dozens of handsome men each week. Tons of men with big dicks, and even extremely successful ones, but none that were actually willing to put in the work required to get and keep me. It seemed that I was always the one doing the teaching and schooling in my relationships and I couldn't help but wonder about all the things Anthony could teach me.

"And what about you?" I asked, "where would you go?"

"I'd most likely go back to Dubai, Thailand, or Bali," Anthony admitted.

"You've been to all of those places?" I asked, eyebrows shooting to the top of my face.

"More than once," he laughed.

"How old are you Anthony?" *I couldn't help myself. I needed to know.*

"How old do you think I am?" he quizzed.

"Well, at first glance, I would have said thirty, maybe thirty-one, but after talking to you, after being around you, I'm not sure anymore," I admitted, "I've never met a guy like you before."

"And what kind of guy is that?" he questioned.

I hesitated before answering. "You're so – *I don't know* – sure of yourself. You command the attention of the room without saying a single word. You know things; you've been places. I imagine you live a life of excitement," I answered.

I heard Anthony take in a deep breath on the other end of the phone before responding. "And none of that means anything when you have no one to share it with."

Four a.m. crept up on me before I knew it and I had just gotten off the phone with Anthony. What the hell was this? We stayed up talking all night like a pair of lovestruck teenagers! He was definitely giving me butterflies in the most magical kind of way.

My phone rang and I heard a familiar voice when I answered.

"Good morning Ms. Hill, I'm outside your door ready to take your suitcase," Tank greeted.

I smiled and made my way to the front door. When I opened the door, I wrapped my arms around Tank's massive body when he walked in and he was visibly caught off guard.

"Uhhh, hello Ms. Hill," he stated with his shoulder pressed stiffly towards his ears as I hugged him tighter.

"Good morning, Tank! Where's Bear?" I asked.

"He's outside with Roman," Tank responded.

"Did it make you feel uncomfortable that I hugged you, Tank?" I asked boldly.

"Uh…well…I…I don't know, I just don't get very many hugs I guess," Tank stammered.

"Well, I'm a hugger, so get used to it!" I shrugged and then smiled before walking back to my bedroom to grab my carry-on suitcase.

I was sure I talked Tank and Roman's ears off on the way to the airport, but they didn't seem to mind. Bear followed behind us the same way he had done the night before. I tapped Roman on the shoulder before giving it a squeeze.

"See you later, Roman!"

Tank opened my door and Bear met us as Tank pulled my suitcase from the trunk.

"Hey, Bear!" I said, as I wrapped him in a hug. Bear raised both hands as if he were under arrest and tilted his head at his brother quizzically.

"She's a hugger," Tank informed his brother nonchalantly with a grin on his face.

They carried my carry-on suitcase and oversized shoulder bag through the airport and didn't allow me to touch my bags until we made it to the front of the security checkpoint.

"Boss will have us pick you up from the airport on Sunday," Bear reminded me. I held both arms out and the twins looked at me and then looked at one another puzzled.

"Come on! Bring it in!" I demanded. The twins moved forward synchronously and I hugged them both at the same time.

Savior had bought me a first class ticket and I was thankful because I needed the extra space to sprawl out into a deep sleep, although Anthony crowded my mind and invaded my dreams on the smooth flight to LA. I was glad I didn't check a bag because it allowed me to move through the busy LAX airport swiftly. I took a moment from the hustle and bustle to check my phone to see I had texts from Rachel and my dad.

Rachel: Did you make it?
Me: Just landed (kissing face emoji)

Dad: Don't forget to let me know when you land, Baby Girl.
Me: I made it (heart emoji)

I was hoping for a text from Anthony, but hadn't received one. I wasn't extremely disappointed because my butterfly levels were still extremely high from our lengthy conversation that had only wrapped up a few hours ago, and that was enough to get me through the weekend. Anthony was turning out to be a pleasant distraction from my life with Savior. Although life with Savior was a bit unconventional, and downright confusing at times, he'd finally admitted he loved me. So...I kind of owed it to myself to see where this two year ball of toxicity could go, *right?*

I was convinced that he wouldn't have confessed his love if he didn't mean it. We had danced this dance for two years and agreed to be honest with one another through all the bullshit. I hadn't pressured him to be in a relationship. Savior came to me because he loved me and wanted to build a life with me, or at least that was the delusional fantasy I told myself that allowed me to stick around for his bullshit. I wasn't surprised that Savior's driver was not there waiting on me because I hadn't given him confirmation that I was actually coming. I had hoped Savior would require the driver to wait there for me just in case I showed up, but I was wrong. I picked up my phone to call his driver. The phone rang and rang, but no answer. I tried calling Savior with no luck. After waiting for an hour, I decided to take an Uber to the address Savior had sent me when he initially invited me to LA. I tried calling him multiple times as the Uber driver neared my final destination. California was beautiful. I admired the palm trees and magnificent homes as we drove through the hills.

"Alright, here we are," the Uber driver informed me as I looked up from my phone to see a sleek, mid-century modern home.

The large front facing windows were absolutely stunning and the wrap around terrace allowed for beautiful views of the mountains. I tried calling Savior one last time before stepping out of the Uber. Again, no answer. I tipped the driver with a ten-dollar bill and pushed my suitcase to the front door. I stood staring at the door for what seemed like five minutes contemplating whether or not I should just turn around and go home. A hollow feeling in my belly and perhaps intuition shifted my perception and made me realize, I shouldn't be here. However, I still rang the doorbell and heard footsteps inside shortly thereafter, but no one answered so I rang the doorbell again. My face wrinkled as I exhaled an exasperated, "what the hell is going on?"

I rang the doorbell one last time and a remarkably beautiful woman opened the door, with a look of irritation across her face. I froze as the woman shifted her weight to one hip. "Can I help you?" the curly haired woman asked.

My eyes darted behind the stunning woman to a handsome little boy wobbling towards the door. He grabbed the woman's leg and looked up at her.

"Mommy, up!" the little boy requested innocently. She smiled at the handsome baby boy before bending down to pick him up, placing him on her hip, and when I looked at him again, I saw it clear as day. I was staring at Savior's son.

The boy's sienna brown eyes and curly hair revealed Savior's secret.

"I'm—I'm a friend of Savior's, is he here?" I fought back the tears stinging my eyelids and straightened my posture, refusing to be defeated by the devastating pain of my heart being stripped from my chest.

The woman's face wrinkled into a frown. "Friend? My fiancé didn't mention anything about a friend stopping by," she stated with a raised eyebrow.

"Fi—fiancé?"

I felt the back of my eyes begin to sting as the tears threatened to burst from the corners of my eyes. Before I could say another word, I caught a glimpse of Savior strolling down the long hallway, his head down as he swiped through his phone. I felt an indescribable fire under my skin as my palms began to sweat. He had seen every single phone call and text message. His phone was in his hand, how could he have missed all of my calls? He was purposely ignoring me.

Savior looked up from his phone and locked eyes with me, causing him to stop in his tracks and for a moment he forgot how to breathe. I didn't know what to do, the thought crossed my mind to burst through his front door and attempt to kick his ass. I also thought about divulging all of his dirty secrets to his fiancé. I wanted to make him hurt, to feel an inkling of the pain and disappointment he had subjected me to over the last two years. I wanted to tell his fiancé that he had just fucked me raw two weeks prior, but what good would it do? What would it change? His fiancé turned to him with suspicious eyes.

"Savior! Who is this and why is she here?"

"Baby! I can explain!" Savior yelled defensively.

I wasn't sure if he was speaking to me or his fiancé, but at that moment I decided not to stick around to find out.

"I'm sorry for interrupting your afternoon, it was a mistake to come here."

I turned around with my luggage and began walking. I didn't have a destination and wasn't sure where I was going. I walked until I couldn't walk anymore, tears flowing from my eyes and the first person I thought to call was Rachel. When she didn't answer, I cried harder, deeper – sobbing and wailing uncontrollably. How had I been so stupid? Of course he had another life here in LA. But why would he invite me to his home knowing his fiancé would be there? Was he intentionally being cruel? Suddenly, my phone dinged with a text message.

```
Savior: I'm sorry Stacey. She wasn't
supposed to be here. When you didn't
respond about coming I didn't know what to
think. Then she popped into town so I
didn't press you about visiting. I would
never intentionally disrespect you like
this. I love you.

Me: Fuck you. It's over and I MEAN
it. Go be a father and husband to your
fiancé!

Savior: Don't do this. At least give
me an opportunity to explain.

Me: Explain what!? The fact that you
have a fiancé and a son?? Or the fact that
you invited me to a house that THEY (your
fucking fiancé and son) clearly call home?
No! Better yet, let's talk about how you
just fucked me two weeks ago and told me
you love me. Let's talk about how we
```

agreed two years ago to never have sex with anyone without protection, but you clearly have a one year old son! So much for being a man of your fucking word. When I get back home I'm going to get tested and if you gave me something, I promise to God I'll make your life hell.

    Savior: I'm sorry. I fucked up. She doesn't live here. She just brought my son down here to visit me. I told you! She wasn't supposed to be here! If I knew she was going to be here I wouldn't have invited you.

I was finished with this conversation. I had cried too many tears. I felt the headache creeping in. I wasn't sure why, but an overwhelming compulsion to text Anthony guided my fingers to our text message thread in my phone. My fingers began moving before I could process what I was doing.

Me: Anthony...
    Anthony: Yes Amor...

I sat on the curb staring into the distance and then wrapped my arms around my legs and sobbed. What the fuck was I doing? Why had I even come to LA? I found it difficult to catch my breath. I was more upset with myself for ignoring the flashing red warning signs that were so bright a fucking visually impaired person would have seen them. Savior was an asshole, had always been an asshole, so why was I expecting him to be anything more than what I already knew he was capable of being? My phone rang and I answered it without looking because I was sure it was Rachel calling me back. I wept into the phone.

"I'm so stupid! I shouldn't have come here! He's engaged, Rachel! Engaged! With a fucking baby!" I dropped my head back, staring into the California sun as continuous tears dripped from my eyes.

I was startled by the voice I heard in response.

"Come home," Anthony commanded.

No, no, no! I pulled the phone away from my face, praying I hadn't made this terrible mistake. Anthony's name stood stationary on my screen. My heart felt as if it might explode. I was humiliated and heartbroken.

"I—I'm so sorry! I thought you were Rachel!" I was completely embarrassed. I cupped my hand over my mouth and cried even harder making an attempt to muffle my cries.

"My assistant is booking you a flight home now. Drop your location, I'm sending a car to pick you up," Anthony informed me.

I was crushed, I mean...how had I lost Savior and the possibility of getting to know Anthony all in the same day? Anthony would no longer want anything to do with me, how could he? He knew I went to LA to see another man. There wasn't a single man whose ego could withstand knowing what I'd done. I ignored ten of Savior's phone calls before a black Tahoe pulled up and rolled down the passenger side window.

"Ms. Hill?" the driver questioned.

I lifted my head, revealing bloodshot eyes, swiped the sleeve of my sweatshirt over my runny nose and nodded weakly, responding with a shaky, "Yes."

"Mr. DeLeon sent me to transport you to the airport," the nice man informed me as he packed my suitcase into the trunk, and extended his hand, lifting me gently from the ground, helping me into the car. I sobbed quietly in the backseat for the duration of the ride back to LAX.

14
STACEY

When I finally touched back down in Houston I had missed fifteen phone calls, ten from Savior and five from Rachel. Tank and Bear picked me up from the airport as promised and were surprised when I gave them both a tear filled hug.

"Uh, you okay, Ms. Hill?" Tank asked, his voice full of concern.

"Need us to kill anyone?" Bear asked nonchalantly.

I giggled through my tears as I wiped my eyes.

"I'll be okay, thanks guys, and *please* don't kill anyone," I said, flashing a closed lip smile to the twins as I slid into the back of the Yukon.

When I walked into my penthouse, Rachel jumped from the couch and ran to me, wrapping her arms around me.

"Stacey! I tried calling you back! What happened!?"

Rachel noticed the redness in my face and immediately knew that Savior had fucked up. Now was not the time for I told you so and although I knew she probably wanted to say it, she was just determined to be there for me. I told her everything that happened when I was in LA.

"And you're sure the baby was his?" Rachel questioned.

"I'm sure, Rachel. Not only did the baby look like Savior fucking spit him out, but he confirmed it through text message."

I was laying on a pillow placed over Rachel's lap, staring at the ceiling, still in disbelief of the day's events.

"That muthafucka! I knew he wasn't shit. I knew it!" Rachel blurted without thinking.

"I know Rachel, I should have listened to you," I admitted, my eyes still misty from the revelation of my two year situationship crumbling before my eyes.

"Stacey, I'm sorry. I didn't mean it like that," Rachel said, looking down at me sincerely.

"Yes you did, but it's okay. You were right, you usually are, and I'd be in a lot less pain had I listened," I admitted, and damn did it hurt to admit.

"But what about Anthony?" Rachel reminded me, actually sounding hopeful.

"It's over before it ever began," I covered my face as tears streamed from my eyes. "He knows everything, he doesn't want anything to do with my dysfunctional ass! Shit! I can't blame him. I'm a mess. A total, complete, hot ass mess."

Rachel sighed. "Stacey, instead of jumping to conclusions, why don't you just call him?"

I locked eyes with her before responding, "Rachel, I'm too embarrassed. I just can't bring myself to contact him."

Her eyes narrowed on me as she scratched her forehead. She gave that typical "Rachel face", which signaled she was about to tell someone about themselves. I sat up and folded my arms.

"I know that face...go ahead! Give it to me!"

I rolled my eyes and waited on Rachel to speak. I mean shit! I'd already been hurt enough, why not, may as well allow her to put the icing on the cake.

"I mean Stace, if you're honest with yourself, you *knew* Savior wasn't the one. You knew two years ago he wasn't the one, but you kept trying to fit his square ass into your circle. Unfortunately sis, that's not how love works. You had every sign to run in the opposite direction, but instead, you entered into a ridiculous agreement with the man to stop using protection, in a fucked up effort to try and claim his heart! And that nigga obviously didn't abide by the agreement, not with that young ass kid!"

Blunt, tell it like it is Rachel was live and in effect, and it was just what I needed.

"Take the time you need, Stacey. Cry a night or two, get him out of your system and then...you gotta let that shit go!" Rachel smoothed my curls as I laid back on her lap.

"He was never the one. Now you can be a fool if you want to and shut Anthony out, but you'll regret it..." Rachel assured me.

"Ms. Hill, the doctor will see you now," a soft spirited nurse called as I gathered my purse to follow her.

Lord, if you let my results come back negative, I'll change my ways!

I'd opted to have full bloodwork done just to be sure Savior hadn't exposed me to any venereal diseases. I had been waiting two weeks to receive the results of my bloodwork. Apparently, the clinic was backed up and taking longer than usual to return test results. Those damned two weeks moved like a snail. Why the hell was it that when you were waiting on something that could potentially be a life changing, devastating ordeal, time dragged? I hoped God had heard my prayer, but wouldn't have been surprised had he skipped right over it! Not like I had the best track record.

After an excruciating wait, I received a clean diagnosis and to say I was relieved would be an understatement. I had thrown in the towel on Savior and made up my mind that we were truly over. Not like, one foot in, one foot out, I meant *done* done! He called and texted every day, but I refused to accept his calls, he could kiss my whole, entire ass! I dropped by the gym to check on my staff and surprisingly fifty new members had joined the gym in my absence. They were holding it down and I felt proud that I could take a leave of absence and my business still ran smoothly.

When I returned to my penthouse I found Tank standing at my front door. I hugged him but was visibly confused.

"H-hey Tank! Is everything okay?" I asked as I opened my door.

"The boss told me to pick you up," Tank informed me.

"What!? I have on sweats and a t-shirt! I'm not going anywhere looking like this!" I replied.

"Uh…Ms. Hill, if you don't come with me then I'll get in trouble and I would very much like to keep my job," Tank said.

I let out a deep sigh. "I need to at least shower first!" I said, folding my arms across my chest.

"No need, there will be a shower where you're going, just grab any essentials you women like to have," Tank said.

I hadn't spoken to Anthony in two weeks and was pretty sure he didn't want anything to do with me. The thought of seeing him after experiencing the most embarrassing moment of my twenty-nine years had me feeling jittery and uneasy. Roman drove until arriving at a gate stamped with a gold cursive D and Tank pressed a remote button that slowly opened the gate. We drove what seemed to be three miles before arriving in front of the largest home I had ever seen. I was accustomed to living in a nice home, my seven bedroom family home was far from average but this…this was a damn castle. Had Anthony invited me to his home?

I immediately felt underdressed. I still wore sweats and a t-shirt with a pair of white, high top Chuck Taylors. My Louis Vuitton crossbody bag was strapped across my chest and I had packed a small bag with panties, shower gel, shea butter, black tights, a white hooded crop top, a pair of fuzzy socks, toothbrush, toothpaste and edge control. I felt rushed when Tank showed up to my penthouse, so I grabbed the first items I could.

"Welcome to the DeLeon estate, Ms. Hill," Roman said before Tank opened my door.

Shit! I knew it!

"Tank, I'm so underdressed. I should have packed a dress!" I rolled my eyes as I handed Tank my bag.

He chuckled. "Ms. Stacey, just be yourself. Boss man will like it," Tank assured me.

I walked up the steps to the glass double doors and when Tank pushed the door open for me, I was greeted by a welcoming woman who introduced herself as Ms. Kelly. She escorted me through the white and gold foyer. The imperial staircase captivated my attention as I took in the stunning architecture of the vaulted ceilings. The exquisite craftsmanship of the gold and crystal chandelier hanging between the double stairs was a dream to behold. This home was breathtaking. I had developed an eye for beautiful architecture over the years from my father and I knew he would appreciate this home just as much as I did. We walked to the third floor, passing a fully equipped gym with mirrored walls, treadmills, stairmasters, ellipticals, squat racks, and an assortment of weights.

Who the hell has a complete gym in their home? I wondered silently as I followed Ms. Kelly.

When we passed what seemed to be the entrance of a club, I stopped in my tracks, noting that the words DeLeon's Place adorned the entry to the room. Ms. Kelly noticed my astonishment.

"It's a club. He has some pretty exclusive house parties here," she informed me.

When we reached our destination there was a sign on the wall indicating it was a spa. I followed Ms. Kelly and was greeted by two beautiful young women once we entered..

"Hello, Ms. Hill. I'm Lori and this is Trish," one of the young woman greeted, "We will take it from here Ms. Kelly. Ms. Hill, right this way."

The women escorted me to a spa shower where I was instructed to get undressed, shower, and to take as much time as I'd like.

"The shower is equipped with a voice-commanded sound system. All you have to do is say 'play whatever' and it'll play anything you want. We've taken the liberty of starting the steam to open your pores, but if at any time the steam becomes too much, just say turn off steam and it'll shut off. We will be waiting on you when you finish," Trish informed me.

As the two women exited the shower room, I took a moment to look around. The steam shower was the fanciest shower I had ever seen. Multiple heads shooting in every direction, steam filling the entire shower. I was thoroughly impressed. I stepped out of my clothes leaving them in a heap on the floor. I felt an immediate release of tension leaving my body under the warm water and steam. I adjusted myself on the long curved seat that was roomy enough for me to fully recline. Water streamed over my body and relaxation set in.

"Play, 'Let's Do It Again' by the Staple Singers."

I was a lover of music , but I got my love of old school from my parents. They would sing and dance around the living room every weekend listening to Al Green, Gladys Knight, and countless other soul music legends. This was exactly what I needed. I washed my body then just sat, allowing myself to be content and worry free. When I finally stepped out of the shower and wrapped a white towel around my body, Trish and Lori entered the shower room.

"Please follow us, Ms. Hill."

I followed the two women into a tranquility room. The lavender and eucalyptus scent of the room made me smile and I noticed a massage table setup in the middle of the dimly lit room.

"Please lay face down, Ms. Hill, and we will grab warm oil to prepare for your massage," Lori said.

I shrugged and placed my towel on a bench near the massage table, comfortably adjusting my body on the table. I closed my eyes and prepared for what I imagined would be pure bliss. One woman began massaging my upper back and the other started on my legs and feet. I felt myself drifting off until I heard the voice of one of the women.

"You know, Mr. DeLeon has never had us work on a woman before."

I lifted my head, resting my chin on my forearms preparing to engage in conversation with the women until another voice caught my attention.

"I've never had you work on a woman before because I haven't come across one that was worth it until recently."

Anthony moved closer to the massage table and the women froze.

"Mr. DeLeon, we're so sorry. We didn't mean it in a disrespectful way," Lori stammered.

He chuckled and gave them a grin.

"No offense taken. I'll take it from here. You're excused."

"It seems to be a trend that your people feel the need to let me know you don't normally bring other women around. I don't know if I should believe them or if I'm calling bullshit." I grinned as Anthony began massaging my back.

"Well, they're just telling you the truth. I won't lie, I have access to a lot of women, but only a certain caliber of woman is able to catch my attention," Anthony admitted.

"Well, if I'm so special, why did it take you an entire two weeks to call me?" I asked.

"Hmmmmm...well, the last time I spoke to you, you were crying tears over a nigga that didn't deserve your time in the first place," he reminded me.

"Ohhhh, so you were debating whether or not you still wanted to pursue me?" I asked.

"I told you, I get what I want. I just needed to give you a little time to get that nigga out of your system so you could appreciate what I have to offer. Wanting you was never something I wavered on," Anthony admitted.

He moved down to my feet and began massaging slowly. I smiled.

"There you go with those feet again."

"Oh, you want me to stop?" he teased.

"You better not," I grinned.

"Oh! And don't think I didn't realize you never told me how old you are when I asked a few weeks back," I reminded him.

"I'm thirty-five," Anthony said.

"Damn, Paw Paw!" I giggled, still resting my chin on my forearms.

He chuckled. "Oh I got your Paw Paw! I've got something for you. I'll step out to let you get decent, there's a robe hanging there on the hook." Anthony pointed to a silk robe.

I wanted to ask him not to leave so he could watch me get up from the table in my birthday suit. I wanted him to see, but I decided to allow him to be a gentleman and to keep my promise of changing my ways. I draped the royal blue silk robe over my body and slid into the fuzzy slippers provided for me. When I looked in the mirror to check my appearance, I noticed my name was embroidered over my left breast. That damn Anthony and his attention to detail. I smiled at my reflection and fluffed my curly fro before exiting the spa room.

"Damn! Maybe that robe wasn't such a great idea, I need to go grab you some sweatpants!" Anthony suggested.

"Why? I think I look good. I love the way a satin robe clings to my little curves," I laughed.

"There lies the problem and Amor, nothing about those curves are little," Anthony stated, admiring my body, moving his eyes from my face, over my breasts, stomach, hips, thighs, legs and landing on my toes. He extended his hand and I walked towards him intertwining my fingers with his.

"You hungry?" Anthony asked.

"Women are always hungry and don't you let anyone lie and tell you anything different!" I joked.

"So where are we going?" I asked.

"To the movie room," Anthony answered.

He led me into his movie room and I gasped.

"An entire movie theater, Anthony!? You said a movie room! This is an entire theater! You're too much."

I sat in the warm leather seat and Anthony pressed a button to elevate my legs. He pressed a button located near his seat and a server entered the theater and handed us both a menu.

"Order whatever you'd like," Anthony said.

I stared at the illuminated menu for a moment before glancing over to him.

"With amenities like these, why would you ever need to leave? You basically have a Studio Movie Grill inside your home!"

"Unless it's about making money, I usually don't, and the food here is way better than Studio Movie Grill," Anthony replied with a smile.

"So what are we watching tonight?" I asked in an effort to shift the energy in the room because staring into this man's eyes was definitely doing something to my lady parts.

"That's up to you. Whatever you want to watch, I can play," he said.

"How about *Love Jones*?" I asked.

"*Love Jones* it is," he answered.

"Tell me something..." Anthony said, causing me to shift my body in the chair, giving him my full attention.

"What do you want to know? I told you everything over the phone," I replied with a shrug.

"You told me surface level shit. That's not what I want to know," he informed me, "Tell me something that shaped the progression of your life, whether it be good or bad. Tell me something nobody else knows about you."

I looked away contemplating whether or not Anthony was trustworthy enough to share my secrets with and when he noticed my hesitation, he said, "It's okay if you're not comfortable yet. I respect that."

Before Anthony could change the subject I blurted out, "I know who attacked me, but detectives are having a hard time finding him."

His face was void of any expression I recognized.

"Are you sure?" Anthony quizzed me.

"I'm sure. I've started remembering events from that day and I'm pretty sure it's a guy I used to be involved with," I said, feeling embarrassed as I lowered my head.

"What's his name?" Anthony asked, still bearing that same unrecognizable expression. If I had to put a name to his expression, it would be a mixture of rage coupled with contemplativeness.

"Quinton Smith," I divulged.

My eyes were low and Anthony lifted my head with his finger.

"Wouldn't want your crown to slip. Don't ever lower your head around me. Even queens have found themselves in unfortunate situations, no need to feel ashamed. But, how do you know he was the one and are you one hundred percent sure? I need you to be sure," Anthony stated, staring at me.

"At first I wasn't so sure, but now I know. He followed me recently and said the exact phrase he said to me on the day he attacked me. He's also been calling and texting over and over again." I ran the pads of my fingertips over each nail nervously. "It's actually starting to scare me a little bit," I admitted, fidgeting with my robe as I shifted uncomfortably in my seat thinking about Quinton. "Where is the closest restroom, Anthony?"

"At the back of the theater. Are you okay?" he asked as he grabbed my fingers and gave them a sincere squeeze.

I looked at him and smiled. "I will be, especially now that I'm here with you," I said as I slowly walked away.

15
ANTHONY

I waited until Stacey had entered the restroom before dialing the number I rarely had to use, but didn't mind using if a situation called for violence.

"Code red, Quinton Smith, handle that shit." There were no other words needed.

When Stacey walked back to her seat, I could tell she was caught off guard when I pulled her on top of me. She straddled me and I wrapped both arms around her waist.

"Thank you for sharing that information with me, I know it wasn't easy," I said.

She shifted her eyes, producing a slight tightlipped smile.

"Yeah, but for whatever reason, I feel comfortable around you." She lowered her eyes and smiled again.

"Stacey, I'm not going to lie. I'm attracted to you. I'm extremely fucking attracted to you," I said.

She smiled. "I'm attracted to you too," she replied as she adjusted her body on top of me causing her vagina to accidentally grind against my sweatpants. When she felt my dick move she looked down. "I think he's attracted to me too," she teased.

It was obvious that she didn't have any panties on, so she tried to keep the robe draped over her vagina because although she was definitely ready for me, which was evident from the warmth radiating from between her thighs, I didn't plan on taking it there. I ran my hand over my beard.

"Yeah…he's been known to have a mind of his own," I chuckled.

"Mmmhmm, has he now?" Stacey asked, "Well maybe one day I'll get to find out just what he's thinking."

She rolled her bottom lip into her mouth and I stared at her with both eyebrows raised because if she kept fucking with me, this good guy demeanor was going out the window. I was going to have her bent over a couch screaming my name if she didn't stop teasing me.

"You're not ready yet," I told her.

"Oh! Really?" she questioned leaning back and tilting her head to the side. "Are you sure it's not *you* who isn't ready, Anthony?"

"Nah, Amor, because once I have you, you're mine and that big girl territory might be too much for you right now," I said as I patted her on the ass. "Let me go see what's taking the food so long."

When I stood, my dick was noticeably hard, so I made sure to position myself in front of her when I reached inside of my sweatpants. The expression on her face told me she was sure I was about to pull my dick out, as she sat back in the leather chair, licking her lips anticipating what she was about to see. I grabbed myself and readjusted my dick to allow me to walk with ease as I stepped away from Stacey and exited the theater. I knew she was stunned when I heard a faint whisper of, "no the fuck he didn't."

As I walked out my phone rang and I answered it quickly.

"Why the fuck are you calling me back? If you aren't calling to tell me the job is done, don't fucking call at all!" I paused for a moment to listen and became infuriated. "You think I give a damn if he's an attorney! Fucking find him! And if I ever hear you question me again, your family will have to find you!"

I hung up the phone dissatisfied with my soldier, but decided to put it behind me now that I finally had Stacey in my presence. I'd slept with many women from all over the world, but the shit was getting old. I needed something more, someone to stimulate me intellectually, someone to talk to, someone who made fucking the cherry on top and not the main entree. In my thirty-five years, I had never experienced a woman turning me down. Stacey was feisty, she had options and she knew it. I knew there was something special about her the moment I saw her smile that day on the trail and I was determined to handle her differently. It had been a while since I was forced to chase a woman, I almost forgot what it felt like. Shit's exciting, and as much I hated to admit it, she had my damn nose wide open. So did I want to fuck her? Absolutely, but I was willing to set my wants aside to see if I could have a future with this woman.

STACEY

I was sitting here practically butt ass naked and he didn't so much as even kiss me! I was used to men not being able to keep their hands off of me—especially my ass; they just had to have a squeeze. But not Anthony! He hadn't attempted anything and it made me question if there was something wrong with me. Never mind the man had just given me a perfectly valid explanation as to why he hadn't tried to fuck me. My twisted up perception wouldn't allow my brain to believe what he said.

I grabbed my phone from the pocket of my robe and dialed Rachel.

"Talk to me!" Rachel answered.

"Bitch! I need to talk and it's gotta be quick!" I whispered into the phone.

"Uh...okay, what's up?" Rachel asked.

"This nigga hasn't tried anything! He hasn't even tried to kiss me! Is there something wrong with me?" I whispered frantically.

"Awwwww, shit! Here you go! No Stacey, there is nothing wrong with you. You just finally got yourself a gentleman and you don't know what the fuck to do!" Rachel informed me. "The nigga is obviously older—"

"He's thirty-five," I interrupted.

"Exactly my point! He's older. He's rich. He's accomplished and the nigga can get pussy from anywhere I'm sure! If he likes you, then he sees you for more than just that hole between your legs. The way you get to a man like that is to be real and honest with him. Share parts of yourself that you haven't shared with other men. Share your heart, your fears, what makes you happy. Shit, bitch! Do something different, other than opening your legs. That shit doesn't work!" Rachel said.

I smiled. "Thank you Rachel! I knew you'd have the perfect words. Gotta go, love you!" I hurriedly hung up the phone just as Anthony was walking back into the theater.

"The food should be out shortly," he assured me.

I sat in my seat watching as Anthony walked past me and sat down to hold my hand. I grinned and shifted in my seat turning to face him.

"Spend the night with me," he requested. "Not on any bullshit. I'm not trying to fuck you."

I raised an eyebrow in offense.

"I didn't mean it like that. Of course I want to fuck you, but not tonight," Anthony admitted, "I want to be near you...that's all."

Those simple words caused my damn heart to skip a beat. He just wanted to be near me? What kind of Shakespearean shit was that? Father don't let this man be a figment of my imagination!

The movie credits scrolled up the screen, but we hadn't noticed. We talked through the entire movie, while stuffing our faces with the delicious meal Anthony's chef had prepared, and didn't seem to get tired of one another.

"Come to my room with me?" Anthony said.

"Of course," I responded.

"Let's take the elevator," he said as he grabbed my hand and led me out of the theater.

When we arrived at the elevator, Anthony allowed me to step in first. He grabbed my hand and pulled me slowly into his chest, wrapping one hand around my waist and grabbing the back of my neck with his other hand.

He stared into my eyes. "You're beautiful."

I grinned and before I could respond, he kissed my lips. An electric current pulsed through my body, different than anything I had ever felt before. His lips were butter soft and he kissed me passionately, no tongue and I felt our souls tie. Anthony pulled away from me slowly and gazed into my eyes.

"Do you want me to stop?" he asked.

I couldn't speak. I just shook my head no and kissed him again, this time slipping my tongue into his mouth. A five minute kiss seemed like an eternity and I didn't want this moment to end. Our hands didn't roam, Anthony was respectful and still, I felt my nipples harden. Anthony pulled away and slid his hand down to his dick, grabbing his manhood in an attempt to calm himself.

"Don't you want to?" I moaned softly as my lips made their way to his neck.

"Stacey, Amor, isn't it obvious?" Anthony asked as he motioned down to his erect penis. "But you're special, I can't treat you like I've treated hoes. I fuck hoes with no intention of it being anything more than that. With you, it's different. This could actually be something, so we have to take it slow."

Anthony's sincere words went in one of my ears and out the other. I kissed his neck before biting and then kissing it again, as I slid my hand on top of his sweatpants to his dick and inched my fingers all the way down to his tip.

He grunted. "You're not going to make this easy for me...are you?"

"Nope!" I responded, kissing his lips softly.

The elevator doors opened and we finally pulled away from one another to breathe.

"Come on."

Anthony grabbed my hand and led me off the elevator into his master suite. My eyes floated around the room in amazement.

"It looks like a hotel room in here," I said as I ran my fingers over a pair of emerald green, velvet chairs sitting near a table in his room.

"I paid a company that decorates boutique hotels in the downtown area to do it for me. I always want to feel like I'm on vacation when I'm in here," Anthony said, rubbing the soft velvet chair.

"They did an amazing job," I replied.

I removed my slippers to sink my toes into the white, fluffy, oversized sheepskin rug. When I walked over to his bed, I trailed my fingers over one of the tall bedposts. I wasn't used to a man having such good taste, his all white duck down comforter resembled clouds laying on top of his bed.

"Anthony?" I called.

"Si, Amor," he responded.

"You want to get to know me and you want me to get to know you?" I asked.

Anthony sat in a velvet chair and nodded his head.

"But...what if you don't like what you learn? What if I'm too much? A man like you can have an easy life. I'm the kind of girl that would complicate life for you." I slid onto his bed and stared at him from across the room.

He smiled. "I didn't get where I am today due to a lack of challenges."

"So tell me about yourself, Anthony. You've asked me questions but have neglected to tell me anything about you," I said with a sudden realization, "I want to know something meaningful, something real, something—"

He cut me off. "I have—had a daughter, her name was Ava," he said.

"Had?" I said.

"She passed away right before her first birthday."

Anthony's words were low, barely audible as he stared at the carpet. My eyebrows furrowed and my face wrinkled as I listened to Anthony.

"It was a febrile seizure. Her mother and I made the decision that it was time for her to start sleeping in her own bed. Ava was pissed." He chuckled at the memory. "But she eventually cried herself to sleep. We checked on her throughout the night and she was fine, but when we woke up the next morning she wasn't breathing."

Anthony placed a balled fist to his mouth. "We tried CPR. We did everything we knew how…but it was too late. Crazy thing is…she had never had a seizure before." Anthony raised his eyes from the carpet, locking eyes with me.

"Pretty fucked up, huh?" he said, "Quite naturally, I blame myself. I could have just let her stay in the bed with us…she was only one year old. I didn't have to insist that she sleep in her own bed. You wanted to know about me. Doesn't get any heavier than that, Amor," he said.

I quickly swiped the tears from my eyes and walked over to Anthony, kneeling down and resting my forearms on his knees.

"I'm so sorry for your loss, Anthony. I can't begin to imagine the heartache you've endured," I said, sympathy lacing my tone.

"She would have been six today and since then I've thrown myself into my work. It was the only way to maintain my sanity," Anthony said.

"And what about her mother?" I questioned.

"We were engaged, but decided to call it off. There was too much pain to move forward. I took care of her for the first few years. Made sure she was good and didn't have to worry about work or money. I just wanted her to have time to grieve," he said, "She's dating someone now, they live together, so we don't really have a reason to keep in touch. So it's been a grind for me ever since then."

"What's different now?" I asked, looking up at him.

"I feel ready now. I can't say the pain is gone, it still hurts like a muthafucka, but I'm in a place where I can love someone again," Anthony said, "Took a lot of fucking therapy to get to this point." He chuckled. "But I'm here," he continued with a shrug, "Your turn."

Anthony glanced at me.

"Uhhh...I don't know. I've told you everything."

I averted my eyes, purposely avoiding eye contact with him, but he shifted my gaze back toward him.

"No you haven't, but I won't force you, you can tell me when you're ready," he said with a warm smile.

I sat contemplating and just as I found the strength to open my mouth Anthony's phone rang. I heard a voice on the other end of the phone, "Hey Boss, I got some news." Anthony motioned for me to give him one minute as he stood from his chair. He walked over to the window and I heard his words but was confused by them.

"You know what to do, I'll meet you at the spot tomorrow, same time."

He hung up his phone, removed the sim card, snapped it into two pieces and inserted a new one.

"Let me guess, entrepreneurship?" I asked.

"Entrepreneurship," he said coyly.

We talked and laughed the entire night and I was enjoying every minute with this man. The fact that I wanted to sleep with Anthony had magically disappeared from my mind as his conversation stimulated me in ways I never thought imaginable. I felt...happy.

16
STACEY

The next morning, I awakened to a tray of fresh fruit, champagne, orange juice, a single, long-stemmed red rose, and a handwritten note.

Had to handle some business. Mi casa es su casa. I'd really like for you to be here when I return, but if you must leave Roman and Tank will drive you.

I sat up and leaned against the headboard as I glanced around the room. My hands shot up to my curls as I rummaged through the matted mess. In an attempt to sleep pretty, I neglected to wear my headscarf...huge mistake. I slid from the bed and tipped over to the bedroom window, gasping when I noticed the infinity swimming pool, mini golf course, and basketball court. If I didn't know any better, I would have sworn I was in a five star hotel. I nestled myself back under the feather soft down comforter and poured a glass of champagne, adding only a splash of orange juice before popping a grape into my mouth. I looked down to see that I was still wearing the satin robe tied snuggly around my waist.

"So much for getting some dick," I sighed.

"But you will soon enough." I heard Anthony's voice enter through the bedroom door.

My mouth dropped and I sat there, motionless as if I were invisible, staring blankly past him. I tried to speak, but was unable to form any damn words. When he stepped in front of me I set my champagne flute on the nightstand and slid under the down comforter, pulling it over my face in embarrassment. I could hear Anthony chuckle and I squeezed my eyes shut hoping I was only dreaming, but when he eased the comforter away from my face, it was pretty clear that I wasn't.

"Anthony! Your note said you were gone!" I mumbled.

"I left that note hours ago, sleeping beauty," he responded through a grin.

"I'm so fucking embarrassed! You probably think I'm some kinda hoe!" I stared at him for confirmation.

"Don't be sorry, Amor. I think it's sexy that you know what you want and trust me, if I thought you were a hoe, you wouldn't still be here. Confidence in your sexuality and going after what you want isn't the same as being a hoe."

I parted my fingers over my face, peeking through at Anthony.

"Really?" I asked.

He placed his hand on my thigh and gripped it.

"Really," he responded, "Now get dressed! We have brunch reservations."

I didn't move. I closed my eyes tightly before popping them back open.

"Anthony! Wait…" I called, surprising myself.

He stopped in his tracks and turned back to me.

"I have something to tell you," I said.

He raised an eyebrow and walked back to me, sitting on the edge of the bed.

"Okay, you've got my attention," he said.

I fiddled with my nails and felt the sweat forming in the palm of my hands.

"You can talk to me Amor, you know that, right?" Anthony said.

"That's the thing, Anthony. I believe you; I just hope that after you learn about all my baggage you won't stop being the person that I can talk to," I admitted.

"That'll never happen," he assured me, placing a kiss on the inside of my wrist.

I sucked in a deep breath and closed my eyes.

"I was molested when I was ten years old. He was a family member by marriage and the abuse continued until I was fifteen when my brother PJ found out about it and almost beat him to death," I said.

I instantly regretted revealing my secret. I had never even shared this information with Savior, and here I was divulging all my deeply rooted issues to someone I had only been on one date with. I looked to Anthony and he hadn't flinched.

"He ended up going to jail and he's still there now, apparently I wasn't the only one."

Anthony grabbed my hand but remained silent.

"But you know what's crazy? I was mad at my brother and my parents for having him sent to jail. In my fucked up immature mind, I loved him," I scoffed in disbelief, "What kind of shit is that? I actually thought I loved him."

Anthony sat quietly, rubbing his thumb over the top of my hand sincerely.

"Amor, you were a child, he manipulated you. You're not to blame for that sick muthafucka. You were a baby!" He defended me and it made me smile.

"I was unfortunately exposed to sex at a very young age, and it's shaped my sexual exploration as an adult. My parents blamed themselves for not knowing. My dad has worked every single day since then to make up for it. Most days he wouldn't even allow me to lift a finger. Even now, he still does everything for me," I admitted, "The guy I was with before you, his name was Savior James."

"The NBA player? Is that who had you crying the day I had you picked up in LA?" Anthony asked.

I nodded. "We had been talking off and on for two years. I wanted it to be something more, but he didn't, until recently." I sighed, searching for the strength to finish my words. "He invited me to LA and when I arrived I was greeted by his fiancé and his one year old son," I said.

"Damn, that's fucked up," Anthony responded, shaking his head disapprovingly.

"Yeah, he's been calling and texting every day since I left LA, but I haven't spoken to him. I'm done with him, and I just needed you to know that," I said, positioning my hands into an X shape and breaking it. "Done-done." I dropped my head, feeling slightly embarrassed.

Anthony lifted my head. "What did I tell you about that crown? Don't ever let it slip." Anthony smiled and kissed my lips. "Let's go, we have somewhere to be," he said, as he rose from the bed.

"So that's it? You don't have a response?" I questioned.

"Baby, you're a woman. A beautiful woman, no fuck that, an astonishing fucking woman and life dealt you a few fucked up cards. But when I look at you, I see a woman who has navigated her way through all of the bullshit," Anthony said, placing his hands on either side of my face, staring passionately into my eyes, "I see a loyal queen, and that's what I need more than anything. So if you were expecting for me to not want you anymore because of a little baggage, then you're sadly mistaken. I want you more because in my world I can't have a woman who breaks easily," he said.

I wrinkled my nose. "In your world?" I asked in a confused tone.

"Yes, in my world," Anthony stated boldly. "Now, get dressed."

After showering, I threw on the black leggings and crop top hoodie I brought with me and met Anthony in the foyer of his estate.

"Where are we going? I'm underdressed!" I looked down at my appearance.

Anthony smiled and said, "you're perfect," before kissing my lips.

"Kelly, please cancel our brunch reservations and call Roman, Bear, and Tank and have them meet us at the jet. We take off in two hours," Anthony said, as if his words were normal.

"Jet! Anthony! What the hell!?" I shrieked. "I can't get on a jet. Where are we going? I have to keep an eye on the gym! I have to—"

Anthony kissed my lips to stop me from speaking.

"The only way you'll really know if this is what you want – *if I am what you want* – is if I give you a glimpse of who I really am," Anthony admitted.

My reservations melted beneath Anthony's stare. "But what about clothes? Makeup? Shit! Panties!?" I asked.

"Charles Renee is gathering items for you as we speak, and will have them on the jet before we arrive, and as far as panties go…you won't need any." He kissed me again and slid both hands down my back and grabbed my ass gently.

Damn! I guess Rachel was right! Being honest and sharing parts of myself I had never shared with anyone else had opened a door for Anthony that I hadn't expected. A driver I had never seen before escorted us to the airstrip and introduced himself as Derrick. There was something off about him and I couldn't quite put my finger on it, but his vibe, his energy from the moment we stepped into the SUV was alarming to me. When we arrived at the airstrip, Anthony could sense I was bothered.

"Amor, what's wrong?"

I shook my head and responded, "Nothing."

"Don't do that, be honest with me, always be honest with me. I'll give you the world if you promise to always tell me the truth," he stated as he grabbed my waist.

I stared into his eyes silently for a moment. "I don't like that driver, his energy was off and it made me feel uncomfortable," I stated truthfully.

He kissed my lips. "Get on the jet," he said.

He joined me moments later and sat next to me wiggling his hand between my crossed legs.

"What were you doing?" I asked.

"I fired Derrick," Anthony stated without blinking.

"Anthony! What! Noooo!" I whined, "Why did you do that? You could have just made sure Roman was the driver whenever I'm with you, you didn't have to fire him!"

I couldn't believe I had just taken food from someone's table.

"Amor, listen and please hear me well. If you don't like something it stops, no questions asked. Do you know how many drivers I go through in a year's time? Roman is the only one who stays because he's blood. Derrick would have gotten fired sooner or later, you just helped expedite the process," Anthony said.

I felt terrible. I eventually dozed off, leaning onto Anthony's shoulder as the jet traveled to a destination I was not informed of. When I opened my eyes the jet was preparing to land.

"Hey, sleeping beauty," Anthony greeted, kissing my forehead.

"Hey," I greeted back, rotating in my seat to stretch out the stiffness in my back from the flight.

"Don't worry, I'll make sure you get special attention to get all of those kinks worked out," he smirked. "Oh! And welcome to Tulum."

There was a limo stocked with champagne, fresh fruit, and an assortment of top shelf liquor when we stepped off of the jet. Roman, Bear, and Tank rode in a separate car following our limo.

"So what's on the agenda?" I asked as I snuggled my body against Anthony smiling from the excitement of it all.

"Whatever you want. This week is all about you," he said.

"Week?" I questioned. "We're staying here an entire week?" I didn't know what to say.

"I could cut it short if that's too long for you," Anthony said, unsure of how to navigate the conversation.

"Absolutely not! I'm past due for a vacation!" I gushed. "But...I can't make any promises that I'll keep my hands off of you during this week."

Anthony peered at me with a smirk and said, "You won't have to."

When we arrived at the private villa the twins and Roman unpacked the limo and I was surprised by the amount of luggage they unloaded because I hadn't packed a bag and I hadn't seen Anthony pack one either. Six of the nine pieces of luggage belonged to Anthony and me while Roman, Tank and Bear each had one. Anthony recognized the surprised look on my face.

"Charles Renee is an excellent packer, he doesn't leave any room for error. I'm confident you'll find everything you need for our week-long stay in one of these six bags," he laughed.

I strolled through the villa admiring the views, each room more breathtaking than the next.

"Wow, Anthony! The beach is literally right here!" I screamed, pointing outside the French doors leading to the white sand beach.

Anthony smiled. "I figured you might like that. I own this villa and you're always welcome. If you and your best friend ever want to get away just say the word. As long as you don't plan on staying gone too long."

I ran onto the beach and twirled around in a circle with my arms stretched wide.

"You're a tad bit overdressed for the beach aren't you?" he asked, prompting me to look down at my hoodie and black leggings.

I smiled at him as I untied my Chuck Taylors and kicked them off. I pulled down my leggings exposing my black thong.

"Hey! Don't make me have to hurt somebody!" Anthony said seriously.

I bit my bottom lip as I swayed my body to the imaginary beat in my head, then I pulled my hoodie over my head exposing my very see through black lace bra.

"Damnit, woman!" Anthony sighed, placing his fingertips to his forehead.

I turned around exposing my bare, voluptuous ass that practically swallowed the thong I wore. I glanced over my shoulder and winked at Anthony before running out to the water. He shook his head as he smiled and gathered my clothes from the sand.

"This little firecracker is going to drive me fucking crazy," Anthony whispered as he grinned and made his way down to the ocean water.

After frolicking in the water and talking until the sun went down, we decided to head back into the villa.

"Can we go dancing tonight?" I requested.

"Amor, we can do whatever you want to do," Anthony responded.

As we approached the villa I could hear Tank, Bear, and Roman laughing and actually making jokes and I was surprised because I hadn't heard them this relaxed. Anthony noticed my surprised look.

"I gave them the night off," he informed me.

As we crossed into the villa the aroma hit me like a ton of bricks as my stomach began to turn flips, I was starving and the reality of how hungry I was had just set in.

"Oh my God! What is that heavenly smell?" I asked, inhaling the air around me.

In an overexaggerated accent Anthony said, "Ay! Mamacita, ven conmigo!" My brain worked overtime to translate. Oh! Mamacita, come with me! I laughed and grabbed his hand.

"I had our personal chef prepare some of my favorites for you! Here we have chiles en nogada, pozole, chilaquiles, mole poblano y sopa de lima! You're going to love it!" Anthony said.

I clasped my hands together. "I have no idea what you just said but I'm pretty damn excited about it! I don't know how the hell I'm going to fit into anything after I eat all of this, but I've never been known to back down from a challenge," I giggled.

We said grace and ate as a family and I felt at home. I didn't feel judged by Anthony for my past. I was able to be goofy with him. I didn't have to eat pretty and dainty, I could just be. It was the most relaxed I had felt in a very long time.

"We leave in an hour, Amor," Anthony informed me after we finished dinner.

"But where are we going?" I asked.

"You said you wanted to go dancing, right?" he responded.

I smiled because I hadn't expected him to really consider taking me to dance. Savior never even took me out for food in public, so I wasn't accustomed to asking to go out in public with a man I liked and actually going. I pushed through the clothes Charles Renee packed that were now hanging in the walk-in closet of the villa. When I spotted a cobalt blue bodycon dress covered in tassels, the rich color and uniqueness of the dress immediately captured my attention. I imagined Anthony spinning me in circles as the tassels lifted from the dress and floated in the air. I decided to pair the dress with a nude python strappy stiletto sandal and a simple Hermes wristlet just big enough for my phone, ID, and lipstick.

I showered as Anthony took his items to a guest bedroom to shower and prepare for the night. He was a gentleman, so it didn't surprise me that he would not invade my space until I had given him permission to do so. I decided to wear my hair in a large puff on the top of my head, off of my neck because I planned to dance the night away. I applied a soft pink lipstick to my plump lips and was almost out of the room when I doubled back for one more extra spray of the Baccarat Rouge 540 perfume Anthony had gifted me. A girl could never smell too good.

"Damn!" Anthony said as I walked from the bedroom.

"You like?" I asked, twirling around revealing my fabulousness. His eyes lingered enticingly on me as a charming grin graced his lips.

"Amor, Queen, you're sensational!" Anthony held his bottom lip between his teeth and moved closer to me, reaching down to catch my fingers as he nodded towards the door, signaling that it was time to go.

17
ANTHONY

When we arrived at the nightclub, music blared through the building, traveling outside, livening the atmosphere. A young, attractive woman with jet black hair greeted me by name and showed us to our private table and I immediately noticed Stacey's eyes cut towards the woman, as her glance traveled the length of the woman's body producing a forced grin. I chuckled silently at Stacey's unfiltered jealousy as I walked behind her, catching her fingertips, stopping her stride, wrapping an arm around her stomach pulling her into my chest. "You're fucking beautiful," was all I said and that forced grin was replaced with an ear to ear smile with a glint of gratification written across her face.

I wasn't flashy. As a matter of fact, I rarely wore anything that was visibly branded. I was one of those subtle millionaires. The kind that wore three hundred dollar t-shirts and custom made suits, but wouldn't be caught dead in anything monogrammed! I remembered my grandfather's words, perhaps the only thing of value he ever taught me. *"Nieto (grandson), when a man has money, he doesn't have to prove it to anyone. The flashiest man is the one with no appreciating assets."*

"Your waitress will be right with you!" the VIP host shouted over the roaring salsa music as she sauntered away to the next table.

"You okay?" I asked, scanning Stacey's body language in search of transparency.

She smiled and leaned over to kiss my lips. "I'm perfect," she said.

"Yes you are," I responded.

She rose from her seat and made her way to the dance floor staying within my visual range. She moved and gyrated her body to the sound of the beat, closing her eyes and raising both hands in the air, swaying smoothly, controlling the roll of her hips. I rested my hand over my dick to hide the half erection threatening to expand because this woman was fucking mind-blowing, and I couldn't exactly pinpoint what it was about her that had me ready to make her half-owner of all my damn assets.

I motioned my head towards her, prompting Tank and Bear to inch in closer. They didn't disturb her, but they stayed within arm's reach.

"Hola papi, what can I get you to drink?"

A half-dressed waitress approached me smiling seductively, purposely entering my personal bubble. When Stacey lifted her eyes to see the beautiful, scantily dressed woman, her expression changed as she cut her eyes at me. I hadn't paid any attention to the waitress, hadn't so much as given her the satisfaction of making eye contact with her. Even as the woman spoke to me, I ignored her, my eyes glued to Stacey, settling within her, proving a point. Roman eventually stepped in to place the drink order and Stacey grinned as my eyes traced her body. Nobody else mattered, and she needed to know that. Contentment graced Stacey's gaze as she caressed the back of her neck, while running one hand up her thigh, bunching her dress around her wrist, as she moved towards her vagina, threatening to expose herself. My demeanor shifted, as I scolded her with my eyes, giving her a *don't start no shit, won't be no shit* stare. She giggled, threw both hands in the air and spun around, relishing in the excitement of the night. I relaxed and sat back in my seat, relieved that I wasn't going to have to run to the dance floor and snatch her ass up.

Fucking firecracker, I thought.

Stacey hadn't noticed the drunk man thrusting his pelvis towards her as he approached with both arms extended and before she ever saw the man coming, Bear had one of his arms and Tank had the other as they twisted both arms behind his back, shoving him in the opposite direction. She was stunned to see the man's body slam into the ground as he slid across the club floor. She turned to me, popped one hip out and placed both hands on her waist. She stared at me through squinted eyes with pursed lips as I raised my eyes and shrugged both shoulders while mouthing, "what?" from across the room as if I hadn't instructed Tank and Bear to intervene. I shook my head and smiled at her as she turned her finger in a circle around the temple of her head, signifying that I was muy loco en cabeza.

Bottles of Clase Azul Resposado and Don Julio 1942 were delivered to the table and I poured a shot for my cousin Roman, as well as one for Stacey and myself.

"What about Tank and Bear? I thought you gave them the night off?" Stacey asked in an attempt not to leave them out.

"I did, but they insisted on being on duty while here at the club," I said.

We toasted and downed the shot together before she pulled me to my feet and into her chest. I instinctively wrapped one arm around the small of her back and swayed as I held onto her. Four songs played before we finally detached our bodies and I couldn't hear or see anyone else in the room. I was intoxicated by this woman. I was showing her the attention, giving her the affection every woman I slept with had begged me for and never received in the past. I wanted to rip her dress off and fuck her in the middle of the club; would have done it too, if she was one of my random toss ups, but she was more than that.

The ride back to the villa was intense and may have even looked awkward to anyone on the outside looking in as we sat in the back of the car trying not to dry hump right there on the seat; an invisible force tugging and pushing at our bodies as we groped one another before being forced apart by this *invisible* thing. The car we rode in wasn't like my SUV with a built in partition and I refused to allow anyone else to see Stacey in the way I planned on seeing her as soon as we stepped foot into the villa. When we arrived, Roman, Tank, and Bear made their way to the three bedroom casita at the west end of the villa. When the double doors of the villa closed, I walked up behind Stacey, pressing my body into her, pretty confident my dick touched her before my hands ever did.

"Wait," Stacey pleaded as my hands cupped her breasts. "When was the last time you got tested?"

"I get tested after every woman I'm with and I don't ever fuck them without protection," I said seriously with a look of disdain spread across my face at the mere thought. "I have my test results on my phone."

"So do I," Stacey countered.

We pulled up our results and swapped phones.

"Ambria, huh?" I chuckled.

"Hey!" She smiled and snatched her phone back. "Wait, it's been two months since you've been with someone? I would imagine you'd get it in every week!" Stacey chuckled.

"Not since I met you. I won't lie, I had more than a few in rotation, but nothing serious, and when I met you... cut them off," I admitted candidly.

Her face twisted in confusion. "When you met me? Why?" she asked.

"Didn't I tell you I get what I want? I knew I'd get you eventually," I said confidently.

"Well, since we'll be using protection—" Stacey said.

I interrupted her, "Says who?"

"You said you never have sex unprotected, didn't you?" she questioned.

"I said I never fucked *those* girls unprotected," I said, with raised eyebrows.

"Well...how do you know I'm not a hoe?" she tilted her neck, quizzing me.

"You know, you've asked me that more than once...if you are and I highly doubt it, your hoeing days are over," I said as I scooped her up and carried her to the master bedroom. When I placed her feet on the ground Stacey just stared at me for a moment. She grazed her fingers down my arms and back up, sliding over my neatly trimmed beard.

"Your body is perfect," Stacey admitted.

I chuckled. "Thank you. I worked hard to get it this way, I tend to pour my everything into something when I want it," I admitted, tilting my head slightly as I placed a finger under her chin, tipping her head back to stare into her eyes.

She removed my tailored blazer which exposed the two pistols I wore in my gun holster, as she carefully removed the holster, sitting it on the dresser. The undershirt I wore stretched against my chest and as she untucked it from my slacks, I helped her lift the shirt over my head. She stepped up on her tippy toes to kiss my lips and I met her halfway because at six foot two, I towered over her small frame as she slipped her tongue into my mouth, moaning while our tongues glided against one another softly. She pulled away and ran her fingertips across my chest and down my six pack as she unbuckled my belt and threw it on the floor. When she grabbed my pants to unbutton them, I restrained her hands and asked, "Are you sure?"

Instead of answering, Stacey continued to unbutton my pants and when I was revealed to her in my entirety she took a step back and her lips parted in amazement.

"I asked if you were sure," I said.

"Yeah but...Anthony, it's not gonna fit!" she said.

I smiled at her reaction. "Don't worry, I got you," I responded, grabbing her hand leading her to the shower.

I washed her body under the streaming water, paying close attention to her most intimate parts before washing myself as Stacey helped wash my back. When we were both clean, I turned to face her, appreciative of the beauty before me. We stepped out of the shower and I took pleasure in drying her body and rubbed her brown skin until she glowed from the shea butter and essential oil mixture. I bent down and whispered in her ear, "can I have you?"

Stacey looked into my eyes and nodded. I kissed her lips before laying her on the king sized bed. Her chest rose and fell with anticipation as I stared down at her naked body. I leaned over her, my tongue finding her neck where I placed soft, elongated kisses as I slid my tongue down to circle her erect nipples. I sucked and tugged gently, using my free hand to rotate her unoccupied nipple with my fingertips. Just the sensation of my tongue and fingers sent her body into a frenzy as she gripped the sheets and moaned softly, as I gently tugged at her nipple ring with my teeth,

"Uh, Anthony."

I slipped two fingers into my mouth and slid them inside of her, a side smirk tugging at the corner of my lips in satisfaction when she arched her back and moaned loudly. Stacey looked down at me to see what type of fucking voodoo I was performing down there. My fingers were inside of her pussy creating what I knew to be an insatiable pleasure based on her body language, and my thumb was on her clit rubbing in a constant circle.

"Anthony! Baby! You're going to make me cum!" she cried out.

"That's the plan," I said as I replaced my thumb with my tongue.

I took my time; I didn't rush with the delicacy of her blush pink pleasure. I widened my tongue and took all of her in, devouring every piece of wetness flowing from her middle. When I felt her juices begin to flow they didn't stand a chance before I cleaned every drop. I grabbed her hands instructing her to hold her legs back, and with both hands I stretched her pussy and ass as far as they would allow and drove my tongue into her center. I was fucking her but not with my dick, not yet. This was nothing short of a tongue fuck and she was losing her damn mind.

I managed to invade her insides with my mouth before moving up to suck her clit until she screamed, "Anthony!"

She began to whisper what initially sounded like sweet nothings, until I tuned in closer to her words as she whispered, "Damn, it's never felt this good before, what are you doing to me?"

I knew she wouldn't hold on much longer as I pulled my tongue out of her, inserted two fingers and rotated her clit again with my thumb. Her body revealed everything I needed to know and I could feel her walls tightening around my fingers as I said, "Cum for me, Amor."

"Oh shit! Ohhhh! Oh-shit-oh-shit!" she whimpered as I forced her body into two orgasms, one vaginal from my perfectly placed fingers on her g-spot, causing her to squirt all over the bed and one clitoral that made her eyes roll to the back of her head.

She didn't have the capacity to worry about how twisted and contorted her face was because it was obvious she had no control over her body. I was the puppet master at that moment. Seeing her lose control stroked my fucking ego creating an elusive feeling that I didn't want to end. As her wet thighs shook, her body experienced the aftermath of my handiwork, as tiny pulses sent shock waves through her body causing her to jump and jolt randomly as she laid on the bed. I kissed her clit softly, enjoying watching her squirm as her tight stomach flinched. I stood to my feet and my dick swayed between my thighs as I grabbed myself and began gently massaging my firm tip. Stacey reached down between her legs to touch herself for a moment before she sat up, scooting to the edge of the bed.

She sat staring at it for a moment before opening her mouth to speak. "Perfection," she said.

I chuckled. "How so?"

"It's long, thick, and everything I need right now," she responded.

As she prepared to take me into her mouth, I lifted her chin. "Amor, you don't have to if you don't want to," I stated in a sincere tone and I could tell she knew I meant it. I would never force her to do anything she felt uncomfortable doing.

She tilted her head and smiled at me. "There is absolutely nothing else I would rather do right now," she said, focusing her attention back to my dick and licking her lips before sliding me into her mouth.

She cupped my balls with one hand while sucking and rotating her hand up and down my dick. I knew I was too big to deepthroat, but she tried it anyway and that shit drove me crazy, so she kept going, gagging between each attempt. She released me from her mouth long enough to catch her breath but kept moving her hands up and down. I was sure she could tell from my body language that I would cum soon and she wanted to ensure that she sent my ass to cloud nine. She bobbed her head up and down and when she heard me groan, "I'm about to cum, Amor!" She placed both of my hands on her head giving me something to grab and she sucked relentlessly until she felt my warm semen slide down the back of her throat. I had planned on pulling out of her mouth but Stacey had other plans apparently. My fingers were wrapped in her curls and I held on tightly as my body jerked.

I moaned. "Fuck! So that's how you doing it?" I asked, glaring down at Stacey as if I wanted to fuck her into a coma.

"I mean, you set the tone, I was just following your lead," she teased with a grin on her face.

I straddled Stacey on the bed before asking, "Are you sure?"

"Anthony DeLeon! If you ask me that one more— Ahhhh." I was inside of her before she could finish her sentence, her moans filling each room of the villa.

I made love to her, kissing her lips, caressing her breasts and taking the time to listen to her body. We both moaned, faces glued together through sensual kisses as I rolled over with Stacey on top of me. Our chests pressed together as we sat upright in the bed and she rode me while I clung to her. I buried my face into her breasts as she slid up and down slowly. I placed my arms under her legs, grabbing her ass and gently pulling her pussy to my dick. Our bodies were tangled in the most beautiful way, sliding, grinding, thrusting and rarely allowing our lips to part. I stood to my feet still clinging to

Stacey, her arms wrapped around my neck as I cupped her ass. I slid her up and down gently and reached around further to give her asshole special attention.

"Ohhhh, right there, right there, don't stop," Stacey softly moaned into my ear causing my dick to jump inside of her.

"Are you on something? The pill? Anything?" I asked through my moans and groans.

"The pill," Stacey whined, "I get the – ahhhhh – the pill."

I placed one of Stacey's legs over my shoulder while the other leg was still wrapped around my waist.

"I didn't even know my body could do this! How the fuck am I even in this position?" Stacey asked in a pleasure induced haze of confusion.

I placed her back on the wall and sank deeper into her depths.

"Oh-shit-oh-shit-oh-shit!" Stacey moaned, "It's happening again!"

I felt the stream of liquid pour from her vagina and I lost myself in her wetness. I looked down as she squirted all over herself and me as I increased my speed, soaking up her juices as I plowed into her with a final thrust before quickly pulling out of her and emptying myself on the floor. Stacey shuddered in my arms and we stared at one another in complete silence, the ocean waves and blowing trees as our music. I stood there, holding her. I didn't move. She didn't move. We were just there...gazing into one another's eyes. I carried her limp body to the bed and rolled us both onto our sides. I lay nestled behind her and kissed the back of her neck before drifting off to sleep.

18
STACEY

I felt the morning breeze brush my skin, the birds chirped and the ocean waves crashed against the white sand beach. Anthony had opened the sliding glass door which led from the bedroom to the beach. I wrapped my body in the white bedsheet and tiptoed outside to find him sitting in a chair peering out at the water. I draped my arms around his neck and kissed his cheek.

"Good morning," I said softly.

"Good morning, Love," he responded.

"Ohhhh, so I'm Love and not Amor this morning?" I asked.

He laughed. "You're both, it just depends on whether I feel like speaking English or Spanish, but you're definitely both, baby."

I loved the way words rolled off that magical tongue of his. Anthony was a damn unicorn, not just because he was a full-fledged Black man that could speak Spanish but because he was young, rich, established—different from any man I had ever met and he wanted me. Broken me. Dysfunctional me. Fall in love too quickly me. He didn't care, he just wanted...me.

"I have some business to tend to today, and it might be best if you stay here," Anthony admitted.

I let go of Anthony's neck and walked around to the front of his chair.

"I'm not staying here; the whole purpose of this trip was for me to understand who you really are." I folded my arms across my chest still holding onto the bedsheet.

He looked up at me nonchalantly and then back to the water before responding, "You're staying," in an authoritative tone.

"No! I'm not!" I dropped the bedsheet and placed my hands on my hips, causing Anthony to shake his head and lick his lips before standing up towering over my sassy ass.

"It doesn't pay to ignore warnings," Anthony stated seriously and I was unmoved by his tone. He looked down at me before scooping me up and heading back to the bedroom for round two.

Anthony placed his muscular arms around my petite frame as I tamed my baby hair with edge control. I placed a thick coat of red lipstick on my lips as he spoke softly. "Baby, you're fucking gorgeous. You can swoop and swish those little hairs all you want, you can put on all the makeup, but just know that you're perfect the way you are," he said before bending over to kiss my neck.

He headed into the kitchen and I admired the man in front of me. He was one of those brothers you saw out in public and just hoped and prayed that he noticed you. His exterior was really just the icing on the cake because his personality was the real gem, and his ink filled skin added to the mystery of Anthony DeLeon and I wanted more of him. I blushed as he walked away. *How did I get so damn lucky?* I was known to fall too quickly and Anthony seemed to expedite my already fast tracked behavior, but I was in no position to stop. If I was going to fall on my face, I was going to do it with a running start and no hesitation. It was how I always lived my life and sometimes heartache was a buy one get one free special that came along with it.

Anthony was the perfect mix of hood bae and sophistication. I couldn't have dreamed up a better combo if I tried. When I was finally dressed and ready to tag along with Anthony to handle business, I noticed him leaning against the bedroom doorway staring at me.

"Is everything okay?" I asked, smiling in his direction.

He paused for a moment before speaking. "I want you to keep this in your purse." He held a small caliber pistol in his hand, motioning for me to grab it.

"But why? I'll be with you and the twins. I don't understand what use I would have for it," I admitted, holding upturned hands in the air as my shoulders stiffened in protest.

"Look, Amor, Mexico can be a dangerous country and I just want to make sure you're protected at all times," Anthony said.

I hesitantly picked up the gun from his palm and placed it into my purse. I wasn't a stranger to a pistol, but I just didn't feel it was necessary on a relaxing vacation with my man. Wait, was Anthony my man? Who the hell was I kidding? The way he handled my body with such precision, oh that negro was mine! He didn't have a choice. There was no way I was giving him back to the streets.

The ride into the city was breathtaking with immaculate views. I sat cuddled up next to Anthony, my fingers intertwined with his as he looked down at me and kissed the top of my forehead.

"Stay with me," Anthony suggested.

I raised my head from his shoulder and looked at him for a moment.

"But I am with you. I'm with you right now, silly," I said as I kissed his lips.

"I mean when we return to the states, come stay with me." His words were confident, calm and reassuring, but his eyes were begging me not to protest.

I playfully tapped him on his stiff chest. "Anthony DeLeon! You play too much!" I giggled, "just silly!" I was tickled and shook my head until I realized Anthony wasn't smiling or laughing and he didn't find humor in my statement.

"Wait a minute...you're serious, Anthony?"

"Do I look like I'm joking? Stacey, I'm not playing about you," Anthony's voice rang in my ears.

I cocked my head back before sliding to my side of the seat.

"But, Anthony!" was all I could get out before he interrupted.

"But nothing, Stacey. Do you enjoy being with me?" he asked.

"Yes but—"

"Do you get the same damn butterflies I get every time we're together?"

"Anthony...yes, but!"

"Do you need me, Stacey?"

"Baby, you *know* I do!"

"Well then it's settled. You're coming with me," he said.

I was at a loss for words. I had barely known this man for two months and he was asking me to come stay with him? I didn't know whether to celebrate or slap the negro for having the audacity to bark out orders as if we were an old married couple. I sat still in an attempt to interpret my feelings in hopes that I would understand why his request made me feel so emotional. Before I could process my thoughts, we pulled into a small village where local vendors sold handmade merchandise. Anthony stepped out of the car when Tank opened his door, and he held his hand out waiting for me to grab hold, so that he could help me step down. I stared at Anthony for a moment, causing him to notice my hesitation. He glanced at me and then he winked, causing me to blush and shake my head as I grabbed his hand.

"We're not finished discussing this," I said with a smile on my face, causing him to grin as he slid his sunglasses over his eyes. "Don't think that nice ass smile is going to make me sweep this under the rug either, Anthony!"

We visited multiple shops until a black SUV approached in the distance.

"Amor, I'm going to go talk to an old friend, make sure you get whatever you want and don't wander off too far, you know I like to keep my eyes on you." He swatted me on the ass before sauntering away.

I grinned and ran my fingers across multicolored handmade dresses. I noticed children in the distance motioning for me to come to their souvenir stand, the cute babies smiled and laughed motioning for me to follow them. I glanced back at Anthony who was still walking towards the SUV with Tank by his side before turning around to follow the children. They showed me toys and trinkets and I bought a few for no reason other than because the kids were so darn cute. I navigated further into a nearby shop, admiring beautifully painted plates and hand carved wooden statues when a shifty looking man caught my attention. His stringy hair and dingy clothes made him appear unkempt. He wore tattered sneakers and flashed a smudged silver tooth that made me cringe internally. After circling the store twice, he aggressively bumped into me causing my shoulder bag to fall to the ground.

"Oh! I'm so sorry," I stated, although I knew I wasn't at fault, as I knelt down to pick up my bag.

The bizarre man knelt beside me and whispered, "Hola, hablas Español?"

I was in a state of discomfort because this fucking man was mere inches away from my face. I could smell the beer on his breath and the fact that he hadn't showered in quite some time was painstakingly evident by the pungent smell exuding from his clothing.

I hurriedly gathered my scattered items as I responded, "No, not really, I only speak English. I'm sorry, I have to go. My boyfriend is—" I stopped, shifting my eyes while still positioned on the ground looking for Anthony or Tank…hell, anyone. The man slowly flipped a black switchblade from his pocket. "Come with me pretty lady," he said in a raspy, bone-chilling voice that immediately caused my heartbeat to quicken.

My intuition urged me to yell, but I was alone in the shop with this man. I had seen the shop attendant step out to smoke a cigarette, so yelling wouldn't help, and time was of the essence. I surveyed the shop searching for an exit route, considering my options as I silently prayed for someone to save me. I was prepared to make a run for it, but my thought of escaping was interrupted.

"Don't think about it. I can slit your throat before you ever make it to the front door," the man said.

The sudden shock made me tense and fear had become a tangible force that washed over my body causing my eyes to prickle with tears. How could I be so fucking gullible? Anthony warned me not to wander too far away. Fuck that! My father had always instilled in me the importance of monitoring my surroundings. Yet, here I was, vulnerable, exposed, alone and without options. The dingy man with the switchblade instructed me to stand up slowly and walk to the side exit of the shop without bringing attention to myself, assuring me that he would stab me in the spine if I made any sudden movements or attempted to alert anyone to what was happening.

"It would be a shame for a pretty girl like you to never walk again because she was too stupid to listen to instructions, wouldn't you say?" he asked in a low, sinister tone with the tip of his blade nudged into my spine.

He stood behind me, close enough that I could smell his revolting breath brush past my cheek and flow into my nostrils. He inhaled my scent with a deep breath as he allowed his lips to graze the nape of my neck. I whimpered and withdrew, becoming despondent when his sweaty palm captured my small arm with enough force to thrust my body forward. As he gripped my arm with his sticky hands and dirt stained fingers, I could feel the sharp blade still pressed against my skin, which inevitably caused me to drive my footsteps forward in hopes that he would release some of the pressure he placed on the switchblade.

I was flung by my arm into the chests of two unfamiliar men who waited outside of the shop. They gathered around me, hiding my body as they led me down an empty alleyway. Bear had stayed behind at the villa and Tank was escorting Anthony to the SUV. He had planned on returning to me once he ensured Anthony was inside the SUV safely but I would be gone when he returned. The men forced me behind a grimy dumpster as the one holding the switchblade began to unbuckle his pants.

"No no-no-no-no-no," I began to sob as flashbacks of my uncle invaded my memory. "Please don't! You don't have to do this, I have money!"

I pleaded with both hands clasped in front of my chest. For a moment I was a ten year old little girl again, only this time, I knew the devastation of having someone inside of me that was never given permission to be there. My legs trembled instinctively, as I remembered the weight of my aunt's husband crushing my tiny body. I was willing to fight for my life and my sanity before I would ever give my body to another man without choosing to do so. A light bulb flickered in my brain as I remembered the gun Anthony had insisted I carry in my purse, and just as I made a mad dash into my shoulder bag, the tall heavy set man snatched it from me, almost taking my arm with it.

"We'll take that too!" the goliath of a man sneered as he began to rummage through my bag. If they found the gun I was as good as dead. I needed to create a distraction to halt his search of my bag. I knew screaming held its own consequences but they couldn't be worse than dying in this filthy ass alley, or having one of these thug's disease infested dicks penetrate me. In a moment of desperation I screamed louder than I ever thought humanly possible and made my own eardrums thump with excruciating pain.

"Help! Anthony! Hel—"

The man holding the switchblade aggressively covered my mouth, shoving his elbow into my neck and scolded me. "You stupid bitch! Didn't I tell you—"

Before he could finish his sentence, three gunshots rang out as Tank and Anthony rounded the end of the alleyway. Tank sprinted towards me, which I wouldn't have believed he was capable of doing just based on his massive size, had I not seen it with my own eyes. He pointed a gun in the men's direction as the thug with his arm jammed into my neck yelled, "Get back or I'll cut this bitches throat!" Spit flew from his mouth into my face as I blinked my eyes closed, gagging silently.

I just needed him as far away from me as possible, he occupied my personal space and made me feel befouled, nasty, violated. Anthony sauntered down the alley as if he weren't pressed for time. He never rushed, never quickened his step, he just strolled, which left me perplexed because I could practically see the anger permeating from his body. Two of the men glared at one another as if they had seen a ghost when Anthony stepped closer and his face came into clear view.

"Oh fuck! Mr. DeLeon. Shit!" One of the two men whispered, as the other dropped my bag to the ground like it pained his hands to hold it any longer.

"M-Mr. DeLeon, we-we didn't know you were in town; we didn't know she was associated with you," one man stuttered and stammered through his words.

Anthony removed the toothpick from his mouth, flicking it in the men's direction before slowly pulling a gun from his shoulder holster and responding, "Mm-hmm, is that so?"

He hadn't even made eye contact with the attempted kidnappers as he pulled a small metal piece from a hidden slot on his holster.

"Let her go!" one of the two men whispered and nudged his friend who was still holding me by the neck.

"This is Mr. Fucking DeLeon, you asshole. Let her go before he kills all of us!" the bag snatcher gritted through his teeth.

Anthony still hadn't looked up to acknowledge the men as he screwed the metal barrel onto the end of his gun.

"Mr. DeLeon, we're really sorry! We don't want no trouble! We didn't know she was with you! Por favor!" the other man cried.

I was mortified by the calmness of Anthony's demeanor and even more terrified by how these two, full grown men were now cowering like two bitches. There must be some cruel inside joke I wasn't made privy to. How had my sweet, passionate, thoughtful Anthony generated so much fear in a matter of seconds? The unanswered questions frightened me more than the series of unfortunate events unfolding in front of my eyes. *What the fuck was happening and how did these men know Anthony?* He braced both feet on the ground before lifting his head to speak, determining that his conversation should remain confidential because I had apparently, seen and heard enough for one day. Anthony spoke in Spanish in an attempt to protect what little piece of adoration I may have still held for him.

"Escúchame. Tus acciones de hoy te han costado más de lo que esperabas, estoy seguro. Esta mujer a la que has intentado dañar, es mía. Tus hijos y tus esposas pagarán los crímenes que cometiste contra mí. Te doy mi palabra de que haré que sus muertes sean rápidas, pero te prometo que morirán ".

Anthony's voice was smooth, calm, and more serious than I had ever witnessed, but I had no idea what he was saying.

"Sir please, we didn't know!"

The silencer Anthony screwed onto the end of the gun muffled the shots as the bodies of the two men hit the pavement. I struggled to catch my breath, and stood there motionless as the man holding me against the wall with his pants pulled halfway around his thighs looked at his friend's slumped bodies in sheer terror. He finally let me go and threw his hands up in an attempt to surrender. I doubled over as I grabbed my neck and exhaled a hyperventilated cry. Sobs fell from my lips as a steady stream of tears washed over my face and then rage set in.

"Ahhhhh! Fuck you!"

I charged at the man, grabbing a fist full of his greasy hair, banging his head against the concrete building. He fell to his knees and I punched, clawed, and kicked at the man's face until I felt Tank's machine-like arm wrap around my stomach and tear me away from the pervert who had attacked me, as I kicked and screamed.

Two more gunshots and this time I felt a wave of sickness crash down over my body. I turned away from the outstretched body and emptied the contents of my stomach onto the ground. Seeing his genitals blown off had proven to be too much for me as I staggered away from Tank and Anthony. Just as my vision began to fade, I felt my body drop.

19
ANTHONY

When Stacey awakened, she was tucked snuggly in the bed inside my villa with a cold towel placed across her forehead. I sat in a chair next to the bed gazing at her with concerned eyes as my stomach turned in knots, anticipating what her first words would be. Would she scream? Would she be afraid of me? I hadn't left her side since bringing her back to the villa. Beneath my tough exterior, I was worried that Stacey might leave me, now that she had gotten a glimpse of who I was, the type of trouble that followed me, and how fiercely I was willing to protect anything and anyone important to me.

She blinked a few times and darted her eyes around the room before settling on me. She smiled and reached for me. I reached out, clasping her hand inside of mine and kissed her fingers gently.

"Will you lay with me?" she asked in a groggy voice.

I was happy to do as she asked, as I cuddled up behind her nestling my nose into the back of her neck. I felt the need to explain, which I wasn't accustomed to doing because I didn't have to. Women flocked to me and I was never pressed for any of their attention, but the thought of losing Stacey pained me, leaving an empty feeling inside my core.

"Love, about today," I spoke, breaking the silence.

"I'm not ready yet," Stacey admitted.

"I respect that. Will you let me know when you're ready?" I asked, my tone was genuine, soft, concerned.

"Of course I will, baby," she replied.

"And please don't leave me," I begged.

What the fuck was wrong with me? Begging? Me? Ah hell no! But I was, and I meant it. She was silent and before I realized it, she drifted back to sleep.

The flight back home was peaceful, and Stacey spent the majority of her time in the air silent, glaring out the window. She wasn't ready to discuss the incident with me and explained that she needed more time to process. She couldn't speak to me until she had her own clear understanding of the situation because it was public knowledge that I had a way of swaying her thoughts. As she so eloquently put it when I attempted to pressure her to speak to me before stepping onto the jet, my seductive eyes, irresistible lips, enticing body, and not to mention the third leg between my thighs and the fact that I could eat her pussy and tell her the sky was purple and she'd believe me was the reason she needed to think without me as a distraction. She claimed to need an unsatisfied vagina to navigate through her feelings without the influence of my dick.

I placed my hand between her thighs to keep it warm and narrowed my eyes in on her, wishing I could peek into that beautiful head of hers to understand what she was thinking. I wished I could simply remove my heart if only for a moment to show her what was inside, to prove to her how crazy I was about her. From the moment I laid eyes on her, I made it my mission to have her, I was determined to make her my queen. If she knew that I was scared shitless of losing her and that I had no choice but to end the idiots that threatened to take away my only good thing. I needed Stacey to know, but I was also willing to respect her need to take time to process.

"I'm going to the restroom, Anthony. I'll be right back," she informed me.

I didn't allow her to walk away until I kissed her passionately and reminded her, "You're fucking gorgeous, you know that?"

Stacey smiled and made her way to the restroom.

STACEY

I was grateful that the jet contained a larger lavatory than commercial planes. There was even a built in cushioned seating area. I didn't need to use the restroom; I just needed a moment alone. I stared at myself in the gold trimmed mirror and ran my hands down my face.

"Get it together, bitch!" I told myself as I braced my weight on the marble countertop.

I was experiencing an internal battle that pulled at my heartstrings and caused me to question my own morality. Although Anthony never lied about who he was, he wasn't completely upfront either. He was obviously dangerous and I was having a difficult time envisioning how he fit into my life. I owned a gym and enjoyed Saturday morning brunch and Sunday Funday, how would being involved with a killer fit into my world? I mean, he was clearly more than a killer, which didn't make the situation any better. What else was he into? Drugs, prostitution, transporting illegal firearms? My mind ran rampant with thoughts of the what ifs. What if his business affairs made their way full circle and came looking for me, or even worse, my family? Was this a risk I was willing to take? I closed my eyes trying to clear the thoughts swarming in my head but before I could look up, Anthony invited himself into the restroom and in a wild stampede of emotion, he scooped me up by my thighs and forced his tongue into my mouth.

He ravished me, licking and sucking my neck, sucking my bottom lip, sucking any part of me he could get his mouth on. I pushed his head away from me, even though he had me elevated in the air with my legs wrapped around his waist. I was angry. I shoved his head in an attempt to stop his kisses, but he persisted.

"No Anthony, you put me in danger!" I whined as tears involuntarily trickled down my face.

"Amor, I'm so sorry!" Anthony admitted between kisses. "I'm so sorry, forgive me!"

Before I realized it, I threw my head back as Anthony kissed my neck. My fighting turned into groping and grinding in no time.

I knew this shit would happen.

I clawed at Anthony's shirt until I was able to pull it over his head. His firm, tattooed chest clenched together holding my body weight. I traced my fingers over a large tattoo. Original Gangster was displayed proudly across his chest. I hadn't noticed before because his entire body was covered in tattoos and the cursive letters blended seamlessly with the rest of the artwork on his body; but today, I saw it crystal clear. As tears continued to fall, I lifted my eyes to meet Anthony's. My hand moved before I realized what was happening and the sound of my palm slapping his face pulled me from the trance that engulfed me.

He stood in disbelief and slid his hand to his face, landing on the sharp stinging sensation. A fire lit behind his eyes and his lips curled turning his apologetic disposition into a scowl. He removed his hand from his face and slowly inched it towards my head before snatching my hair at the roots aggressively, causing my head to fall back as I moaned. He leaned in and licked from my neck, up my chin, over my lips, and up my cheeks clearing away my tears. My nipples hardened.

"Fuck you, Anthony!" I yelled into his face.

He was still holding my body against his and I had yelled so close to his face that he raised an eyebrow in bewilderment. I hadn't meant to yell so loudly, but I couldn't hold it in. I was pissed, but wanted him to fuck me at the same time. So yes, fuck him for making me feel this way! He put me down and looked at me before walking towards me, backing me into the cushioned bench. I was visibly angry and still crying, but I didn't want him to stop. I fell back, plopping onto the bench as Anthony got down on both knees staring at me without speaking as he pulled my baggy joggers down. He broke eye contact with me to admire my body. The blush crop top I wore stopped right under my breasts and the imprint of my hard nipples was visible. He rubbed his hands up my thighs, navigating over my waist and then under my shirt, firmly gripping my breasts. I closed my eyes and exhaled a deep breath.

"Fuck it!" I said as I sat up grabbing his face with both hands and forcing my tongue into his mouth as he returned the favor.

I stood up to roll my panties down and sat back on the bench, propping both of my feet up.

"I thought you said fuck me?" Anthony asked with a slight smirk.

"You say you're sorry, right?" I asked. "Well then...show me how sorry you are."

Anthony pushed my crop top up to my chin and snatched my bra down causing my titties to bounce out of the bra. As he caressed both of them in his hands, he slightly tugged at my nipple rings, causing me to gasp. He leaned over, kissing my stomach delicately as I sank my fingers into the plush curls he'd decided not to subdue into waves. He slipped his tongue into my belly button and I fought back a smile as he kissed my inner thighs and hugged them forcefully with his muscular arms.

ANTHONY

I wanted to feel her wrapped around me as I kissed and lightly bit the inside of each of her warm, soft, yet firm inner thighs. Stacey's pussy was pretty fucking beautiful to look at and I wanted her to cum all over my face, the apology that kept on giving. I wanted to make her forget the bad parts of the week and remember how our kindred souls connected before all the bullshit unfolded. If I had to eat her pussy every single day, shit, multiple times a day, I was more than willing to do that. I licked my lips and kissed her entire pussy. I hadn't even opened her lips yet and she was already about to lose her shit. I tongue kissed her pussy, making love to it with my mouth. When I split her lips with my tongue and rotated her clit in a circular motion, her legs quaked and trembled. I allowed my saliva to slide down her clit to her pussy opening and slid one finger inside her tight walls as she met my thrust and began fucking my finger.

I loved the taste of her. She always smelled like coconuts and vanilla and her taste? She tasted like fucking pineapples and honey. Everything about this woman was above average and I had no plans of letting her go. I moved in and out of her enjoying watching her juices glide up and down my finger while my tongue worked her simultaneously. I felt her walls tightening and knew she would cum soon, so I decided to fuck with her due to that little slap she decided to land on my face moments earlier.

"You said fuck me, right, that is what you said, isn't it?" I asked in an arrogant tone, still thrusting my fingers in and out of her.

"Uh...yes, but," Stacey panted as she bucked her body against my finger.

"But what? You were talking some big shit just a second ago," I reminded her.

"Baby, I'm sorry," she moaned.

"Nah, but you will be," I said as I inserted another finger into her walls and sucked her clit.

"Oh shit!" Stacey screamed, "Fuck! Baby!"

She didn't give a damn about anyone else onboard the jet. I was certain they could hear her screams and moans but all that mattered was the apology I was giving between her legs. She pushed at the top of my head which was her signal, letting me know that the intense feeling growing in the pit of her stomach was about to explode. Her legs locked around my neck and her nipples were so hard they resembled small pebbles. I could tell she wanted to yell stop, but she didn't and I was unyielding in my effort to make her cum.

My fingers were still moving in and out of her at a steady pace and I sucked her clit like a damn machine. I felt a gush of her wetness wrap around my fingers and kept moving them in and out of her and intensifying my sucking until she locked my head between her thighs and began convulsing as she screamed, "Fucking shit, Anthony, it feels so *good*! I'm cumming, I'm cumming, I'm cumming! Fuck!"

My face was wet and I didn't give a damn. My beard leaked with Stacey's juices and I didn't even attempt to wipe it away as I kissed her lips, allowing her to taste the sweetness that I had just had the pleasure of enjoying as I said, "I'm sorry, Amor…now stand up."

STACEY

I could barely move, how the hell did he expect me to stand up! I managed to drag myself to my feet and looked up at him.

"Turn around," Anthony instructed.

I did as I was told but wore a confused expression. He slapped my ass cheek aggressively as he watched it jiggle causing me to gasp, my shoulders jerking in surprise. He cocked my leg up on the bench and pulled my body back into his stomach as he grasped the front of my neck and whispered into my ear, "You're the only person to ever put their hands on me and get away with it." He reached between my legs sliding his fingers around my wetness.

I drew in a breath. "Baby, about that, I'm really sorry," I whined trying to turn and face him, but he held me in place by grabbing the back of my neck and pushing me down, causing me to brace my hands on the back of the bench.

"I told you earlier than you'd be sorry, didn't I?" Anthony said as I looked back at him.

He spit into his hand before rubbing it all over his tip and shaft and sank into my wet walls as I screamed his name. I alternated between screaming his name, screaming that I was sorry, and screaming please don't stop. He held his bottom lip between his teeth, watching my full ass bounce on his dick, grabbing a fist full of curls, yanking my head back as he pumped vigorously admiring the deep arch in my back.

"Keep your fucking hands to yourself, do you understand me?" he grunted as he beat up my walls.

"Ahhh! Okay, baby! I promise! I promise! Shit! I promise!" I moaned.

Anthony repositioned me, making me touch my toes and as he plowed even deeper and my knees began to buckle. He was fucking my pussy up! I felt his pace quicken as he grunted an animalistic growl before pulling out and releasing his seed onto my ass. He stepped back into his underwear, not even bothering to wipe my juices off of him and he captured my chin, kissing me intensely.

"I love you, Stacey," he admitted gazing into my eyes, "Don't say anything, I just needed you to know."

He stared at me for a moment longer before kissing me again and bending down to pick up my thong to hand it to me.

"Come out whenever you're ready, I'll be waiting for you." He grinned and kissed my cheek before stepping out of the restroom.

I fell back onto the bench and just sat there, reliving what Anthony has just done to my body. He was going to have to be my last because there was no way anyone would ever be able to top the dick this king was dishing out. Even Savior's ass had never done it like this and that was saying a whole fucking lot. How had what was supposed to be his apology end up being my apology? Had me apologizing like a damn fool. I thought I was crazy for wanting to tell Anthony I loved him. I was sure it would send him running, but now I knew it wouldn't because he said it first. I couldn't contain my smile as I rolled my panties back over my sticky behind and slipped my joggers back on. *Maybe this is what love was,* I thought. Maybe it was complicated and awkward and ugly at times, but if two people loved each other, they could figure out all the ugly stuff, right?

I walked shyly past Roman, Tank, Bear, and the stewardess and sat next to Anthony who reached for my hand and gently kissed my wrist.

"Baby, I'm so embarrassed. I'm pretty sure they heard me," I said, burying my face into his shoulder.

He chuckled. "What? You think they ain't never made love before?"

I tilted my head back and smiled. "Oh! Is that what you call what we just did? Making love? Because I'm pretty sure you just fucked my pussy into a coma," I said.

"Well, I love you, so yeah, I'd say it was making love. I just did it the DeLeon way," he replied as he smirked.

"Mmmhmm, I love you, too," I said, causing Anthony to quickly turn and look at me. "I do love you," I repeated. He smiled and leaned in to kiss my full lips.

"I promise to tell you everything when we get home," Anthony said, which prompted me to hold my pinky finger out to him.

He looked at my finger, then into my eyes, and then at his finger before wrapping his pinky around mine. We both kissed the end of our hands with our pinkies intertwined to seal the deal. He kissed my forehead and placed his hand between my warm thighs.

20
STACEY

It had been a few weeks since we returned from Mexico and my father was adamant about me coming to dinner with Anthony. The idea terrified me because I had gotten used to enjoying Anthony in the comfort of my own little bubble. I hadn't had to share him with anyone and I felt like that might be why things seemed so perfect when we were together. The more people involved, the messier a situation could become. I appreciated having King Anthony DeLeon all to myself.

He crept up behind me and wrapped both arms around my waist, causing me to jump as he tickled me playfully, placing multiple kisses on my neck.

"Oh! You scared me," I shrieked with a giggle.

"I have something for you," he said as he pulled my body close to his gripping my ass cheeks and rubbing them softly.

"Well, if it's what I think it is, then we'll never make it to dinner in time!" I teased.

"Oh, you're gonna get some of that later," Anthony laughed, "but I was referring to something else. Come with me and close your eyes."

I grabbed his hand as he led me from his bathroom into the master bedroom where three gifts wrapped in white polka dot wrapping paper with gold bows tied around each package sat on his bed.

"What is this for?" I asked excitedly.

"Just because," he responded as he slapped my behind.

"Somebody can't keep their hands to themselves tonight, I see," I responded with a smirk.

"Go ahead, open them," he said as I picked up the first package and ripped the wrapping paper to reveal a pair of Air Jordan 1 retro high top Travis Scott sneakers.

"Anthony! These sneakers cost over two thousand dollars, are you serious? You didn't have to do this for me." I was extremely grateful but the gift was too much.

"I overheard you and Rachel talking about them, so I decided to cop you a pair," Anthony stated nonchalantly.

I smiled a toothy grin. "Thank you baby, you trying to get you some pussy tonight, huh?" I asked, teasingly grabbing at his dick.

"We gone fuck around and miss dinner if you grab my dick again," Anthony responded seriously, "Open the other two."

I opened a brand new Tiffany & Company charm with the initials S.D. printed on it. My current charm only held the traditional Tiffany & Company heart.

"I got the S.D. because I'm gonna marry you one day," Anthony said matter of factly.

My eyebrows shot up in surprise and my jaw dropped.

"Really now? I might be more than you bargained for Mr. DeLeon," I teased as I prepared to open my final gift.

"Now don't lose your shit over this last one. I can explain," Anthony warned.

I opened a box and the most stunning, seven carat, solitaire, diamond ring I had ever seen was glistening inside the box. I sat down on the bed voiceless, never removing my eyes from the diamond ring.

"Okay, so let me explain, Amor." Anthony's voice was shaky.

It was the first time I had ever heard him sound afraid.

"So, you know I love you, right? I mean…shit! Of course you know that already. What I'm trying to say is that…well, Stacey, I got you this ring because I love you and I want to marry you. Not right now! But I know I want to. So, I got you this just in case there was any doubt in your mind about where I stand. Don't wear it until you're ready, it doesn't matter how long it takes, whether it's two months from now, or two years from now, two hours from now would be nice, but…I just needed you to know where I stand."

Anthony's cheeks were a blush pink color, which wasn't an easy task behind his chestnut brown skin.

"Ahhhhhmmm – I…I—um. *Shit, Anthony*! Really?"

"Really – Amor."

Unshed tears crowded my eyes as I stared at him in disbelief, my bottom lip hanging as my eyes bucked from his words of confirmation. It wasn't that I didn't want Anthony because I did…I really *fucking* did. But…the timing, it was quick— it was…too quick. *What if it didn't work out?*

I hadn't noticed the tears sliding down my cheeks until I was pulled from my daze by the gentle touch of Anthony's thumb sweeping the droplets of water from my face.

"Hey—you know how I feel about those tears," he reminded me, causing a giggle to escape my lips as I wiped my face with the outside of my wrists.

"What about when they're happy tears?" I asked, gazing at him with a grin.

"I mean, happy tears are alright I guess," he teased.

"Escuchame Amor, just—think about it…be sure because—once you say yes, I'm not letting you go."

"Well, this is it," I said as we arrived at my parents' house, "My dad already likes you, so I doubt you'll have to try very hard."

I had a hard time focusing on dinner because I couldn't tear my mind away from the diamond Anthony gifted me with and the Mexico conversation was well past due. I had been avoiding it for fear of losing Anthony, but I had the feeling that tonight he wouldn't take no for an answer when it was time to have the conversation. I appreciated the fact that the dinner with my parents was going more smoothly than I expected. My mother and father seemed as if they hadn't missed a beat.

"So Anthony, what do you do?" my father asked.

Anthony wiped his mouth with the Hill monogrammed napkin and cleared his throat before speaking.

"Actually Mr. Hill, I'm a real estate investor. I own multiple buildings throughout the city and I also dabble in the stock market. I was blessed to have a few investments handed down to me through a family trust, which allowed me to grow my business."

My mouth dropped at the elaborate lie Anthony was able to create on such short notice. Well, maybe all of it wasn't a lie. Hell. Maybe none of it was a lie, but omission was equivalent to telling a lie, wasn't it?

"Baby Girl, I like him!" my dad stated, "Now that's the kind of man I would like to welcome into this family one day."

I hid behind my hand in embarrassment as I squeezed Anthony's thigh. My parents had managed to keep the cringeworthy baby stories to a minimum and my father thankfully neglected to mention how much of a juvenile delinquent I was as a teenager.

"So Anthony, do you have children?" my mother asked, while placing a perfectly cut piece of green bean into her mouth.

I noticed Anthony shift uncomfortably in his seat and I wanted to intervene. Just as I sat up in my seat and prepared to come to his rescue, he gripped my thigh gently, as if to say, "I've got this."

"Well actually Ms. Hill, I had a daughter, but she passed away unexpectedly as a toddler from medical complications. Now I just pray that God blesses me to one day become a father again," he said with a tight lipped grin.

My eyes lingered on Anthony and my heart broke for him as I placed my hand on top of his, giving it a gentle squeeze.

"I'm so sorry to hear that, son," my father said, his brows furrowed with sympathy.

After dinner, I was ready to have Anthony all to myself again. And when my father asked, "So Anthony, you two getting physical yet?" That was my cue to get us the hell outta there.

"That's a really great question honey, I'd like to know, too." My mother smiled widely and I rolled my eyes at her nosy ass.

"Okay parentals, enough of that, dinner has been great and we've really enjoyed chatting with you both, but we have a few more stops to make before the night is over," I informed my parents as I stood from the table.

"Anthony dear, please don't be a stranger, you're always welcome in our home," my mother stated, kissing his cheek.

Once back in the SUV I couldn't contain my anger.

"How the fuck did you lie so well back there?" I blurted out with my arms folded across my chest.

"What? I didn't lie, Love. Everything I said to your parents was the truth," he stated nonchalantly.

"Sounded like a lie to me!" I shot back.

"I don't fucking lie, Stacey," he scolded.

"So then what, Anthony? You just omit shit and you think that's better?" I yelled, becoming more infuriated at his laid back demeanor.

"Stacey, I've been trying to talk to you about this shit for weeks! Don't act like I'm the one that's been avoiding the damn conversation! If you'd put your big girl panties on we could just talk about the shit and be done with it!" Anthony said through gritted teeth.

"So now I'm being childish?" I questioned.

"Don't put words in my mouth, Love. That's not what I said!" Anthony said, still remaining calm, leaving my energy unmatched and my frustration rising.

"Fine, Anthony! Let's talk. Since you want to talk about it so badly, then let's do it!" I said.

"Amor, I don't like this, we're screaming at each other…well, you're screaming, cursing, this isn't us. We don't do this. I love you, Stacey."

Anthony was right, this wasn't us, and I didn't want it to be us. It was hurting my heart that I felt angry, my eyes softened as I reached for his hand.

"I love you too, baby. That's why I've been so afraid to have this conversation, I don't want what you tell me to ruin us Anthony. I don't want us to be over." There it was, my reason, the reason I had been avoiding the Mexico conversation.

"Love, the only thing that can ruin us is us," he said as he kissed my wrist.

Roman parked the SUV in front of my penthouse apartment and raised the partition.

"So how about this," Anthony began, "I'll stay with you tonight so that we can talk and I'll also help you grab a few things that you'd like to keep at my house. How does that sound?"

I smiled as I rested my hand on his tight chest. "I like the sound of that, but are you sure you don't want us to just go back to your place tonight? My penthouse is cool, but it's definitely a downgrade compared to your spot," I admitted.

"Nah, Amor, you always come to me, let me come to you." He leaned in to kiss my lips and responded, "You taste like candy."

I giggled. "Do I?" I smiled while biting my bottom lip, gushing at how quickly he changed the subject and positively shifted the energy in the SUV.

"Yep and your pussy tastes like pineapples and honey," Anthony growled, sliding his hands between my thighs.

I threw my head back and laughed at him. "You're so nasty! Stop it before you get me going!" I pushed his hand from between my legs and kissed his lips.

Tank walked me and Anthony up to the penthouse and Anthony reminded him, "You can pick us up tomorrow around...." He trailed off, looking toward me for confirmation.

"Around noon should be good," I confirmed before wrapping both arms around Tank and saying, "See you tomorrow."

Anthony lifted both eyebrows staring in Tank's direction. "Say, nigga! Do I need to fire your big ass?" he asked in a joking tone.

I jokingly popped Anthony on the shoulder. "You better leave my friend alone, get in this house!" I shoved Anthony through the doorway.

"See you tomorrow, Tank," I said, closing the door.

"Hey, y'all!" Rachel shouted from the living room sofa.

"Hey, girl!" I said as I walked over to kiss Rachel on the cheek.

"How you doing, friend?" Anthony asked Rachel.

"I'd be better if you two lovebirds found me a damn man so I can stop sitting here by myself all damn day," she blurted.

"My boy Tank is available," Anthony responded.

Rachel snapped her neck around to look at him. "That nigga is huge! I got a fly mouth; he'll fuck around and knock me into a wall!" Rachel laughed.

I shook my head, and grabbed Anthony's hand, leading him into my bedroom. After getting comfortable in the bed, positioned between Anthony's legs and leaning back onto his chest I finally asked, "So, what do you really do Anthony? Give me the real, I'm ready."

He paused for what seemed like an eternity, but in actuality was only about two minutes before sucking in a deep breath and saying, "I'm the head of the DeLeon Cartel."

"Cartel! Like drugs and killing and hiding out from the police and all the shit I see in the movies?!" I sat up and flipped my body around to face Anthony. I could feel my stomach twisting as goosebumps began to flood my skin.

"Uh, not quite like the movies, but similar," Anthony responded hesitantly.

My reaction was making him nervous and Anthony didn't get nervous, but somehow, I was able to pull emotions out of him that he wasn't accustomed to feeling.

"Love, breathe," he reminded me because I hadn't taken a breath since he mentioned the word cartel.

I inhaled a deep breath.

"So...do you kill people? No, that's a stupid question. I've seen you kill someone, but do you do it all the time?" I couldn't figure out a better question because my brain was rattling inside of my head as I tried to process the information Anthony had just given me.

"I usually don't. I have people who will do that for me," he admitted boldly.

"Anthony, I'm going to be honest, I'm two seconds away from running out of that door." I pointed to my bedroom door. "You're going to have to make this shit make sense to me."

I sat in my bed facing him with my legs crossed between his legs. He ran his hands down his deep waves and over his beard.

"Amor, I'm gonna be honest, my stomach is in knots right now, and I've never felt this shit before in my life," he said, looking genuinely hesitant to speak. "There's no politically correct, or pretty way to explain my occupation and I can feel you slipping away Stacey, each time I open my mouth, you're slipping away." Anthony clasped his hands together and placed them on top of his head.

"Well, I need you to try to explain, try, for me," I said, placing my hands onto his legs as I inched closer to him.

"It's complicated, Amor. The business is multifaceted. Yes, a portion of the business is run off smuggling drugs, another sector is run off the transportation of illegal firearms and the last sector of the business is our real estate. I don't do anything illegal through the real estate. I've worked diligently to keep that part of the business legit, and no, we don't fuck around with human trafficking. If I found out anyone in my organization was, I'd—" Anthony paused.

"You'd kill them?" I asked, in a low voice as I dropped my eyes. He raised my head with his fingers, allowing his eyes to meet mine.

"Yes, I would and I don't want that to scare you because I would never hurt you, Love. But I need you to know who I am and what I'm capable of," he said.

We sat there silently staring at one another.

"Talk to me, Amor. Tell me something, be upset, hit me, scream, do or say something, but please don't just sit there," Anthony pleaded.

I glanced away from him because I could feel my eyes burning and knew the tears wouldn't be too far behind.

"Anthony, you made me love you. You let me fall in love with you, knowing you had this secret, what am I supposed to do?" I asked, shrugging helplessly.

I noticed a tear escape Anthony's eyes, and a familiar expression crossed his face, one I remembered from the day he told me about his baby girl, Ava. Another tear formed and slid down slowly, surprisingly; he made no attempt to disguise his anguish.

"Just love me," Anthony struggled to say.

I peered into Anthony's eyes and could feel his pain. He wanted me, he needed me. He wasn't a crying man, and I knew that this moment was especially for me. The tears, the delicacy of his emotions were reserved for my eyes only. He needed me to see how vulnerable he was with me, how much he loved me. I crawled onto my knees and leaned forward, gently wiping away his tears and kissed his soft lips. In that moment, I made the decision to love him through his faults. I didn't have a clear understanding of how loving Anthony DeLeon, the head of the Cartel, would change the trajectory of my life, or what it meant for our relationship moving forward. What I did know was that

I loved the shit out of this man, and I was willing to go the distance with him.

"Nothing will make me stop loving you, Anthony DeLeon."

ANTHONY

I placed both hands into her fluffy curls and kissed her passionately, melting away her fears and anxiety.

"Make love to me, Anthony," she requested and I did as I was asked, multiple times until she creamed all over me and I put her to sleep, safely in my arms.

That night our souls tied and I knew I had found my queen. I had never exposed who I was to any woman I had ever been with, not even Ava's mother. I was taking a risk by disclosing my true business dealings to Stacey, but she made me feel safe and I didn't want our relationship to be built on lies. I lay awake in bed, staring at her angelic face and admiring her breathtaking curves beneath the white bedsheets. I couldn't take my eyes off of her. I was willing to risk my life and the business I spent my entire adulthood building for the heart of this woman. She was worth every hypothetical risk I drummed up in my brain. Somehow, I knew trusting Stacey with my secret was a crucial stepping stone in our relationship, and I had no regrets in regards to trusting her. My mother on the other hand might have quite a bit to say about it, but that was a headache for another day. I received a text message that drew my attention away from Stacey as I glanced down at my phone and back to her sleeping body before sliding from the bed and sauntering into the bathroom.

"What do you mean you couldn't find him?" I asked as I immediately became annoyed by the incompetence of my associate. "Look, nigga! I'm going to say this one time and it'll be the last time I say it. Find him and bring him to me! Alive!"

I hung up the phone and turned to see Stacey teetering towards me, rubbing her eyes sleepily.

"I'll slap that hoe." She stretched her arms to both sides, and yawned, her eyes hardly open as she walked past me.

I threw my head back and bellowed a roar of laughter. "Love, what are you talking about?" I asked in an amused tone as I tilted my head to gaze at my woman.

"Whoever that was you snuck out of the bed to talk to, don't make me slap that hoe," Stacey repeated in a calm, yet half-awake tone.

I smiled as I gripped her face gently and kissed her forehead. "Amor, I promise to never put you in a position to have to slap a hoe. I was just handling business," I assured her as I embraced her tightly.

21
ANTHONY

I awakened to the aroma of breakfast and strode into the kitchen with my bare, ink covered chest and black Nike sweatpants. I snuck up behind Stacey and wrapped my arms around her waist as I planted multiple kisses in the crease of her neck.

"Good morning, baby," she grinned as she swooned in my embrace. "How did you sleep last night?"

"Great, until a little crazy woman threatened to slap an imaginary hoe she thought I was on the phone with." I chuckled as Stacey smiled shyly.

"Sorry about that, I guess it's safe to say I can be a real fool actor if it comes down to it." she shrugged her shoulders as if to say, *oh well!*

"Damn! Is your whole back made of muscles?" Rachel blurted out as she made her way into the kitchen. "And y'all are nasty! Making all that damn noise last night! I thought someone was going to call the police the way you had this heffa screaming!"

She grabbed a cup of coffee and rolled her top lip to her nose, turning away from Stacey and I. We looked at one another and snickered under our breaths at Rachel's revelation.

"You know Rachel, I can hook you up with my boy, don't miss out." I laughed, teasing her.

The doorbell rang and Rachel inched closer to answer it.

"I already told you, big man wouldn't be able to handle a woman like me, even though he is...solid, thick, and kinda sexy," Rachel said as she giggled.

When she opened the penthouse door her smile quickly converted into a mixture of terror and confusion. Savior pushed his way past Rachel and stopped when he noticed me, shirtless and standing far too close to Stacey for his comfort.

"Savior, get your ass out of this house before I call the police!" Rachel yelled as she planted her feet and crossed her arms over her chest, while hurriedly shuffling in front of Savior, blocking him. "I can hear the breaking news now. NBA player gets fucked up for breaking and entering," Rachel whispered in a low threatening tone.

Stacey was frozen, unable to move, speak, or co-sign Rachel's words. She ripped her eyes away from Savior to see me standing firmly with both hands tucked into my sweatpants. I knew Stacey could feel the anger I made no attempt to conceal and it was obvious that I was ready to fuck Savior up for the disrespect.

"You just left LA a few weeks ago and you're already fucking somebody else?" Savior roared charging towards my woman. My fucking woman.

She screamed and threw her hands up to protect her face as she shrank in anticipation of the blow, but before he got close enough to make her fear a reality, I shoved him in the chest with such aggression that he stumbled backwards almost tripping over his feet. I stood in front of Stacey, my tone low and guttural directed towards Savior, "If you value your piece of shit life, I suggest you walk out that door while you still can, homeboy."

STACEY

I snapped my neck in Anthony's direction, his tone reminding me of the words he'd said in the alleyway of Mexico weeks ago, and undoubtedly made me fear for my ex's life.

"Savior! Please! Go!" I screamed.

It was the only way I could think to warn him that his life was in more danger than he could ever fathom. He no longer held a place in my life but I didn't want to see him die because of his own arrogance.

"So this is what you want? You're going to throw two years away over a misunderstanding?" Savior sounded and appeared hurt.

"Muthafucka! The audacity! You fucked over her for two years! You had a fucking baby! Are you serious right now?" Rachel's high pitched voice rang throughout the penthouse as she approached Savior aggressively. She was fed up with his bullshit and refused to hold her tongue.

"Rachel, you better learn to shut the hell up!" Savior warned.

"Or what?!" Rachel challenged as she flicked Savior off with both middle fingers.

In a fit of rage Savior turned on his heels as if he were preparing to leave, but quickly turned back to face Rachel and backhanded her hard, causing her to fly over the couch.

Tank heard the commotion and rushed through the front door just as Rachel hit the couch and flipped onto the floor. Before Tank could reach Savior, Anthony had his gun drawn placed firmly against Savior's head. Tank rushed around the couch to check on Rachel. Her eye was swelling as Tank inspected the rest of her body to ensure she was okay before he picked her up and sat her on the couch. Savior blinked rapidly as his hands trembled and his eyes glossed over.

"Get on your fucking knees," Anthony instructed, forcing the gun into Savior's mouth.

I sprinted across the room to Rachel, cradling her as I rocked slowly, watching as Tank strolled over and placed his hand on the gun positioned inside Savior's mouth. Anthony removed the pistol from Savior's mouth, and released his hand from the trigger. Tank's massive body towered over Savior as he rubbed his knuckles with a sinister grin on his face, before landing a powerful, neck jerking blow to Savior's jaw. He pounded Savior's face until bloody teeth flew from his mouth and I yelled, "Enough!" causing Tank to halt his movement mid swing.

I was astonished that Savior hadn't passed out, but maybe the shock of what was happening kept him alert.

"Savior!" I screamed, dragging him out of a woozy daze, "We're over! Done! Don't ever come here again, you had your chance, I'm with Anthony now."

I rounded the couch to stand next to my man. I captured his hand shakily because truth be told, I was scared shitless of what would happen next. Here I was, standing between my first love and my new love, saying words I never thought I would hear exit my mouth because once upon a time Savior was my everything.

Tank lifted Savior and pulled him in closely as a grizzly voice escaped his lips, "If I ever see you around here again, your basketball days are done because I'm going to break every single bone in your fucking legs."

He tossed him halfway down the hallway before making his entrance back into the penthouse. He slowly moved towards Rachel and dropped down to both knees in front of her on the couch. Even with Tank positioned on his knees, his large body still practically towered over Rachel, as he cupped her face with both hands. "Let me have a look at you," the giant insisted.

The breakfast I'd planned was now cold and even if I made an attempt to warm it, I hadn't cooked enough for Tank's massive appetite. Anthony could see the disdain in my eyes as I glanced at my ruined breakfast, and I hoped he could also sense my pain and feelings of being overwhelmed. Although I stood firm next to him in the presence of Savior, it hadn't been an easy task to dismiss someone I saw a future with not too long ago. Anthony was empathetic to my feelings as he grabbed hold of me and whispered, "I know you're struggling internally, and it's okay, what just happened was a lot and it's okay to need time to process. Get dressed, Love, we're going to brunch."

"Really?" I asked as I gazed up at him.

"Yeah, I'm taking us out, you can cook another time," he said smiling at me.

A mile wide smile stretched across my face. Anthony knew feeding me would help alleviate some of the stress I had experienced that morning, and wanted to remove me from the penthouse where a murder had almost been committed moments earlier. I needed fresh air and a reminder of how much Anthony loved me didn't hurt either.

"Say, big nigga," Anthony called to Tank.

"Sup, Boss?" he answered, pulling his eyes from Rachel for a moment to face Anthony.

"Take the day off and come to brunch with us, call Bear, and have him take your place today," Anthony requested.

"Uh, Boss, you sure about that?" Tank questioned.

"Yea nigga, I'm sure!" Anthony laughed and excused himself back to my bedroom.

Tank gazed at Rachel. "You sure you okay?" His words were soft and sincere and Rachel couldn't help but to smile.

"Yeah, I'll be okay. That muthafucka is lucky I didn't have my gun, old no basketball playing bitch!"

Rachel was definitely back to her usual antics, even a slap to the face couldn't stop her from talking shit. Tank chuckled at Rachel.

On the way to brunch Tank and Rachel sat positioned with a large gap between them as Anthony and I cuddled and practically sucked one another's faces off the entire ride. Surprisingly, there was not a peep about what happened to Savior and that put me at ease. I felt terrible about what happened to him, but there was no room for sorrow regarding his situation while also trying to love Anthony. I was going to have to choose because Anthony would notice if my energy were off and I didn't want to make the situation any more complicated than it already was. By no surprise at all, Anthony was able to secure a private dining room for brunch, which proved beneficial because Tank ordered enough food to cover two tables, so the extra space was much needed. We drank and ate until Rachel and I excused ourselves to the ladies room.

"Bitch! Do you see how Tank has been staring at me all day?" Rachel asked with an unfamiliar toothy grin.

I was surprised to see my friend actually smiling.

"Actually, yeah! I have noticed! But the real question is, what are you going to do about it?" I nudged Rachel, rubbing shoulders with her hoping for a straightforward answer.

"I don't know, he seems really cool, but..." Rachel paused.

"What's wrong?" I asked.

"He seems kinda...dangerous," Rachel said as she turned to face me, scanning my eyes for reassurance.

However, I was unwilling to substantiate Rachel's claim for fear of exposing Anthony. She was going to have to navigate this one solo.

"I mean, you saw what he did to Savior, but that was only because he was protecting you," I reminded her. "So, can he be dangerous? Maybe, but, then again, who knows?" I did know and I didn't warn her.

"Well, I could use a big, healthy brother like that, he looks like he can handle all of these curves," Rachel teased as she wound her booty in a circle.

I laughed at my friend. It was refreshing to see her in such a good mood, despite the bruise Savior planted over her eye, her spirits were high and I was elated to see her smile.

"Come on girl before Anthony comes into this restroom looking for me!" I laughed as we pushed the door open and found Tank's big ass standing there waiting on us.

Rachel jumped and squealed. I giggled.

"Yeah, go ahead and get used to that!"

As we sat back at the brunch table, it apparently dawned on Rachel that I hadn't mentioned anything about my vastly approaching birthday.

"Uh, Stace, why haven't I heard you mention anything about your birthday?" she asked in a concerned tone with a lifted eyebrow. "That's not like you Ms. Dancing Queen!"

I sighed. "I don't know, I guess I'm just over this year already. My parents separating, then getting back together, being attacked, police have yet to find who did it, and now this shit with Sav—" I hesitated, unsure of how anyone at the table would feel at the sound of his name. "The shit with Savior was just kind of the icing on the cake, it's just been a helluva year, so I've decided to just lay low this year."

"Lay low!" Rachel screeched with discontent. "In all the years I've known you, lay low has never been a part of your vocabulary! Hell no! You're having a party and I don't want to hear shit about it! You're turning thirty and we're turning up whether you like it or not!"

22
STACEY

In the weeks leading to my birthday, I experienced surges of varied emotions and needed someone to talk to. My big brother always knew how to make me feel better and spent the majority of his life protecting me. As the phone rang, I prayed he would pick up.

"Hey, little big head girl!" PJ greeted as he smiled through the other end of the receiver.

"Hey, Peanut Butter Jelly," I said, using the nickname I'd called him when we were kids.

My voice was low, almost inaudible, which caused PJ to wonder what or who had me in such a somber mood.

"Uh oh, what's going on? I know that tone," PJ said. "What nigga has you in a mood? It better not be Savior, I told you to leave his ass alone a long time ago—"

"It's not Savior," I interrupted PJ's rant.

"Oh," PJ said.

It was always Savior, so PJ was pleasantly surprised to find out this time, it wasn't.

"So what's going on? What's got you sounding so blah?" he asked.

"I met a guy," I said shyly.

"Yeah, and," he said.

"And I really like him...I mean like...really, really like him," I said.

"Okay...again...and?" PJ was still confused, but I guess I wasn't doing a great job of explaining myself.

"Fuck it! I love him and he loves me and he wants me to marry him PJ."

I paused to catch my breath and listen for the verbal lashing I was sure would follow. But, to my surprise, he didn't fuss, he didn't yell, and he didn't ask me a ton of annoying big brother questions.

"Congratulations, sis!" was all he said.

"That's it?!" I shrieked, as I threw my hand in the air, confused.

"That's it," PJ said.

"What kind of shit!" I responded, beginning to feel frustrated with my brother.

"Look Stacey, you're grown. You're not a little kid that needs protecting every minute of every day. Are you surprised that a man wants to marry you? Build with you? Start a family with you? Because I'm not surprised, little sister. You're going to make an amazing wife and it's not my job to stand in the way of that."

I blinked and removed the phone from my ear to stare at it for a moment.

"So when do I get to meet your fiancé?" PJ questioned.

"Well, that's the thing, I haven't officially accepted," I said, regretfully.

"Why not, is there something wrong with him?" he questioned.

"No, nothing wrong with him, we just haven't known each other for an extremely long time," I responded, fiddling my fingertips together as my nerves invaded the conversation, causing me to become skeptical of what I had with Anthony.

"Well, you know mom and dad only dated for three months before getting married and now look at them," PJ reminded me, "I mean...I've known Pilar for years, but we have only been officially dating for six months and I know without a doubt she is going to be my wife. Does he have a job?"

"Yes."

"Does he have a house?"

"More than one."

"Does he have kids, baby mama drama?"

"Nope. None."

"Is he good to you?"

"The best."

"Well then, little sister, I think you know what you need to do."

PJ was right, what the hell was I waiting on? Here I was with a man that wanted me, despite the fact that my fucked up past relationships kept running back haunting my new relationship. Even after Quinton and Savior, Anthony's feelings for me were unwavering.

I sat silently holding the phone before responding, "Thank you PJ, I figured you could help, I love you."

"I love you too, spoiled brat," he said.

As we hung up the phone, I had an overwhelming urge to go to my man. I needed to see him; I needed his warm, full lips on mine. Shit, I just needed a hug and if I happened to fall on his dick in the process, that was okay too. Before texting Anthony, I changed his name from Anthony to Baby and added a heart emoji at the end to signify that shit was getting real. I smiled thinking about him and made the decision that I was willing to jump head first into whatever Anthony DeLeon had to offer. I was turning thirty years old and had no time for regrets.

```
Me: Hey Baby
Anthony: Hola Amor. I miss you.
Me: Do you? How much?
Anthony: Too damn much. Having a hard time getting any work done.
Me: Can you take a break? I kinda...need you.
Anthony: Is everything okay? Do I need to send someone? Tank should be close to that side of town. I can send him and be on my way to meet you.
Me: Not that kind of need, baby. I need you and my extremely large friend between your legs.
Anthony: I'm on my way to get you. (running emoji)
```

I smiled as I peeled my clothes off, dropping them to the floor and running to turn on the shower water as I pulled my curls into a loose top bun. I quickly washed myself in anticipation for his arrival, then hopped out to moisturize my skin. Once my body was glowing from the shea butter mixture, I dressed myself in a matching canary yellow lace bra and thong panty set and slipped a short, loose, silk spaghetti strap dress over my curvy frame, paired with high top Chuck Taylors and pulled my curls into a high ponytail and waited for Anthony to call. It was rare that he drove himself, so I was pretty surprised when he showed up in an Aston Martin DB11. He hopped out of his seat and trotted over to my side of the car, planting a juicy kiss onto my lips and giving me a quick tap on my behind before opening the door for me.

"This is the first time I've ever seen you drive," I admitted, smiling as I glanced around the inside of the vehicle.

"Yeah, I gave the guys the day off. You ready to roll?" he said, as he grabbed hold to my thigh meat and squeezed it as he stared into my eyes.

I smiled seductively. "Ready."

He pulled away from the curb and sped down the street heading towards the highway and I exhaled, embracing the free-spirited sensation and release of tension evading my body at the mere presence of this man.

"Can we let the sunroof back?" I asked, eyeing the double wide clear roof in the exotic automobile.

"We can do whatever you want, Love," Anthony said, pressing a button on his dashboard causing the rooftop to retract.

The wind sent my ponytail into a frenzy as it whipped around my neck. I closed my eyes and smiled as I lifted my arms towards the sunroof, the summer sun beaming down warming my face and legs. I glanced over to Anthony, his eyes on the road, one hand on the steering wheel, the other hand gripping my thigh firmly as if there was a fear I might blow away. I grinned and knew that Anthony could feel my eyes burning a hole through him as he peeked in my direction momentarily and rolled his bottom lip into his mouth, holding it in place with his teeth.

"I love you," I said softly, never taking my eyes off of him.

He smirked and then licked his lips before responding in his smooth, baritone voice. "I love you too."

I could feel my nipples throbbing and my panties were beginning to feel moist as I looked down at the bulge in Anthony's shorts and licked my lips, my mouth watering. Chills rolled over my body, despite the warm weather and I felt an insatiable desire to put his velvety smooth dick into my mouth. I turned my body in the leather seat, still constrained by the seat belt, but managing to maneuver the top half of my body in such an angle that left the bottom half of my body still secure in the seatbelt, as I leaned over Anthony's lap.

"Whoa! What are you—" Anthony started, but quickly closed his mouth when he realized what was happening.

I leaned over and tugged at his Nike shorts and he elevated his hips, sliding the shorts down a few inches, just enough to expose his boxer briefs. When I released his dick from the hole in his boxers, I just stared at it for a minute. Taking it in, admiring it, rubbing it. I could feel the saliva begin to crowd my mouth as I slid my tongue over my lips and wrapped them around his tip.

"Ohhhh shit," he groaned, clenching from the pleasure of my warm mouth as I meticulously stroked him with my tongue.

I slid my tongue around the tip of his dick before burying him deep within my throat, bobbing my head up and down as I closed my eyes and gave my best effort to suck his soul through his dick – trying to make him feel my love through my lips. He managed to force his eyes to stay open, although a few prolonged blinks almost caused him to pull over on the side of the highway.

"Ohhhh shit, Love," he moaned again, as he wrapped a gentle hand around my ponytail, forcing his dick further into the back of my throat. After a few seconds of me gagging, he loosened his grasp, I moaned and pulled away, as a string of saliva trailed my lips and then I spit on it. My moans matched his because just watching his glistening dick stand at attention in my hand made me want more of him inside my mouth. I bobbed my head up and down again until I felt Anthony's grip on my head intensify, as he raised his hips from the driver side seat and thrust into my mouth.

"Got damn, Love! Shit!" he grunted as his seed flowed effortlessly down my throat and I loved it. I devoured every drop, sending him into a foggy headspace causing him to stare at me a moment too long.

"Baby, watch out!" I screamed as Anthony's automatic brakes activated and his quick reflexes allowed him to swerve instantly, dodging a stalled car on the highway.

"Sorry," I said, as I wiped the evidence of what I had done away from my face.

"You're about to kill us, Amor." Anthony chuckled at the realization that we were safe. "But damn, if I had to go, I wouldn't mind going out like that." He smiled, but kept his eyes on the road this time.

When we arrived at his home, he rounded the car to open my door and when he pushed the doors to his home open, I was surprised to see an older Latina woman standing in the foyer. She was visibly annoyed as she tilted her Chanel sunglasses down the bridge of her nose to peer at me. She wore a black fitted dress with black peep toe Christian Louboutin stilettos. Her Chanel bag hung on her forearm and her hair was cut into a blunt bob with bangs. Anthony's light hearted, playful mood immediately changed when he saw the woman standing inside his home as she removed her sunglasses and glanced in Anthony's direction.

"Well, aren't you going to greet your mother, son?"

Anthony blew out a deep sigh as he positioned himself between his mother and me.

Gripping his forehead he said, "Mother, this is my lady Stacey, Stacey, this is my mother Valentina."

I was surprised to see Valentina, especially since Anthony had never mentioned her before. I thought it was odd that his mother would make a grand appearance out of the blue, yet Anthony had never so much as mentioned her name. I smiled genuinely as I approached Valentina with an extended hand.

"It's so nice to meet you."

I waited anxiously for Valentina to acknowledge my hand as I stood there feeling foolish, but she never did. Anthony recognized the embarrassment spread across my face as he approached me, cupping my extended hand between his own, producing a weak smile that I recognized as an apology on behalf of his mother's rude behavior.

"Love, why don't you wait for me in the bedroom, and I'll join you shortly," he stated as he kissed my lips softly and smiled as he gently rubbed his thumb across my cheek.

I walked back toward the direction of the bedroom but didn't go all the way there; instead ducking off to eavesdrop.

Anthony glared at his mother with a raised brow and tight lips. "You were unnecessarily rude to her, Valentina," he scolded his mother.

"Oh honey! You've got to have tough skin to be in the line of work we're in. Don't talk to me about being rude, and stop with the Valentina nonsense. I breastfed you for twenty-three months, you'll call me mother, am I clear?" Valentina warned.

He sucked in a deep breath and held it to keep from disrespecting his mother.

"Valent—Mother, what are you doing here?" he asked, lifting both hands palms up, making no attempt to conceal his discontent for his mother's unannounced pop-up.

"We need to discuss the transport from Mexico to Houston scheduled for next week, so get rid of your little plaything so we can get down to business," Valentina said, focusing her attention on her freshly manicured nails, with no regard for Anthony's feelings towards her statement.

"She's not a plaything, Mother. I love her!" he informed Valentina, pointing his finger at her for emphasis.

She glared at her son's finger and then into his eyes as she chuckled.

"I taught you everything you know, your temper, you got it from me. Your ability to kill without remorse, got that from me too. Your ability to run a multimillion dollar drug cartel, oops! *Guilty!* Me again! So before you make the decision to disrespect me, remember how the hell you arrived in the dream life you live!" his mother reminded him.

ANTHONY

I was annoyed, but my mother was right, had it not been for her, I would have nothing. Valentina risked her life to birth me. When her father found out she was pregnant by a Black man, he threatened to have my father killed and tried to force her to have an abortion. She elected to disappear until I was born and out of her father's grasp. She was unwilling to abandon me to appease her father. My grandfather would have to love his only daughter and me, we were a package deal. When I was born Valentina fell in love with me instantly, or so she says. When she laid eyes on my chestnut brown skin, she knew her father would never accept me. When she finally made the decision to rejoin her family—with me, she knew that I would never be safe as long as her father still had breath in his lungs.

My mother devised a plan to kill her father and was able to successfully execute the plan with the help of her loyal soldiers, who still remained employed with her thirty-five years later. Valentina DeLeon was the most powerful woman to ever run a male dominated cartel and although I was technically the boss, I still answered to her in many regards.

"I'm sorry, Mother, but you popping up here just caught me off guard, and your attitude towards Stacey is unfair. She's my woman and I would like for you to treat her with some respect. She's not leaving but we can discuss the Houston drop in the study," I said as I motioned towards the French doors to my office space.

"I've gotten word that the drop has been compromised. You need to notify your men and provide them an alternate route to secure the package. We don't want to jeopardize our relationship with the Jimenez Cartel," Valentina said as she crossed her legs staring sternly at me.

"Shit! I know Adrian is behind this!" I growled, remembering my cousin's most recent pop up at the club.

"I did say he needed to be dealt with years ago," Valentina said facetiously, admiring her nails, neglecting to make eye contact with me.

"Not today, Mother! I'm not in the mood for this today. My decision was made, and it's final. Your comments and smug remarks are not needed, and I would truly appreciate it if you kept them to a minimum," I said as *respectfully* as I could.

Valentina giggled. "My beautiful, empathetic boy, you're so much like your father – a heart of gold," she said as she caressed my face, causing me to remember how much I truly loved her, despite how strained our relationship seemed at the moment.

I hated it when she mentioned my father. Never having an opportunity to meet him was punishment enough. Before my grandfather's death, he'd kept good on his promise of killing my father. I closed my eyes as remembrance crept in, reminding me of the nights my mother would rock me to sleep, caressing my cheek after I had cried on her shoulder because not a day went by when I wasn't called a nigger. She instilled in me that I was a beautiful Black man and that being born

Black was a gift and not the curse my family tried to make me believe it was.

"I'll handle the Houston drop, mother. Thank you for the warning," I said, as I prepared to escort her to the front door.

23
STACEY

"Is your mother gone?" I lifted my shoulders, my high pitched voice sounding puzzled.

"Yeah, finally." He pushed a deep breath through parted lips and placed both hands on top of his head as he fell into the velvet chair.

"I didn't even get a chance to tell her bye," I sulked as my eyes fell to the ground with furrowed brows.

"Probably for the best," Anthony said.

I recognized the irritation in his voice and approached him hesitantly.

"Are you okay? I've never seen you this...annoyed before." I placed a hand on his shoulder, attempting to comfort him.

He chuckled. "Valentina seems to be able to bring that out of me," he admitted as he shook his head in disappointment.

I dropped to my knees in front of him, crossing my arms over his legs and leaned forward to place my chin onto my forearms.

"Wanna talk about it?" I asked, smiling sincerely in an attempt to lighten the mood. He glanced down at me and smiled.

"Not really. We just needed to discuss work related issues; I'd really like to keep you as far away from that part of my life as possible, if that's okay with you," he said, his tone begging me not to press the issue. "There is something else I would like to discuss with you, though."

"Uh, okay," I said as I focused on him.

"About this thirtieth birthday."

He gripped his chin before gently stroking his beard as he shifted his eyes into the air as if he were devising a master plan. My head fell back as I rolled my eyes.

"Not you too! Between you and Rachel, I get the feeling that y'all are plotting and scheming," I said as I playfully hit

Anthony's leg. "You don't have to do anything for my birthday. With you, everyday feels like my birthday. All I need is you. Nothing more, nothing less."

I kissed his lips and allowed my tongue to slip into his mouth. I stood from his lap and strutted over to the sheepskin rug and sank my toes into the plush, white fur, dropping my dress from my shoulders, allowing it to gather around my feet. I stared over my shoulder at Anthony.

"You coming?" I said as I walked towards the master bathroom. He raised slowly from the velvet chair, grazed his hands over his pants and followed me into the shower.

When I opened my eyes the next morning, the scent of fresh flowers filled the room, and I smiled as I peered at the three dozen red roses sitting on the nightstand next to a handwritten note from Anthony.

Had to run a few errands, four days until your birthday, smile. I love you.

-Anthony

I grinned and leaned over, taking a whiff of the gorgeous roses before falling back onto the pillow, placing my hands over my heart, smiling from ear to ear. Anthony was damn near perfect, well, aside from the fact that he was a dangerous, drug dealing cartel boss, but other than that, he was pretty perfect. I traced my fingers around the ring box sitting on the nightstand before snatching it and flipping the box open. I stared at the glimmering diamond ring in amazement, still stunned that Anthony actually wanted to marry me. I had yet to give him an answer and still, he hadn't pressured me, not one time.

The man had the patience of Job and the more I thought about the immeasurable amount of love and affection Anthony showed me on a daily basis, the wider my smile became. I removed the ring from the box and placed it onto my finger. How had he gotten the size so perfect? Had the negro measured my ring finger in my sleep? I was learning not to question how Anthony managed to do the things he did, and to just savor the moment while learning to appreciate such a thoughtful man. I was pulled from my love-stricken trance when my phone began to ring.

I scrambled upright in the bed.

"H-hello! Detective Williams?"

I hadn't heard from him in weeks. It wasn't like I had ever been involved in a crime before, so I was oblivious to how it could actually take to find a suspect.

"Ms. Hill, I apologize it's taken so long for me to reach out to you. This Quinton fellow is hard to catch. We thought we had a lead on him last week, but he continues to evade us some kind of way," Detective Williams informed me.

I rubbed my forehead in disbelief as the news I heard snatched my nostalgic mood, inciting fear and anxiety where butterflies had just resided moments earlier.

"So you're saying he's still out there? He's a lawyer! How could he possibly be that hard to find?!" I could feel my hands begin to sweat as Detective Williams' voice began to fade to nothingness in my ear.

"Ms. Hill, Ms. Hill, are you there?" Detective Williams called, snapping me from my trance.

"Yes…yes, I'm here." I blinked, shaking my head to clear away the distractions.

"I know this isn't what you want to hear, but we're doing everything we can," Detective Williams informed me before hanging up the phone.

ANTHONY

Roman drove as I rode in silence. Tank, Bear and a dozen additional men accompanied me as I prepared to meet my cousins traveling from Sinaloa, Mexico. When Valentina informed me that the drop had been compromised, I proceeded to warn my cousins before their scheduled arrival to the Houston drop point. I was the odd man out amongst my family. Although I was technically the boss, many of my blood relatives never accepted the fact that my mother ruined their pure blood line when she slept with a Black man and conceived an indisputable Black son.

I traveled with an entourage for my own safety against my family because although I was making an attempt to protect my cousins – who had never cared for me – interrupting their route would be met with hostility, especially when they realized I was behind the disruption. Roman trailed behind the eighteen-wheeler with six brand new Audi SUVs attached to the bed of the truck. Two of my SUVs split the back of the trailer, speeding past the eighteen wheeler as they sped in front of the massive truck and slammed on their brakes, causing the truck to come to a screeching halt.

I signaled for my men to rush the eighteen-wheeler as I approached slowly with Bear close by. The two men inside the truck jumped out with their guns drawn, prepared for war, until my familiar voice caused them to lower their weapons.

"Cousins, nice to see you again," I called, causing them to turn cautiously. My words were far from genuine, however, regardless of the trajectory of our relationship, I didn't want to see them killed.

"You're probably wondering why I'm here," I stated boldly, pacing towards my cousins known by their street names as Joker and Spider, the brothers of the devil himself, Adrian.

They glared at me, faces wrinkled in anger and confusion.

"You better have a good reason for this shit, Blacky," Joker said with a growl.

I hated that name. It was the name my family taunted me with when my mother wasn't around to defend me as a child. It was the name I fought over countless times as a teenager. However, now as an adult, the cut didn't feel as deep, it didn't hurt as bad. I chuckled, "Hm... Still the same asshole you were when we were kids I see," I responded unflinchingly as I stood face to face with Joker.

Joker filled his chest with air, his hand still curled around the trigger of his pistol.

"I'm here for one purpose and one purpose only. The drop is compromised, I came here in person to let you know."

I took a step away from them in an attempt to diminish some of the hostility.

"Who is it? Who would be stupid enough to fuck with our shit?" Spider asked, his body language displaying his tense mood.

"I'm figuring it out," I said as I rubbed the side of my nose with my thumb.

Joker scoffed under his breath, "Some fucking help you are!" Before he could utter another word, my pistol was out of the holster and pressed against Joker's skull.

He threw both hands into the air in protest, "Primo! Cousin! What the fuck?" Joker's voice rose two octaves, as fear captured his words.

"I didn't catch that," I said. "Say it for me one more time," I said, still pressing the pistol firmly to the front of Joker's head, leaving a small circular imprint.

"I'm sorry, man. I was just fucking around!" Joker winced as his eyes shifted from side to side. Spider watched nervously as he attempted to reason with me.

"Anthony, you know he didn't mean shit by that, let's just calm down," Spider reasoned, and rightfully so because they had over a dozen guns pointed in their direction.

I chuckled as I removed the pistol from Joker's forehead.

"Bitch ass, watch how you speak to me, we aren't kids anymore and don't forget, I run this shit."

I placed my gun back into the shoulder holster.

I glared from Joker to Spider. "Have either of you heard from your brother, Adrian?"

They looked at one another and then back to me.

"Not in a few weeks," Spider said, and he surprisingly sounded like he was telling the truth.

I was done with this conversation and prepared to walk away but slowly turned back.

"Change your fucking driving route because if the shipment doesn't arrive, it won't be an idle gun being held to your head next time," I warned, as I turned to walk away, "And make sure you check in when the drop is complete."

I rode silently anticipating the phone call I knew would come from my mother when she got wind of the run-in with my cousins, and I didn't give a damn. I walked on pins and needles and allowed my entire family to treat me like shit. I didn't begin to notice the blatant racism and disregard my family had for me until I was eight years old, when I began to understand I looked different from the rest of them. Tank's voice caught my attention, pulling me from my walk down memory lane.

"Where to, Boss?" he asked.

I gazed out the window.

"She's waiting on me, take me home."

I felt an instant shift at the thought of Stacey. I was an outcast, a killer, a businessman. I was ruthless, but in this moment, all I felt was in love. The thought of her, her beautiful brown skin, her head full of curls, her scent, the idea that I might actually be with her for a lifetime made me want to give up my current life and create a new one with her. I had never met a woman important enough to make me reconsider how I maneuver in life, but she had done that. She was special and I was willing to do anything to prove that to her.

STACEY

I heard Anthony's voice trail up the hallway and I quickly returned the diamond ring back to the box, placing it back onto the nightstand as I forced a smile across my face. I refused to pile my problems onto him because he lived in a world of dangerous problems already, so now was not the right time to mention Quinton.

When Anthony entered the doorway of the bedroom I noticed the weight of the world melt from his shoulders as he grinned when my eyes locked with his. He climbed on top of the comforter and found his sweet spot, his body resting snuggly between my legs and his head nestled comfortably on my soft breasts. He sighed as he released his breath and allowed his body to melt into mine. I gently circled my hands over his back and kissed the top of his head.

"I missed you," he said, placing his head nose down into my chest, breathing in as much of me as he could.

"I missed you, too." I smiled as I began to trace his deep waves with my fingertips. "You okay?" I asked, brows furrowed at the sound of his voice.

"I will be," Anthony murmured, his face still planted in my chest.

I giggled and placed both hands on his cheeks, lifting his head. "You're going to suffocate in there!" I said playfully as I held his face in my hands and stared into his deep brown eyes.

Anthony's side smirk caused me to smile even wider as I stretched my neck, allowing my lips to meet his.

"Baby," I called and then paused.

"Yes, Love," he responded.

"I want you to be able to tell me any and everything. I know it may take you some time, and I don't want to rush it. I want it to happen organically," I said, treading lightly at the realization that this wouldn't be an easy subject for him to discuss.

He raised an eyebrow and tried to look away, but I wouldn't loosen my grip.

"It's just that…on days like this, I can tell that you're holding something back from me and I don't particularly like that feeling," I sighed as I explained myself the best way I could.

"I just—I don't know, it's like you're trying to protect me from…you…and that's not what I want. I want all of you, even the ugly parts." I stared at Anthony, my eyes beginning to gloss over and he knew I was being honest.

"I'm not rushing you, baby, but I just wanted to put it out there that I want an open, honest, transparent relationship with you. I mean, if we're going to be married one day, it's important to discuss even the unpleasant situations, right?" I asked, shrugging my shoulders, waiting on confirmation from Anthony.

He smiled, actually showing his teeth. "So you plan on marrying a nigga one day, huh?" He began kissing my chest playfully.

I giggled and squirmed. "Anthony DeLeon, is all you heard that I would marry you one day?" I threw my head back onto a pillow as I laughed. "You sure do have a selective hearing, baby."

He stopped kissing me for a moment. "When my mother visited yesterday, it was to inform me that our Houston drop was compromised," he said, changing the trajectory of the conversation. "Someone discovered the location of the drop and planned on robbing and most likely killing my cousins who were making the drop. I had to go warn them today."

I focused my eyes on Anthony as I adjusted myself to get a better look at him.

"Well, it sounds like you did the right thing, you wouldn't want your family members to be harmed," I said as I continued to stroke his head.

He exhaled a deep sigh as he closed his eyes, wrapping his arms further around my warm body.

"That's the thing, I shouldn't even care, they've never given a fuck about me. But I couldn't take the chance of letting them fuck up something I've worked so hard to build."

"Fuck it up? What do you mean?" I asked, confusion ceasing my tone.

"If the drop would have been hit, the business would be out of millions and word would get around that we were weak, which would cause another set of problems that I'm not ready to deal with." Anthony rolled off my body and onto his back to look at the ceiling as he locked his hands behind his head.

I sat upright, pushing my back against the headboard as I looked at my man. "What makes you think they don't care about you, baby? Family members fight, but that doesn't mean—"

"They tried to kill me," he interrupted.

My mouth dropped in bewilderment as he stared at the ceiling.

"They tied me up when I was thirteen years old, beat me until pieces of my flesh ripped from the bone and left me tied up to die. They never came back for me."

His voice trembled and for a moment, tears threatened to stream from his eyes until he remembered I was sitting there. The deep breath Anthony sucked into his lungs allowed him to regain his composure long enough to will the tears away to continue his conversation with me.

"Who found you?" My voice was low, filled with sorrow for the pain he endured.

"Nobody found me. I ripped myself from the ropes that bound me. The rope burns were deep, they cut through my skin leaving permanent marks."

He removed his gold, diamond embezzled Rolex watch from one wrist and pulled the sleeve of his shirt up, uncovering his other wrist as he held both arms above his head leaving them eye level for me. The deep scars wrapped around his entire wrist and were permanently ingrained into his skin. I gasped at the revelation of how brutally Anthony had been treated at such a young age. I immediately had a revelation as I opened my mouth to speak.

"The tattoos?" I asked.

"To cover the marks," he responded.

Anthony's body was covered in tattoos. It never crossed my mind as to why, because I found them extremely sexy, but now my heart broke with the realization of why he covered his body in ink.

"My cousins were surprised when my mother received a call about my condition." He sat up and placed his hands in his lap.

"They didn't expect me to live and due to the nature of our family business, I couldn't go to the hospital." He elevated both arms, locking his fingers on top of his head.

"My mother set up a makeshift hospital room in our home and had nurses and doctors checking on me around the clock," he said, his eyes still turned to the ceiling, as if he were reliving the moment.

I swept the cover from my legs and crawled over to Anthony, pressing my warm skin against his back as I wrapped my arms around his neck and nestled my chin over his shoulder.

"But I don't understand, why would they do this to you?" I asked, unable to hide my confusion.

He chuckled but not because he thought my question was amusing, his chuckle was one of disbelief, one of embarrassment.

"Because I'm Black and in their eyes the Cartel is no place for a nigga." He squared his shoulders and turned his head slightly to look at me. "Imagine the disbelief when my grandfather died and everything was passed down to my mother, only for her to pass it on to me," he scoffed as his lips curled into a lopsided grin.

"So they work for you now?" I asked.

Anthony nodded in agreement.

"Oh hell no! Why the hell would you ever allow that?" I said.

Channeling my best friend Rachel's energy, I slid from the bed and walked around to stand in front of him. I planted my feet and folded my arms over my lace bralette. I was visibly angry and Anthony let out a soft laugh.

"Damn you're cute when you're mad!" he said, groping at my thighs and ass.

I raised an eyebrow and leaned over to one side, popping my petite hip out to the side, waiting on Anthony to answer me and to see that I was not playing with his ass. He traced his bottom lip with his tongue and stared at me with a grin on his face before pulling my little ass into his chest.

"Because, we live by a certain set of principles and family over everything is one of them. I'm a man, and I was taught that a man is to be honorable. I'll never allow how someone else treats me determine who I am as a man, or how I operate." Anthony's words were genuine and heartfelt. "Spider, Joker and their older brother Adrian..." he paused and swallowed hard, "They, Spider and Joker were just following their brother's orders, and I don't blame them because Adrian would have kicked their asses for not obeying him. But Adrian, he was the ringleader."

Adrian...Adrian...Adrian... I thought, trying to remember why the name was so familiar.

"You mean the muthafucka you introduced me to in the club that you made part owner of your club!? Anthony, what the entire fuck!?"

"I made that move when I was a young adult, still seeking the approval of a family I later realized would never accept me. And so—" he paused.

"What is it, baby?" I asked.

"So I made the decision to create my own family built on the foundation of love, trust, honesty, and an unbreakable bond. I thought I was going to have that with Ava and her mom, but when Ava died and her mother left, I thought maybe I was fucking cursed to be alone, until I met you."

His eyes met mine. I could feel the deep lines in my face begin to smooth because I had just gained a better understanding of Anthony.

"Family over everything has been a motto for my family since before I was ever thought of, and I believe in it, even if some of my family doesn't, but maybe with you, it'll be different," he said.

I was awestruck by this man. I had never been with anyone as intoxicating as Anthony. He was a man and didn't allow himself to be bogged down with trivial bullshit, and I could appreciate his character.

"Love," he called to me, his arms still wrapped tightly around my waist.

"Yes, baby," I responded, before palming his face and looking into his eyes with a heartwarming smile.

"I need you. Right now," he said as he returned my gaze, sliding his hand between my thighs.

I welcomed him and parted my legs without hesitation as Anthony's fingers found my clit. He buried his face into my neck, inhaling my sweet scent of coconut with a hint of vanilla as he pressed my love button, causing me to moan softly as he slid two fingers into my sleek middle.

"You're already wet for me, Love," he growled into my neck as he found the soft, gushy spot inside of me that made my knees buckle when his fingers circled and stroked it.

"Ahhhhh," I moaned as I covered his hand with my own, trapping his hand between my legs as I rocked against his fingers, "She's always – oh, shit! – wet for you."

My brazen moans captivated him and he just stared at me. My head tilted back, overtaken by extreme pleasure, moaning softly, licking my lips, biting down on my bottom lip when the intensity jolted my limbs. My face twisted as my chest rose and fell and explicitly sweet nothings fell from my lips. Anthony was satisfied simply watching me.

"You're fucking perfect," he whispered.

24
ANTHONY

    I showered as Stacey rested her exhausted body from the lovemaking session we engaged in earlier. I'd become aroused again just thinking about her. The damn girl was tantalizing. I craved her. The intensity of my feelings for her made me feel delirious and I didn't live the type of life where I could short step. Getting too comfortable could cost me my life, a lapse of judgement could crumble my empire, but letting my queen go was out of the question. When I stepped out of the shower, I called Tank and requested that he and Bear meet me at the house. I felt the need to increase my security team as I allowed myself to freely feel the love Stacey and I shared. I wouldn't allow my lifestyle to rob me of this moment.

    I paced over to Stacey and brushed the curls from her face as she slept, blanket and sheet tucked snuggly between her legs. I admired her exposed thigh as I ran my fingertips from her ankle to her hip, causing her to stir as she stretched and smiled at me with sleepy eyes.

    "Tank will be taking you shopping and I've arranged for Charles Renee to accompany you," I said, standing over her, wrapped in a bath towel, beads of water still glistening on my skin.

She pulled the sheet down, exposing her nipple rings and turned over to her back before asking seductively, "What's the occasion?" Shifting her eyes from mine and down to my growing penis hidden beneath my bath towel, Stacey smiled sinfully at the revelation that she was able to get me hard instantly as she slid her hand under my towel.

    I let out a soft, "Fuck, Love, how am I ever going to get anything done?" I complained but didn't ask her to stop.

    "You can ask me to stop at any time," she informed me as she continued to grin, gently jerking her hand up and down my dick.

"That's not fair," I growled, but this time dropping my towel to the floor. "Tank and Bear will be here in less than five minutes.".

She leaned over licking the tip of my erect penis.

"Well then you better hurry," she said, smiling.

STACEY

Tank accompanied Charles Renee, me, and Rachel, who I invited last minute to join me on my shopping trip. Anthony had given me his American Express black card and told me to buy what I wanted before kissing me on the lips and leaving to handle business of his own. Tank and Rachel locked eyes on several occasions as both blushed, making an awful attempt to hide what they were doing.

"Heffa!" I looped my arm around Rachel's as Charles Renee grabbed her other arm. "Spill the damn tea!" I whispered, only loud enough for the three of us to hear.

Tank paced behind us, allowing enough space for privacy, but close enough to protect us if necessary.

"What?" Rachel asked coyly grinning as she looked from me to Charles Renee.

"Bitch! Don't what me! What's going on with you and Tank?" I quizzed Rachel, elated at the opportunity to finally poke and prod into her love life, in the same manner she had always done to me.

"Yas, honey! Spill the beans! Because I know that big sexy ass man has some mandingo warrior in his pants!" Charles Renee said as he added a little extra sachet in his walk.

Rachel and I glanced at each other puzzled and both said in unison, "*You know?!*"

Charles Renee stopped walking and glared at us. "Oh girl! Not like that! I don't *know* know. I'm just assuming because Bear *definitely* has that daddy long dick!"

Charles Renee licked his tongue out seductively and swirled it around the straw of his cold brewed coffee.

The screams and laughter that erupted from us caused bystanders to stop and stare as Tank walked behind us nonchalantly grinning.

"So Bear is gay!?" I whispered.

"As a goddamned daisy in May honey!" Charles Renee teased.

Rachel and I clutched our imaginary pearls as Charles Renee informed us, "You're safe with Tank, but baby Bear is swinging in my territory."

Rachel giggled. "We've just been texting and talking a lot he swung by last week and we watched a movie. I like him, y'all!"

Rachel grinned and placed both hands over her face at the embarrassment of it all. She hadn't so much as given a man a chance in over a year. She'd much rather be alone than to worry about a lying, cheating asshole disrupting her zen or her yoni PH balance with his dirty dick, as she so *eloquently* put it.

"So when are you going to give him some because everyone is tired of your stale ass attitude!" I blurted out.

"Some dick would do your body good!" Charles Renee chimed in.

Rachel's jaw dropped. "Fuck both of you bitches! I'm selective with who I give my goods to! You loose pussy hoes can do whatever you want, but my pussy and I are just fine!" Rachel informed us as we all giggled.

I tried on multiple dresses and jumpsuits, all with an added flare. Sequins, rhinestones, glitter, feathers, Charles Renee was not about to let me rock a boring outfit.

"Y'all! I don't even know the occasion!" I admitted.

"Doesn't matter doll, you shut that shit down, no matter the occasion!" Charles Renee reminded me.

Tank stood close by as we occupied the private dressing room of the exclusive boutique. Anthony's unlimited funds had awarded a stellar shopping experience and I, along with my two guests, was enjoying every minute of the experience.

"Bitch! This is it! This is the showstopper right here!" Charles Renee boasted as he found the white lace bodysuit and white high waisted, wide leg pants.

He glared at the outfit as he lifted it in the air admiring the expensive fabric. He hung the outfit on a rack and stood back with his hands folded across his chest, before he placed a hand on his chin as he just looked, as if he had some superpower outfit put-together machine implanted in his brain.

"Yep! This is it! Go put it on!" he said as he shoved the white material towards me.

The thong bodysuit was practically swallowed by my big ass and gave me a ridiculous amount of cleavage. The see-through lace made my silver nipple bars visible through the bodysuit and my mind flashed to Anthony, he would lose his fucking mind! I wiggled into the slightly stretchy high waisted pants and called for Rachel to zip the back of the pants that sucked my waist in and made my butt look even more plump that usual.

"Stace! You look like a damn hourglass!" Rachel shrieked as she dragged the zipper to the top of the pants.

When I slid the heavy dressing room curtain back, Charles Renee dramatically threw himself onto the plush couch and placed a hand over his forehead.

"Girl! I can't take it! You're fine as hell! If I liked kitty kat, I'd be all over that!"

I smiled and lowered my eyes to the ground as I blushed.

"Stop it, y'all!" I said.

When I heard Tank's deep baritone voice a few feet away say, "Looks nice on you, Ms. Stacey," I knew that this was the outfit because Tank hardly spoke, but for him to speak on my appearance, I knew this was it.

"Well, I guess we're bagging this up!" I said. Even though I didn't know exactly why I was getting all dolled up, I figured it had to do with my birthday.

ANTHONY

I pulled into the driveway of the club where the surprise birthday party was set to take place the following night. My security team inspected entrance and exit doors, and spoke in detail to waitstaff, bartenders, and bottle girls about my strict expectations. Rachel was in charge of the guestlist, and anyone who showed up that was not on the list was to be sent away, no exceptions. I had an itching suspicion that Quinton might show up, so I dispersed his photo and let my team know that he was allowed to enter, but that I was to be notified as soon as they spotted him. I spared no expense for my love on her thirtieth birthday and was looking forward to seeing the excitement on her face. The bar would be open and there would be four buffet stations setup throughout the club to limit the long lines for food. I thought of every detail, down to the entertainment, LED lightshow and customized dance floor. When my phone began to vibrate I smiled to see Stacey's face flash across his screen.

"Hola, Love, find something amazing?" I asked, as a smile spread across my face.

"Mmmhmm," her sultry voice echoed from the other end of the phone. "You plan on making it home anytime soon?"

Her voice was more of a demand than a question, and I figured I'd better wrap up my business quickly because I was missing her just as much as she was missing me. I received word that the Houston drop was a success, which provided relief and would allow me to relax and enjoy the birthday party, but there was another issue pressing my conscience. Unbeknownst to Stacey, I issued a manhunt with a sizable reward for the capture of Quinton, but all of my men had come up emptyhanded. I managed to suppress my frustration and anger in the presence of Stacey, but remained vocal and outwardly brutal towards my men because I didn't do failure and this...being unable to find the man who committed a crime against my woman was failure. I glared at my phone as it vibrated in my hand again.

"You better be calling me with some fucking useful information," I said through clenched teeth.

The man on the other end of the phone hesitated.

"Uh…well you see, Boss, we're working on it. We had him, but the muthafucka is slick. I asked around and apparently he has friends in high places from his NFL days. He keeps managing to go underground, we could—"

"Shut the fuck up!" I hissed, annoyed, "Don't call me again until you've got your hands on the nigga."

When my phone rang for a third time and my mother's face flashed across the screen, I became even more annoyed.

"Yes, Mother," I answered in a stale voice, making no attempt to cloud my contempt for my mother in my tone.

"Well hello, son. My day has gone well, thank you for asking," Valentina said facetiously, matching my monotone voice. "Must you be such a little shit every time we speak? Have I not given you the world?"

"Mother, I don't have time for this today. I'm handling important business," my voice boomed through the phone.

"And what might that be? Because the last time I checked, planning your little girlfriend's birthday party should be the last thing my son – the leader of the most powerful Mexico/Houston cartel –would be involved in. Don't you have more pressing business to tend to?"

My mother's voice was condescendingly crass. But I was not at all surprised that she was keeping tabs on me. I was her only child and I learned everything I knew from her. She was the reason I was ruthless. She made me and I owned the fact that I was a monster created by Valentina DeLeon. I loved my mother, but she was far from perfect, and that part I didn't mind too much. It was her inability to protect me as a child, more so, her unwillingness to protect me. The way Valentina saw it, misfortunate experiences were character building stepping stones and I had used those stones to climb my way to the top. Now, as an adult I understood what my mother was trying to do, but as a child I felt overwhelmingly lonely and abandoned after my attack. I credited my childhood for the lack of love in my life. I bottled those broken feelings and allowed them to mold my relationships.

    It was my daughter who gave me a new set of lenses to see the world through. Had her mother not accidentally gotten pregnant, I was positive I would still be running the streets and she would have been just another notch on my belt. My precious baby girl Ava made me give the family life a chance. I was willing to settle down if it meant Ava would have a stable home. When she died, I gave up hope of ever being a family man. I was almost certain this was the reason Ava's mother had left me and made the decision to find her own happiness because I was unable, rather unwilling, to give her the love she deserved.

    "Mother, is there a particular reason why you called me?" I said, as I pulled myself from memory lane.

    "Well actually, son, I was hoping we could do dinner tonight, your place, say around seven p.m.?" Her question was not really a question at all, more like a warning, informing me that she would be there regardless of my response.

    I sighed before responding. "Stacey will be there and I expect for you to be on your best behavior," I warned.

    My mother chuckled. "Of course dear, I look forward to chatting with your little lady. You have to have tough skin to be a part of this family. Tonight will prove whether she is DeLeon material or not because I know you well enough to know if you're keeping her around, she must be special," Valentina responded.

    "Mother, here you go! What makes you think being a DeLeon is even in the cards for her?" I asked defensively.

    "Don't insult my intelligence, boy! Did you really think your uncle would not call to tell me you removed three hundred and fifty thousand dollars from the offshore account to purchase a ring?!"

She scoffed, and I could hear the irritation in her voice.

"Don't you ever get tired of keeping tabs on me, Mother? You do know that I am a grown ass—I'm sorry. You do know that I'm a grown man, right?"

"He's our accountant, Anthony! I wasn't keeping tabs on you, the man we pay to handle our finances was simply doing his job," she informed me.

I blew air through my lips and placed a hand on my head in an attempt to soothe the headache I could feel migrating to my brain out of thin air. "Okay Mother, I'll see you at seven." I finally gave in to get her off the phone. I figured I'd better text Stacey to warn her of the tornado that would be making an appearance for dinner.

25
STACEY

"So if you're feeling him, why don't you just call him, Rachel?" I asked, trying to talk sense into my best friend.

Rachel grew quiet as we sat on the patio overlooking the pool in Anthony's estate.

"I don't know. He works a lot," she said, finding any excuse to *not* call Tank.

"Bitch! Are you serious? Is that all?" I asked, raising myself from the pool chair onto my elbows as I tilted my sunglasses down.

"I mean, yeah. He's always working, so clearly this isn't going to work," Rachel confessed as she fell back onto her chair and slapped her forehead for mustering up such a piss poor excuse.

"Okay! Done! I'll tell Anthony to give him more days off," I said, grabbing my cell phone, thumbing to Anthony's name, causing Rachel to pop up and make an unsuccessful swipe at my phone.

"No! Don't do that!" she said, with an outstretched hand, as if she could stop me. "I don't want Tank to be upset with me for intervening in his personal business!"

"Too late! I already texted Anthony asking if he could give Tank additional days off to be with you. He said he will find someone to cover his position on his new off days," I said.

Rachel dropped her head into her hand. "Damnit!" she said, "Well, I guess I better call his big ass now that you've inserted me into his life!"

"You're welcome," I said, taking a sip from my margarita.

When Anthony finally made it home, I had wrapped up my midday happy hour with Rachel and was wrapped in one of his t-shirts with a pair of his socks that came up to my knees as I read a book waiting on him to arrive. When I locked eyes with

Anthony, I placed my book on the nightstand and walked over to him. I wrapped my arms around his neck and he effortlessly lifted me as I wrapped my legs around his waist. He stared at me for a moment, causing me to tilt my head and smile.

"You okay, baby?" I asked, still grinning at Anthony's adoring gaze.

"Yeah, but I need to tell you something and I really don't want you to be upset," he said, causing me to unwrap my legs and slide down his body until my feet reached the floor.

I felt the palms of my hands begin to perspire as I backed away from Anthony and gazed up at his eyes, those damn eyes, how were his lashes so long and perfect? I didn't know that there was anything this man could tell me to make me run for the hills. He was absolutely breathtaking. I had already made up my mind that whatever bomb he was about to launch into my world, I would just have to deal with it because Anthony DeLeon was mine.

I sucked in a deep breath before exhaling. "Okay I'm ready, but just so you know, I'm not going anywhere. You said you love me and I believe you, so whatever fucked up mistake you've made, we can get through it together. Just please don't tell me you got someone preg—"

"Love, slow down! Calm down! I would never do that to you. I just wanted to let you know that my mother will be joining us for dinner," he said.

"Oh my God!" I rushed Anthony, wrapping my arms around his toned midsection. "Thank God!" I exhaled as I felt tears sting my eyelids threatening to release themselves from the corners of my eyes. Anthony chuckled for a moment before he realized where I was going with the conversation.

"Wait a minute," he said as he gently pulled me away from him and gazed at me disappointingly, "You really think I would do some shit like that to you?"

His face wrinkled as his brows tilted inward and a glimpse of hurt crawled across his face. I felt embarrassed for even placing Anthony in the same category as Savior, they were nothing alike. Anthony had proven himself to be loyal, and yet, I was unable to move past the hurt I experienced. Shit maybe it was karma for all the hearts I'd broken over the years. I wasn't exactly sure, but what I did know was that he had given me no reason to accuse him of anything this foul.

"Baby, I'm sorry. I just…it's…just that…shit. I don't know, I guess I'm still a little hurt from my last situation," I said.

"But have I not proven that—"

I interrupted him. "Yes Anthony! Absolutely you have! You've proven that you're nothing like him, and I'm so sorry for even letting it cross my mind for a minute that you might be," I said.

When I lifted my eyes to look at Anthony, I could no longer fight the stinging sensation pricking the back of my eyelids. As a tear rolled down my face Anthony swiped it away with his thumb.

"None of that, not with me, smiles only."

He flashed a lopsided grin, which caused me to giggle as I hugged him tighter.

"Thank you for being so amazing to me, Anthony." I embraced him as if I were trying to keep him from leaving me, when in actuality, he wasn't going anywhere.

"Love, you're mine. What kind of man would I be if I didn't take care of you?" he asked, as he kissed the top of my forehead.

In the moment I had forgotten what caused us to arrive at this point, and when it dawned on me that Anthony mentioned his mother coming to dinner, I jolted backwards, separating our bodies.

"Your mom is coming to dinner!? But she hates me!"

My palms began to sweat again as I rubbed them on the t-shirt I wore.

"Damn sweaty ass hands!" I cursed as I paced back and forth.

"Amor, wait, wait, wait. It's okay," he assured me, holding my shoulders tightly to stop me from pacing.

"But it's not okay! What am I going to wear? I need to comb my hair! I need to cook! Oh my God! What if she hates my cooking!?"

I was completely frantic.

"Love, stop, please," he begged as he backed me into the bed. As I continued to ramble, he pushed my legs apart and kissed me gently on top of my panties.

"Anthony, what are you—" I started, but when he aggressively snatched at the waistband of my panties, dragging them down to my ankles and throwing them onto the floor, I stared at him in disbelief.

"It's the only way I know how to calm you down," he said, looking up at me from between my legs.

"Baby, what are you...I have to get ready! We don't have—"

Anthony covered me with his lips and closed his eyes as he used his tongue to open me up. I gasped for air.

Who the hell stole all of the air from the room? I thought to myself.

"*Shit*," I moaned as I propped myself up on my elbows and allowed my head to fall back.

He gripped my legs, wrapping his fingers around my thighs, caressing them deeply. Anthony licked, slurped and entered me with his tongue, sucking away my anxiety, licking away my fears. He placed two fingers inside of me as he rotated my clit with his thumb.

"You listening to me?" Anthony's deep voice boomed and I could feel his breath on my pussy as his fingers slid in and out.

"Uh huh," I moaned in response to his question.

"This is my house, which makes it your house," he informed me.

"Ahhhhh, okay," I responded.

"Don't ever feel like you have to be anyone other than yourself, especially in your own space," Anthony said as he thrust his fingers deeper.

"Yes! Yes baby!" I responded.

"So calm your little ass down! Wear what you want, you're not cooking, we have staff for that, and you don't need to comb your hair because you look fucking beautiful, do you understand me?" he asked.

"Ahhhhh, I understand!" I responded.

"Don't ever let me see you lose yourself like that again. You're the prize, I'm just the lucky one that was smart enough to see it," Anthony said, causing me to moan loudly as I thrust my body against his fingers.

"Now cum for me," he demanded, replacing his thumb with his mouth and I lost my fucking shit.

I opted for a black, ribbed, off the shoulder, calf-length, bodycon dress and a pair of nude heels with the Cartier diamond studs Anthony had gifted me months ago. I was preparing to wear my hair in a sleek bun, but reconsidered when Anthony walked past me as I stood in the bathroom mirror, struggling with my impossible curls and said, "I like it better when it's out" referring to my lion-like mane.

I dropped my arms, letting go of the bun, causing my hair to fluff instantly. Buns made my head ache terribly. I had always been extremely tender headed and Anthony's confirmation was all I needed to unleash my curls. He walked past me again on the way out of the bathroom and smacked me on my butt causing me to yelp and then giggle.

"Mannish," I said as I laughed and shook my head. Before heading downstairs to meet his mother Anthony pulled me aside.

"I love you, you know that, right?" he asked.

I nodded my head and flashed him a smile.

"These past two and a half months have been the best thing I've experienced in a very long time. Please don't let my mother change that tonight." Anthony placed his hands on either side of my face locking eyes with me. "She's tough, I won't lie but—"

I placed a single finger over his lip shushing him.

"I've got this," I said as I winked at him and led the way to the foyer.

"Ms. DeLeon, so nice to see you again."

My voice echoed throughout the marble foyer as I approached Valentina, touching both of her cheeks with my own. She raised a brow and stared me down from head to toe before finally parting her lips.

"Sarah, right?"

I chuckled. "Oh Valentina, aren't you a funny one? It's Stacey, might want to remember it, I'll be around for a long time." I smiled as I walked away. "Feel free to join us in the formal dining room," I called over my shoulder as I strolled confidently grabbing Anthony's hand with a grin on my face.

"I guess someone found their lady balls tonight," Anthony leaned in and whispered into my ear.

I shrugged. "My house too, right?" I said.

"Right," he said as he kissed my forehead.

I surprised myself by holding my own in the presence of Anthony's mother. There was no denying that Valentina was an intimidating, stone cold bitch, but if I wanted a real shot at being with Anthony, I couldn't be afraid of his mother. I had to prove to Valentina, Anthony, and my damn self that I could cut it in this family.

"So, what is it that you see in my son?" Valentina's cold tone caused chills to rush down my arms.

"Uh well, what is there to not see?" I smiled as I looked beside me at Anthony's handsome face.

"I mean, aside from his money, dear. The money will always make the hoes come running," Valentina said as she pushed the food around her plate, staring into my eyes with a slightly sinister grin.

I paused, placing my fork onto my plate and folding my hands together before placing them flat on the dining table and leaning forward to ensure I heard her properly.

"Hoes?" I questioned; my head tilted in disbelief as I chuckled at Valentina's brazen disrespect. "Ms. DeLeon, I have my own money, I've owned my own business for many—"

Valentina cleared her throat interrupting me. "I know all about your gym in Third Ward. I know about your father and his successful architecture business. I know that you went to the finest private schools and live a pretty upscale life, but let's not pretend that anything you have is remotely similar to the life my son can afford you," Valentina said as she pursed her lips together, waiting on my response.

She was right. I was living an extremely modest life compared to the life Anthony had created for himself and I found myself at a loss for words in rebuttal to Valentina's statement. Just as I had conceded defeat, I heard Anthony's voice swoop in,

"Mother, I pursued her. She didn't even know who I was, so don't paint her out to be some gold digger, *I* wanted *her*!" he informed his mother.

I smiled and interlocked fingers with Anthony as I stared at him, ready to rip his clothes off and straddle him on the dining room table, and had Valentina not been there, I would have done just that.

"Son, give Stacey and I a minute," Valentina said as she motioned for him to leave.

Anthony hesitated. "I don't think that's a really good idea," he said, gripping my hand securely.

"It's okay, baby," I reassured him with a smile and a nod.

As Anthony started to exit the dining room, I noticed a *slight hesitation,* as he turned heavy steps away from me. *Why the hell was he afraid to leave me with this woman?*

"Stacey, you seem like a really sweet girl. You have no children. You own your own business. You come from a pretty decent family based on my research. Why would you want to get yourself tied up with my son?" Valentina asked, and surprisingly, she seemed genuinely concerned.

I shifted uncomfortably in my seat, heart thumping against my chest. "I love him," I responded as I slightly shrugged my shoulders.

Valentina chuckled. "Love?"

"Yes, I love him, Ms. DeLeon." I shifted my body forward and folded my hands over the dining table looking into Valentina's eyes.

"How far do you think that love will carry you when his life within the cartel begins to spill over into this house?" She whirled her finger into a circle looking around the room. "Huh? How far will that love carry you when you worry about the safety of your unborn babies? Because in this life, you'll never sleep with both eyes closed."

Now I see why Anthony hesitated to leave me with her. Damn, Valentina was crass as fuck...and unborn babies? What the hell!?

There was a seriousness to Valentina's tone that made my limbs feel numb. She wasn't bitchy like she had been in our initial meeting, her words almost sounded like a warning. Valentina was in a class of her own in the petty department. I had come to dinner ready for war, but at this moment, I sensed a sincerity from Valentina and suddenly felt a deeply rooted desire to know more. I closed my eyes for what seemed like an entire minute before speaking.

"Ms. DeLeon, thank you for your honesty. Really, I mean it, but I need you to know that I love Anthony. Don't know that I've ever felt this kind of unconditional love in my entire life, so I guess the only real question would have to be how do you suggest I make it in this life? Because I have no plans of going anywhere."

Valentina's eyes bulged at my declaration and I saw something I never imagined I might see from her—a smile.

"I must admit, I was skeptical about you, but loyalty weighs heavily among our family and you seem to be just that." Valentina grabbed her purse as she slid her chair back.

Her words made my skin itch and I felt my palms begin to sweat again.

"Loyalty?" I scoffed. "With all due respect, Ms. DeLeon, how can you speak of loyalty when you allowed Anthony's cousins to nearly kill him?"

The room was still for a complete two minutes and Valentina was visibly bruised by my words as she stood from her chair and walked over to me.

"You have no idea what the hell you're talking about," she hissed as deep veins protruded from her forehead and neck.

I could feel the tension squeezing me as flames grew in Valentina's eyes, but I was unwilling to silence myself because I may never get the opportunity to speak candidly to her again.

"Why did you allow them to live after what they did to Anthony?" My bold voice was unrelenting as I took a step closer to Valentina.

"You think that was my choice? You think I would have ever willingly allowed those little shits to live after what they did to my precious boy?"

Tears unconsciously fell from Valentina's eyes and at that moment I realized it was Anthony who had ordered her not to kill his cousins. Anthony wasn't hurt by the fact that his mother didn't retaliate, he was scorned because she wasn't able to protect him during the time of the incident. I reached my hand towards Valentina's face and wiped her tears. I had no idea what possessed me to do such a thing and was even more surprised that she actually allowed me to do it.

"Maybe you can accomplish something I was never able to do," Valentina stated honestly.

I squinted my eyes and cocked my head to the side in confusion.

"Protect him. Make him see that family over everything goes out the fucking window when that family makes the choice to betray you," she said as she leaned over to hug me.

My arms shot out beside me in shock by the embrace when Valentina's voice soothed me. "Take care of my son, please."

I embraced her and we were both startled by Anthony's deep voice.

"Look, Mother! I love her, and you're just going to—"

His words were halted and his feet planted as he witnessed his mother and I in a heartfelt embrace.

"What the hell?" Anthony said, completely shocked by the view.

Valentina slowly released me from her embrace and grabbed my hand.

"Son, you've got you a good one. She loves you, take good care of her, and darling, wear the ring," Valentina said before winking at me, causing me to smile. "Well, looks like I need to be heading out, I'll catch you two lovebirds another day, and thank you for the amazing dinner."

She kissed Anthony on the cheek and headed toward the front door. Anthony stood staring at me perplexed and I just smiled, throwing my hands palm up as I shrugged my shoulders. I surprisingly made it through what I thought would be an excruciatingly painful dinner unscathed.

"So, what was that all about?" he asked once we were in our bedroom and he unzipped my bodycon dress.

"Oh nothing, we had a really great conversation, and I don't think moving forward your mom and I will have a problem seeing eye-to-eye," I grinned as I spun around on my heels to kiss Anthony's lips before strolling to the drawer to grab a black lace lingerie slip and sliding it over my head.

"You know, anytime you're ready, you can have a full set of drawers," Anthony teased as I flashed him a squinty eyed glare.

"Mmmhmm," I responded with a side smirk.

He stripped down to his boxer briefs and crawled into bed with me, his warm body cradled mine as we fit together like puzzle pieces. I could feel Anthony's warm breath on the back of my neck as I closed my eyes and sank into him.

"You know that I love you, right?" Anthony asked in a reassuring tone.

I turned to face him, gripping his face in my hands, gently stroking his full, neatly trimmed beard. I stared into his eyes and smiled before responding, "I know, and I love you even more."

"Doubtful," he responded, returning my smile before kissing my lips and wrapping his arms around my body to slide me closer.

I nestled my head under Anthony's chin, wrapped my warm thigh around his legs and closed my eyes as he held me tightly. Just as I felt myself dozing off, I heard Anthony whisper, "Thank you, God."

26
STACEY

I awakened the next morning to an empty bed, which I had become accustomed to. Anthony was an early riser and often left home to handle business before I got out of bed, but he liked to be back before I got up to get my day started. I looked towards the nightstand and reached for my diamond ring, which I hadn't decided if I would wear or not. I removed the ring from the box and placed it onto my finger as I pushed my hand away from my face admiring the brilliance. When I heard my phone buzz, I placed the ring back into the box and swiped my phone from the nightstand. I felt my heart skip a beat when Savior's name scrolled across the screen. I had not heard from him since the day Anthony and Tank threatened to kill him. I closed my eyes tightly, sucked in a deep breath, exhaled and opened the text message.

Savior: Happy Birthday Beautiful! I know we're not okay, I don't expect for us to be. I just couldn't let today pass without telling you that I'm sorry, I love you and what we had wasn't bullshit, I handled you wrong. I hurt you, and for that I'm truly sorry. You deserve the world. All I ask is that you don't allow that gangster to trick you into thinking he is the one. I've seen dudes like him. He's going to cause you a world of trouble. But anyway. Happy birthday and I'm always here if you need me.

I was stunned. The fucking audacity of this man! How dare he have the nerve to speak on Anthony when for two whole years, Savior had done nothing but break my heart. I scoffed in disbelief. Just as my fingers prepared to move across the screen to rip Savior a new asshole, Anthony poked his head into the room. "Get dressed, Love," was all he said before vanishing back into the hallway.

I took my time grooming myself before throwing my hair into a messy bun and sliding on a pair of black tights and matching black sports bra. My skin glowed from within and I topped everything off with a slab of Vaseline across my lips. I was effortlessly beautiful and smiled at my reflection. I drifted from the master suite through the foyer and was surprised to see my mother, father, brother PJ, Rachel, Charles Renee, Tank, Bear, and a host of other people I hadn't expected to run into.

"Happy Birthday!" they all screamed, causing me to jump and cover my mouth with my hands in surprise.

It was hard to hide my excitement as I scanned the room for Anthony. When he approached me, I playfully slapped his hard chest.

"You did this for me?" I asked, as I wrapped my arms around him.

"Anything for you, Love," he said, kissing the top of my forehead as he embraced me.

I glanced around the room to see two private chefs and various stations setup with my favorite foods. Shrimp and grits, fried catfish, chicken and waffles, chicken benedict with hollandaise sauce, a mimosa bar, and the room was decorated with pink and gold balloons. There was decor on every wall and a photobooth station with props and a DJ tucked off in the corner. Anthony really outdid himself, which wasn't particularly surprising because he always managed to glamorize everything he touched.

I rounded the room socializing and smiled when I reached my parents. They wrapped me in an embrace as my father whispered, "we have a lot to discuss young lady," with an awkward smile on his face that I didn't recognize.

"Don't mind your father, dear. He's just not used to anyone having more than he has and he wants to know what exactly it is that Anthony does," my mother stated, wrapping her arm around my father's arm.

I grinned shyly and quickly changed the subject to deter my parents from asking uncomfortable questions that I was unwilling to answer at the moment.

"So! Anthony reached out to you two?" I asked inquisitively.

"Yes," my mother responded, grinning from ear to ear, "He wanted to let us know how smitten he was with you and how much he would love to have us over for brunch, but we had no idea that the young man was so established."

"What is this I hear about a ring?" my father asked, lifting my bare hand.

Damnit, Rachel! I cursed internally.

I knew she was the culprit without my parents ever confirming the source. She was more than my best friend; she was more like a sister and had built a strong bond with my parents over the years. It was no surprise that Rachel would spill the beans about Anthony proposing to my parents, but luckily, I hadn't decided if I would marry him or not, so there was no ring on my finger...which made the conversation easy to evade with my parents.

I hugged and mingled with friends and family before Anthony walked over to me and whispered into my ear, "I have something special planned for you tonight," causing me to jerk my head to look at him because what he had already planned was enough.

"But baby!" I said, before Anthony kissed my lips to quiet me.

"It's your birthday, Love. I don't want to hear anything you have to say, this is nothing."

I rolled my eyes before displaying a wide grin on my face.

"Listen, enjoy your family and friends, I have to handle some business and then Rachel and Charles Renee have scheduled for you to have your nails and toes done," he said.

"Make sure you're ready to go by nine p.m., sound good?" Anthony asked.

"Sounds great," I responded as he kissed my lips.

He turned around to make a speech to the room. "Excuse me lovely people, but I have to run, business calls, but mi casa es su casa, make yourselves at home and mingle with the birthday girl as long as you would like. DJ! Give my love something to dance to!" Anthony winked at me and headed to the front door with Bear trailing behind him.

He had allowed Tank to stay and keep an eye on the party, but I knew it was really so that he could be close to Rachel. I danced and sang and pranced around the house enjoying my family and friends until a text message chimed and caught my attention.

```
Savior: No response? We're better
than that Stacey.
```

I rolled my eyes and walked into the master suite clear of distractions to address Savior.

```
Me: Savior, I'm truly flabbergasted
by your arrogance. You really think I owe
you anything with the way things ended for
us?
Savior: Stacey, I tried to apologize. You
weren't supposed to find out like that. I
had every intention of telling you and I
feel like shit that I didn't tell you soon
enough.
Me: Don't feel like shit, because ridding
you from my system gave me space to let
someone in that truly deserves me.
Savior: That nigga from your apartment?
Stacey! A blind man could see that he is a
thug! Is that the life you want for
```

```
yourself? The type of nigga you want to
take home to your parents?
    Me: (laughing emoji) My parents
happen to LOVE him and he's done more for
me than you EVER have! In EVERY area
(smirking emoji)
Savior: You're upset and I get it, but
you're being irrational. I'm in town. Meet
me. I just want to talk.
```

"Girl! What are you doing in here all cooped up? Ohhhh, so this is where all the magic happens!" Rachel laughed, as she invited herself into the master suite, which didn't bother me.

I rolled my eyes and shoved my phone towards Rachel. She took the phone from me. "Oh bitch, hell no!" she said in response to the messages.

"Mmmmhmmm," I said.

"Can you believe him?" I was shocked.

"So are you going to meet him?" Rachel asked, with raised brows.

I shot up from the bed. "What! No! Absolutely not!" I responded with a scowl on my face.

"Okay, okay, I was just checking, you know this man was your weak spot not so long ago. Just making sure that chapter of your life is over," Rachel said.

"Oh it's done done! You hear me!?" My words sounded convincing but deep down I had a desire for closure, whatever the hell that meant.

As the party wound down I received a phone call from Anthony.

"Hey mi amor, how is everything going?"

I smiled at the thought of knowing Anthony made it a habit to think about me while he was away.

"Everything is perfect, just about everyone has left with the exception of Rachel and Charles Renee. I think I might take a nap to prepare for tonight," I said, hoping Anthony bought my lie. I hung up the phone with Anthony to see Rachel throwing plates and cups into a black garbage bag.

"Hey girl, you can leave all of this mess, Anthony has a professional company coming to clean," I informed her, causing her to drop the bag full of garbage.

"Well shit! Why didn't you say that to begin with? Got me messing up my manicure," she scoffed playfully.

"Where is Charles Renee?" I asked.

"Oh, the last time I saw him, he was outside on the patio taking a phone call," Rachel informed me.

"Well, I think I'm going to close my eyes for a bit, you know, to prepare for tonight. See y'all later for my nail appointment? I don't know what Anthony has up his sleeve, but I would surely hate to fall asleep on him." I let out a forced yawn as I stretched my arms out to my side signifying that I was ready for them to excuse themselves.

"Bitch! You ain't gotta tell me but one time. Charles Renee, get your Betty Crocker ass up and let's go," Rachel called outside to the patio where Charles Renee sat on a lounge chair talking on his cellphone.

He sashayed past me and blew me a kiss before catching arms with Rachel and heading out the door. Tank trailed behind the both of them, which wasn't in his job description and I was sure it had everything to do with Rachel.

When Tank entered back through the double doors, I said, "Tank, I'm actually about to take a nap, so there is no need for you to stay here with me. Go ahead and enjoy your day."

I had hoped that my attempt to dismiss Tank would be successful, but I could tell by his glare that it most definitely was not.

"Ms. Stacey, you know the boss man will kill me if I leave you here alone," Tank said with a raised brow, "You know I don't want to lose my job, or die." Tank shrugged.

I sucked in a breath and blew it out before forcing a smile and responding, "okay," as I walked into the master suite.

Think Stacey! Think! I told myself. How the hell was I going to get past Tank's big ass to get to my car? I paced the length of the room trying to concoct a strategy that would allow me to leave the house without being seen, but when I thought about Anthony's wrath towards Tank if I were to do something that reckless, I reconsidered. Fuck it! *I guess it's time to see just how loyal Tank is*, I thought. I barged from the master suite and stormed up to Tank.

"Listen! I'm not taking a nap. I lied!" I said.

Tank stood there stoically, visibly confused.

"Okay, you know Ms. Stacey, however you decide to run your nap schedule is perfectly fine with me," Tank teased.

I shook my head. "Tank, I was trying to get out of the house without you," I admitted boldly.

His face wrinkled in confusion. "But why? I'll take you wherever you need to go," Tank responded.

"I know Tank, but I just didn't want you to go to this place." I held my head down, looking at the ground embarrassed. "Just come on," I said.

When Tank and I arrived at the coffee shop, he rotated his head, looking from side to side, obviously trying to make sense of why we were there. When he saw Savior emerge from the coffee shop and sit on the patio I noticed a change in his demeanor.

"Tank, before you say anything, I just need you to know that I need this closure. I gave him two years of my life, but I need him to know that we're done," I said as I held up my left hand, holding the unmissable diamond in plain sight. "I just need him to know that he and I will never be and I'm going to be Mrs. DeLeon," I smiled.

When Tank flashed me a slight grin, my heart felt at ease.

"I'll be right here if you need me," Tank assured me as I gave his arm a gentle squeeze.

"Thank you, Tank," was all I said as I slid from the SUV.

Savior noticed me before I was in plain view. How could he not? He gazed at me as I walked closer and immediately, the look on his face spoke volumes. *How did I fuck this up?* was what I imagined he was thinking.

"Hey Savior," I greeted as I approached and pulled my chair out.

He stood and raised an eyebrow. "I don't get a hug?"

I looked over at the black SUV where Tank was parked and hesitantly walked into Savior, allowing his arms to wrap around my body. Damn he smelled good. There was no way I could deny that, but not as good as Anthony, I reminded myself as I pushed away from him with a forced smile and took my seat.

"Your face healed nicely."

I winced at my comment because I hadn't meant to say that; it just kind of slipped out. It was true, I didn't know what would come of Savior's beautiful face after the beat down delivered to him, but I had to admit, as I glared into his sienna brown eyes, I was relieved to see that he was just as beautiful as I had remembered. I averted my gaze and dug into my purse looking for absolutely nothing. When I pulled my hand from my bag Savior noticed the ring on my finger and his body stiffened.

"So, you asked me to meet you. What do you want to talk about?" I asked nonchalantly.

"Uh, I mean. I just wanted to clear the air, we didn't leave things on the best of terms," he admitted reluctantly, running his hand down the back of his neck with a shameful demeanor nestled across his face.

I suddenly remembered the heartache Savior caused me, a heartache I hadn't fully processed because Anthony swooped in to save me. As I peered at Savior, remembering the broken promises and wasted time, I felt a tinge of pain rush through my chest, and I was happy that Anthony had been there to help relieve some of the hurt from Savior's bullshit.

"Savior, I'm not upset with you. You did what you wanted to do. You always have," I shrugged and sat back in my chair.

"The baby wasn't planned, Stacey," he said halfheartedly.

"Didn't stop you from hiding it though, did it?" I shot back with a glare. "A fiancée, Savior? Really?"

"Man, she was threatening to take my baby away from me. I had to do something to buy some time until I could figure out how to handle this situation," he said, reaching his hands toward mine as I shook my head.

This explained the harsh treatment he unleashed on me, but I was no one's damn punching bag! So I felt no remorse.

"You know what's crazy as hell?" I said, reaching forward to grab his hands, making sure my left hand was clasped on top of his, leaving my ring visible. "If you would have just been honest with me, I would have forgiven you for everything."

Sliding my hand away slowly, I watched the sunlight dance across my diamond ring, creating the most brilliant glimmer. I watched Savior's head shoot up, his eyebrows lifted and there was a flicker of hope that I recognized because I had once held that same feeling in her heart.

"Our time has passed, Savior, and I don't regret anything we had. You taught me more about myself than I ever thought possible, and you also taught me what I don't want, so thank you," I said as I pushed my chair back.

"Stacey, please! I know we can get past this; we always get past the bullshit." He grabbed my fingers, looking at me with those bright, mesmerizing, sienna brown eyes pleading for me to stay.

"Not this time, Savior. Not this time."

I slid my fingers from his grasp and walked away. Tank stepped from the car staring at Savior with a smirk on his face as he rounded the SUV to open the door for me.

"You okay, Ms. Stacey?" Tank's baritone voice boomed.

"I'm better than okay." I smiled, feeling a weight drop from my shoulders.

I was quiet the entire ride back to Anthony's place. I wasn't sure if Tank would snitch on me, but I surely hoped he wouldn't. He didn't strike me as the loose lipped type, but I also didn't sign his checks. When Tank and I entered the house, I expected for Anthony to still be handling business, but I was wrong, he was waiting for me.

"Tank, your location was off on your phone. Where have you been?"

Anthony wasn't the jealous type, but anytime he left one of his men in charge of looking out for me, he liked to know where we were. His lifestyle was dangerous and he needed to know where to find me if anything ever happened. Tank stood with his legs gapped apart and his hand clasped, one on top of the other. *Here we go,* I thought. Tank is about to snitch. I shifted uncomfortably and stepped towards Anthony, prepared to reveal my truth when Tank started talking.

"Sorry about that, boss. I must have forgotten to turn it on. Ms. Stacey just wanted to go look for some shoes," Tank said as he looked in my direction.

"Yea, but I couldn't find any," I smiled and walked towards Anthony, wrapping my arms around him.

Shit! Fucking shit! Why the hell did I just lie like that!?

"No problem, Amor. As long as you're okay, no explanation is necessary."

Anthony smiled and pounded fists with Tank before swooping me off my feet and cradling me in his arms as he carried me into the bedroom.

"He likes you a lot," Anthony informed me.

I grinned. "What makes you say that?" I asked, glancing at him lovingly as he carried me over to the bed.

"I think he views you like a little sister," he replied, tossing me playfully onto the bed before crawling between my legs, until he reached my neck, kissing it gently.

I giggled as I turned my head in the opposite direction of him, allowing him to gain better access to my neck because his kisses felt heavenly.

"What makes you say that?" I giggled softly as Anthony continued to kiss and tickle me.

"Because he's never lied to me before today and he did it for you," Anthony said.

I knew he felt my body tense and my heartbeat thumping against his own chest. I instantly felt foolish for not telling him the truth. He was a leader of a cartel, of course he had ways of finding things out. What the hell was I thinking? I elevated onto my elbows.

"Baby, I'm so sorry! Please don't be mad, I promise nothing happened," I said as my eyes began to fill with tears. *My crybaby ass.*

"Aht! What did I tell you about that crying shit, Stacey. Not with me. You needed closure. I understand, and I'm not upset, but please know that you can tell me anything. I'm not these other niggas you use to fuck around with. I'm a grown ass man and you are a grown ass woman. If there is ever a decision you have to make, you do it, but be honest about it. I'm going to love you regardless," Anthony said, wiping the tears from my face.

I let my head fall back as I tried to force away the tears, but they fell anyway. When I lifted my left hand to capture the droplets of water, Anthony's eyes widened. He slid from the bed and stared at me. I sat upright confused and when I saw tears building in the corners of Anthony's eyes I became concerned.

"Baby, are you okay?" I asked, looking at him desperate for answers.

"You're wearing the ring," Anthony managed to mumble, causing me to look down at my hand and then back up to him with a smile.

He dropped to his knees and slid me to the edge of the bed as he wrapped his arms around my waist and buried his head into my stomach.

"Thank you, Amor," Anthony whimpered.

I grabbed his face and pulled his head up as I looked into his eyes.

"No baby, thank you," I said, and this time, I was wiping away a tear from Anthony's eyes as I said, "*Oh no, no, no! No crying with me, only smiles.*" We both chuckled and embraced one another as joyful tears fell from our eyes.

Anthony stood to his feet. "Nope! I gotta do this shit the right way."

He grabbed my hand and pulled the ring off my finger.

"Let's go," he said.

We drove thirty minutes to my parents' house.

"Anthony, what are we doing here?" I asked, looking around, as Anthony waited for me to give him the gate code.

He rounded the car and opened my door, extending a hand for me to grab. When we rang the doorbell George greeted us, welcoming us inside.

"Anthony, Stacey, what a pleasant surprise! Honey, come downstairs. Stacey and Anthony are here!" my father called from the foyer.

My father shook hands with Anthony and hugged me tightly as my mother approached and wrapped Anthony in her arms before kissing me on the cheek.

"Mr. and Mrs. Hill, I apologize for the unannounced drop in, but I have something very important to say."

My parents looked at one other before glancing at me causing me to shrug my shoulders because I wasn't sure what the hell he was doing either.

Anthony cleared his throat. "Mr. and Mrs. Hill, I love your daughter and I would like to ask your permission to marry her," he said, standing tall.

My mother's hands flew to her mouth as she let out a muffled scream of excitement.

"Mr. Hill, I know that she is your everything, and I promise to take care of her and always do right by her," he informed my father.

My mother was now hugging me as we both smiled and spun around in a circle.

"Please tell me you will give me your blessing, Mr. Hill," Anthony asked.

My father strolled closer to Anthony. My mother and I stopped moving and focused our attention on them.

"Son, I knew you would marry my daughter the moment I met you in the hospital and it would be an honor to call you my son-in-law," my father said, as he extended his hand and pulled Anthony into an embrace.

My mother and I screamed even louder as Anthony turned to approach me. When he reached me he got down on one knee and held up the ring.

"Stacey Ambria Hill, will you make me the happiest man on earth and be my wife?" I nodded as Anthony placed the ring back onto my finger and swept me into a hug, elevating my feet from the ground.

"I had to do it the right way, you deserve it," he whispered into my ear.

"You have to allow us to host the engagement party!" my mother said, grabbing Anthony and me by our hands. "We will spare no expense! It'll be everything you ever dreamed of!"

I smiled and looked at Anthony.

"How could I say no to that?" Anthony responded.

As my mother and I disappeared into the house gushing over details, Anthony joined my father on the patio for a celebratory cigar.

27
ANTHONY

"You know, son, my daughter is a handful and I'm afraid that's my fault," Patrick admitted, lifting his gold torch lighter to the end of the Kuba Kuba cigar before passing it to me.

I chuckled. "She's perfect to me, Mr. Hill," I said with a smile large enough to brighten the dimly lit sky.

Patrick returned my smile. "Yea, that's what we all say until they start to get on our damn nerves," he said, as he tilted his glass of whiskey in my direction for a friendly toast.

I nosed the whiskey, inhaling the aroma before taking a small sip and responding, "Vanilla, oak and a hint of nutmeg, let me guess, Whistlepig Whiskey aged fifteen years?" I asked with a raised brow, awaiting confirmation.

"Actually, it's eighteen years," Patrick responded and was unexpectedly surprised. "A man who knows his whiskey is my kinda man!" Patrick chuckled heartily as he patted me on the back, holding his cigar between his teeth.

"Mr. Hill, thank you for giving me your blessing. I wasn't sure if—" before I could finish speaking Patrick interrupted.

"Keep her safe," he replied as he peered out over the sprawling land of his backyard, his face engulfed in cigar smoke.

"I would never let anything happen to her," I said, my body tensing as the thought of harm coming to Stacey caused me to become internally furious.

Patrick met my stare as he puffed on his cigar. "Make sure your business dealings don't collide with my daughter's happiness. I'm a businessman, and trust me, I've seen it all. Keep her away from your shit, are we clear?" Patrick asked in a way that wasn't really a question.

"Crystal clear," I responded as I exhaled a massive cloud of smoke.

As Stacey and I made the drive back home, I found myself deep in thought. I was seasoned when it came to matters of the streets and business. The two seemed to intersect more often than most people realized. Even successful family and business men like Patrick had gotten their hands dirty a time or two. There was a mutual respect between my future father-in-law and I. Businessmen didn't dabble in the details of another man's business unless they were working together in some aspect. The fact that Patrick had not inquired about the details pertaining to the nature of my business evoked the street saying, what's understood doesn't need to be explained.

I hadn't experienced true happiness outside of the day my Ava was born until the day I met Stacey. I'd be lying to myself if I said I wasn't concerned with how I was going to keep my treacherous world separate from the imminent fairytale life I was determined to create with Stacey. The feelings I possessed for her were hard even for me to explain and they were my damn feelings.

Lust.
Love.
Infatuation.
Adoration.

I wanted to put a smile on her face every day, to give her the world. I wanted this woman to have all my damn babies and never have to lift a finger again unless she chose to. I had never entertained the idea of leaving my line of work until this woman came into my life like a damned earthquake shaking shit up. She was the game changer, the new factor introduced into my situation that was causing me to rethink my life. How was I expected to head the cartel when all I could think about was burying my face between her thighs every waking moment? Daydreaming about her pussy was going to get my head blown off. I chuckled to myself at the thought of living thirty-five years just to be taken out because I couldn't keep my mind clear of my fiancée. I was going to have to find some balance.

I licked my lips and glanced over at Stacey to find her gazing at me with low sultry eyes as she bit the corner of her bottom lip, which caused me to chuckle even more. This right here was exactly why I couldn't get her out of my head. She was an aphrodisiac and I found it impossible to resist her salacious demeanor. The girl could look at me and cause my dick to jump but it wasn't just the sex with her. I could be honest, vulnerable and transparent without fear of judgement around her. I felt safe with her and she didn't want anything from me, which was why I was willing to give her everything.

She made my complicated life more manageable and discovered a path through the impenetrable wall I had amassed around my heart, and she wasn't even trying. I wasn't sure how and I didn't want to cross-examine the feelings because I rejected any thoughts attempting to persuade me that I should decelerate my feelings for Stacey. She was it for me. She loved my complicated ass and as incomprehensible as it was to me, rather than inquire why, I made the decision to thank God – which I didn't do often – and just love her as passionately as I knew how.

STACEY

On the ride home I felt a wave of emotions cover my body like a warm blanket, a sensation I had never felt before.
Security.
Stability.
Love.
Maybe this was how life was intended to feel. Just gazing at Anthony's side profile as he maneuvered through Houston traffic gripping my thigh caused chills to travel through every inch of my body. India Arie's "The Truth" floated through the car speakers, causing my heart to palpitate fast enough for me to notice the change in rhythm. I couldn't help but to realize that Anthony was indeed the truth. Enthralled by how flawlessly Spotify radio had captured the

moment with the perfect song, doubt began to creep in causing me to wonder was this actually happening?

Was I going to marry this man? Was it too soon? Would our relationship last?

When he flashed me a side smirk and gripped my thigh tighter, I felt a gush between my legs that immediately swept away the skepticism threatening to shatter my cloud nine high. I was engaged to a man I absolutely adored and I would be damned if I would authorize any uncertainties to wreak havoc on my thoughts. When Anthony drove through the inscribed rod iron gate of his estate, he hadn't fully opened my door before I pounced on him, caressing his lips with my own. I threw myself into the air and wrapped my legs around his waist as he caught me midair, cupping my ass, pulling my body close to his.

He spun around, pinning me against the car, our lips still merged together, as my soft moans were whisked away into the cool night's breeze. He pulled away from my lips and slowly kissed down the center of my chest as he cupped both breasts aggressively, causing my head to dart around the property grounds nervously, as I moaned in a faint whisper, "Anthony, what if someone sees?"

"Fuck 'em," he growled, pulling my breasts free as he bit my right nipple, causing my knees to buckle as a blissful groan escaped my lips.

His moist lips coupled with the frigid night air brushing against my skin caused me to pant breathlessly as I gripped the back of his neck, relaxing my body, allowing my head to fall back, resting on the car. Anthony slipped his tongue down my midsection until he found his sweet spot right between my legs. He kissed the top of my panties softly before draping one of my legs over his shoulder as he slid my panties to the side. I braced myself in anticipation of the warmth of his tongue but looked down surprised when I felt nothing. Instead, I glimpsed down to see Anthony staring up at me holding his bottom lip between his teeth.

"What's wrong, baby?" I moaned as my body involuntarily gravitated towards his face.

He smiled at my reaction. "Whose pussy is this baby?" he asked as he gently caressed my clit with a single kiss before pulling away.

I was two seconds from grabbing his head and shoving it into my vagina as I managed to let out a soft moan.

"It's yours, baby, this pussy belongs to you and only you, now stop playing and—ahhhhh!" I moaned as Anthony wrapped his lips around my clit, gently sucking, slurping and pulling. "Shit, Anthony!" were the only words I was able to articulate as he did his damn thing. I placed both hands on top of his deep waves and allowed them to follow his head as it moved in a circular motion.

"Damn, Love, this pussy tastes so good, and it's so wet, mmmmmm."

The way Anthony groaned, kissed, licked and sucked, would have caused anyone listening to think he was the one receiving the pleasure. He was devouring a pussy buffet and indulged in every moment of my goodness. When Anthony wiggled two fingers into my center, I all but climbed onto the hood of the car as I let out a loud, "Fuck!"

I was wet, open and ready for my man. I reached between my legs clutching his head as I pulled him up to my face and kissed his lips before licking them to taste myself as I whispered, "Baby, I want you to fuck me."

I searched his eyes for a hint of hesitation and when I found none, I grinned. He returned my grin as he forcefully flipped me around causing my palms to land on the hood of the car. I saw his hand rise into the air from my peripheral vision and I was sure the neighbors, although over a mile away, could hear the smack as it landed on my ass.

"Mmmmm!" I let out a muffled, pleasure-filled moan and felt Anthony's penis slap against my butt as he rubbed himself for a moment before coating himself in my juices.

He entered me slowly allowing his toned stomach to press against my back as he settled into me, wrapped in my warmth. He raised himself from my back, gripped a handful of my curls and gave them a slight twist, wrapping my hair around his knuckles, yanking it, causing my head to fly back.

"Ahhhhh," I moaned as his pace increased and he plowed into me.

The sound of skin smacking together, paired with the splish and splash of my wet pussy when Anthony's dick met my juicy walls caused his knees to buckle.

"*Shit*," he muttered under his breath, as the *I'm about to cum* look splattered across his face.

The sound of my voice as I screamed, "I'm cumming!" caused Anthony to bite his bottom lip as he tightened the death grip on my waist and gave me every inch he had to offer.

My legs began to shake uncontrollably and my body went limp causing Anthony to react by placing one hand on the car and catching me around my midsection with his free arm. He never pulled out, never stopped stroking, he filled me with his dick and his seed.

28
STACEY

After showering, putting on my makeup, which Anthony fussed about because he didn't understand why I didn't just allow him to call my glam squad over, and fluffing my curls, I stepped out in the white bodysuit and high waisted white pants Charles Renee had found for me. When Anthony turned from his top drawer where he kept his firearms, he observed me for a moment with lifted brows and an expression of shock stole his usual relaxed, mild mannered appearance. His expression immediately caused me to feel insecure as I tried to cover myself with my hands and arms, mainly my breasts, because my silver barbell nipple rings were slightly visible through the delicate lace.

"What's wrong? You hate it don't you? I knew it was too much! I'll go change," I said as I attempted to turn around hurriedly but was stopped by Anthony's hand around my wrist.

"No, Love, you look fucking incredible! Are your nipples showing?" he teased, causing me to pout as I tried to loosen his grip around my wrist.

"See, I knew it was too much!" I brooded.

Anthony chuckled as he pulled me into his chest. "Love, when have I ever dictated what you can and can't wear? You're a woman, *a fine ass woman*, you could have a fucking oversized dashiki on and niggas would still try their luck," he said, palming my ass.

I tried not to smile as I slightly bit my inner cheek, looking down at the ground, tucking my chin shyly. He smiled and kissed my matte red lips.

"But damn! You're definitely trying to get a nigga killed tonight with this outfit!" Anthony said as he slapped my ass.

I playfully pushed him in the chest. "Shut up, silly!"

"You think I'm playing! Don't make me have to end a nigga's life over you tonight, Stacey Ambria DeLeon!" Hearing my name meshed with his made me drop my purse and stare at him with a wide smile on my face.

"What?" he asked, adjusting his dick in his slacks, which he had to do often because the man was well endowed.

"I hope you don't think you're hyphenating your name; you'll be a DeLeon 'til the day you die," he said, sliding his custom leather belt through the loops on his slacks.

"Oh, I don't mind dropping my last name, baby. It just kind of caught me off guard to hear you call me a DeLeon," I said as I bent over to pick up my clutch, switching my items from a big shoulder bag to a small gold clutch I would be carrying for the night.

Anthony and I hadn't discussed the details of our wedding. Hell, I'd just made up my mind to marry the man earlier today. I didn't know if I wanted a large or small wedding. I hadn't thought about local versus destination or about the fact that I would have to change my last name. I hadn't even thought about how long of an engagement I wanted to have or kids. Oh god! He would want kids!

Anthony immediately noticed the dubious expression plastered on my face and approached me, wrapping his large arms around me reassuringly.

"Amor, we can move as slow or as fast as you want, I'm not in a hurry," he said as he pushed my curls aside, kissing the nape of my neck softly, causing me to melt into his firm body.

"Thank you, baby. You always know what to say." I smiled genuinely as I leaned into him feeling his dick harden against my butt. "Uh! Anthony!" I scoffed.

He lifted both hands turning them face up in a failed attempt to appear innocent.

"What! You know how fine you look in those pants? How the hell am I supposed to keep from getting rock hard when you've got your whole entire ass sitting on my dick?" he said with a wide, guilty grin.

"You're so nasty!" I giggled as I snatched my clutch from the bed. "Oh! And we're going to talk about what happened outside when we get back tonight. I hope you didn't think I wouldn't notice the nut running down my legs on the way back into the house." I pursed my lips and raised an eyebrow, waiting on his excuse. "I mean, I know this pussy is fucking spectacular, but you better pull out next time," I said as I slapped Anthony in the chest with my clutch giving him a side smirk.

The truth was, I didn't care where he decided to release himself. My mouth, my stomach, my ass, or inside me, I just wanted him to know that I noticed and in some twisted, deranged, unexplainable fashion, it made me feel even more loved by him. He loved me enough to cum inside of me, that made me special, right? I shook my head dismissively at the realization of how nonsensical my thoughts were. As we traveled through the foyer of Anthony's – correction, *our* – massive home, Tank, Bear and Roman met us at the door. I knew we were in for a night of fun if the entire team was on the clock. A smile spread across my face as my imagination ran rampant with thoughts of what the night might hold.

Halfway into the drive Anthony pulled a satin scarf from his pocket, dangling it in the air for me to see. I reclined my neck and raised a brow as I peered at the scarf.

"Uh-uh, nope, not gonna to happen!" I retorted as I folded my arms across my chest.

"It's not a request," he stated boldly, his facial expression unchanging as he licked his full lips. "Now turn around."

I rolled my eyes and slightly shifted my weight in the leather seat, turning my back to him.

"And not too tight! I finally got my eyelashes on perfectly; you better not knock them off!" I fussed, using my hands to guide the blindfold onto my face, making sure Anthony didn't ruin my makeup with the placement of the scarf.

"Can you see anything?" Anthony asked playfully, knowing his words would irritate me.

ANTHONY

"You know I can't Anthony!" she bickered through clenched teeth.

I transitioned to the seat parallel to her, allowing me the opportunity to revel in her beauty. Her curly tresses flared from her scalp, falling well past her shoulders, imparting the appearance of a crown adorning the top of her head. Her breasts sat perfectly, with no assistance of a bra, unaffected by the consequence of gravity. Her waist dipped inward, making room for her wide hips that spread across the seat. She had not been hitting the gym as consistently, which resulted in a small pooch right above her pussy that I treasured and found myself holding onto at night, despite her disgruntled pleas that I not grab her fupa because it made her feel insecure. But I didn't care about any of that shit. She was everything.

In my astonishment, I couldn't resist the urge to slide my hands between her legs. The white high waisted pants she wore accentuated every curve she possessed and if it weren't for the fact that we were only five minutes from our destination, I would have ripped those pants off of her and buried my face between her legs, my favorite place to be. It had been a long time since a woman was able to endure my sex drive. I wasn't ashamed to admit that I wanted sex more frequently than the average man, based on conversations I had with some of the fellas. Some had even considered me a sex addict, which I resented and refused to accept.

This was why I tended to have a different woman every night of the week. Because after wearing one out, typically multiple times in one night, she wasn't ready to go another night and I needed someone new and fresh. But it perplexed me to see how Stacey, such a small woman, had been able to dominate me—never rejecting me, never complaining of a *headache*, or being *too tired*, and always managing to keep her pussy tight as if it were the first time I ever entered her.

As my hand navigated between her thick thighs, parting her legs, she gasped through the darkness that enveloped her as she sucked her bottom lip between her teeth, unprepared for the powerful grip I placed on her thighs. I placed the heel of my hand against her vagina and pressed firmly, watching her chest rise, as the silver nipple rings became strikingly visible as her nipples hardened. She stretched her arms out to each side, giving herself a better position in the seat as I knelt down, wrapping both arms under her thighs, giving her a slight tug, positioning her middle right in front of my face.

"Oh!" she yelped, from the sudden movement as a grin spread across her face.

Roman would be announcing that we had reached our destination at any moment, but I could not withstand the good fortune of having my woman's pussy in my face, so I closed my eyes and placed my warm mouth over the top of the white pants. I kissed with forceful lips and rubbed her clit through the pants, careful not to leave a wet mark from my mouth. When her back arched, I reached up, grabbing her silver barbell nipple ring and gently twisted, causing her mouth to fall open in gratification. I felt the SUV come to a halt as I removed my mouth and whispered, "we'll finish this tonight."

She reached between her legs, cupping her vagina as she squeezed her legs around her delicate fingers.

STACEY

I could feel the blood rushing to my clit as my entire vagina tingled uncontrollably in anticipation for what I couldn't have right now.

"Shit," I whispered as I slid my body back up the seat and reached up towards my blindfold.

"No," was all he said to make me put my hand back down.

Anthony walked around to open my car door and gingerly guided me from the SUV.

"Just hold on to me Love, I've got you."

I wrapped both hands around Anthony's thick bicep and leaned into him delicately. "I know baby," I whispered as he allowed his footsteps to guide me over the threshold of a building.

I jumped when an ear-splitting air horn blared from speakers all around me, the thunderous noise echoed, reminding me of how a DJ might signify that a person of VIP status has entered the building. The blindfold was removed from my face and what seemed like two hundred people screamed, "Happy birthday, Stacey!" as the DJ dropped Uncle Luke's infamous "It's Your Birthday" song.

"Wha – oh my gosh – how did…where did…Anthony!" My smile stretched from ear to ear as I turned towards Anthony with tear filled eyes. "You got all of these people here for me?" I asked sincerely.

"With the help of your parents and Rachel, yes." He returned my smile as I attacked him with kisses.

"Thank you, thank you, thank you baby!" I said.

"The entire club is yours for the night," he replied, each word interrupted by one of my kisses.

"Ahhhhh! Turn up!" Rachel's uproarious voice captured my attention as I hugged her, as if I hadn't just seen her earlier in the day.

I looked back at Anthony, as if asking for permission to wander off with Rachel. He smiled and waved his hand in the boisterous club, motioning for me to go as he mouthed, "Have fun, Love."

I saw faces I hadn't seen in years, family members, first, second and third cousins, high school and college classmates, and even my gym family. I couldn't believe Anthony had managed to pull this off without me knowing.

"Girl! If you don't marry this nigga, I—"

Before Rachel could complete her sentence I twisted my lips and threw my hand towards her face. "Bam!" I yelled over the music as Rachel cupped both hands over her mouth, muffling a scream that would have surely caused a panic in the club.

She threw her arms around me as we both bounced up and down in celebration.

"Stace! Oh my God! When did you say yes? Ahhhhh!" Rachel screamed again, which caused me to erupt into laughter.

"I accepted this morning," I said with a wide smile.

And this right here was why Rachel was my girl, her sincere positivity and well wishes for me was soul warming because I knew without a shadow of a doubt, that she was genuinely happy for me.

"Come on, someone came a long way to see you," Rachel informed me as she grabbed me by the hand, guiding me through the club. We approached a large roped off section where my mother, father, and brother PJ sat conversing among one other.

"PJ! Mom, Dad!" I shrieked.

PJ rose from his seat and scooped me from the ground, embracing me in a bear hug that flashed me back to our childhood.

"I'm so glad you could make it!" I cheered with arms glued around my brother's neck.

"I wouldn't have missed it for the world," PJ said as he lowered me to the ground.

He moved closer to my ear in an attempt to drown out the club music as he said, "Seems like you finally got a good one. Bro is cool as hell."

"You've met him?" I asked, confused.

"Yeah, he sent his private jet for Pilar and me, and I met him when we touched down." Just then, a tall, mahogany skinned woman with a blonde buzz cut approached with two drinks.

"Hi, Stacey!" the woman gushed handing both drinks to PJ and wrapping her arms around me as if we were familiar friends.

Her energy was contagious and I returned her embrace as I flashed PJ a thumbs up behind Pilar's back. I was pulled away from Pilar by a commotion in the middle of the dance floor. Guests were cheering, slapping one another on the shoulders as they doubled over in laughter and disbelief yelling, "Aye!" holding their drinks in the air, and I needed to know what was happening. Upon pushing my way through the crowd, there before my very eyes was Ms. Ann, in a hot pink, snakeskin catsuit, dropping it low as she *looked back at it*. Heat rushed to my face as if I were looking at my grandmother out on the dancefloor. Between bouncing her ass, standing up straight to shake it, and then dropping it down again, she noticed my stunned face in the crowd.

"Stacey!" she yelled, bouncing up from her squat stance, as if her sixty plus year old knees were unbothered.

She wrapped me in a snug embrace and I couldn't help but to giggle as I held onto her arms and slightly pushed away from her to admire the skintight catsuit she wore.

"Well damn Ms. Ann! You're in here looking like a whole snack!" I yelled over the music.

"And you better believe I'm ready and willing to teach these young whipper-snappers a thang or two!" she said, throwing her hips in a circle. "That Anthony of yours is zaddy material! You better be slobbin' on that knob every night because if you aren't, someone else will!" With those wise words she kissed my cheek and returned to the dance floor.

I cupped my hands around either side of my mouth, calling out to her over the music. "I'll come back around to check on you," I said, stretching my neck hoping she heard me because she had moved away so quickly, I wasn't sure she could.

I made my way through the club hugging and welcoming my guests, feeling more loved and appreciated than I had ever felt. Everything I ever wanted in a man, Anthony was that and more.

"Anthony!" I said as I instantly gazed through the crowded club looking for my man.

I had allowed the excitement of the night to sweep me away when I realized it had been nearly forty-five minutes since I first left his side. I peered at the aerial contortionists swinging from the silk fabrics affixed to the ceiling rods as they spun, flipped, landed in air bound splits and moved their bodies in ways I could only dream of. The private sections setup through the club with various girls serving bottle after bottle of top shelf liquor with large sparklers springing from the tops made me smile because this was all for me. I stepped up on my tiptoes, attempting to look over the heads of my guests to spot Anthony, but at five foot two, virtually everyone was taller than I was. The multiple shots I had taken at my parents' table, along with the two drinks I had downed with my future sister-in-law Pilar, were beginning to take hold.

I hadn't meant to leave Anthony and wasn't sure how I managed to wander off without Tank. I decided to make a pit stop at the restroom before continuing my search because those drinks had run straight to my bladder. I quickly shuffled to the restroom, gold clutch in hand as I passed two of my cousins on my way out of the restroom.

"Stacey! Girl! This birthday party is amazing!" my cousin Ashley said as she high fived our other cousin Tammy.

"Yea girl! And who is that man you walked in with? I haven't been able to keep my eyes off of him all damn night!" That was Tammy's thirsty ass. I rolled my eyes slightly and held up my hand.

"My fiancé bitch, so slow your roll," I said in a joking tone but meant every single word.

My two cousins inclined their necks and looked at one another.

"We would be the same way if we had a nigga that fine! Congratulations, girl!" Tammy said as they threw their hands into the air and made their way back to the dance floor.

I shook my head as I thought about all the women I might have to check in the future as our relationship progressed. *I'm going to have to beat these bitches off with a stick!* I thought as I squatted over the toilet of the massive marble floored bathroom. Just as I unrolled a handful of tissue, I heard what sounded like a door lock. I grinned at the idea that Anthony had found me in the restroom. *Oh, he must be coming to finish what we started in the car,* I though, as the phantom tingling sensation returned to my vagina at the mere thought of Anthony.

When I swung the restroom door open, my clutch fell from my arms as I stood face to face with Quinton. Before I could scream, his hand was aggressively pressed over my mouth as he backed me into a wall and placed one hand around my neck.

"You're a hard fucking woman to find, Stacey Hill," he whispered in a tone that immediately made me feel that I wouldn't walk out of this restroom alive.

I would never get the opportunity to marry Anthony or give him children because Quinton was not going to let me go tonight. My terrified, muffled screams caused Quinton's hands to tighten around my neck as I felt the room closing in on me. When he noticed my eyes begin to roll backwards as my pupils disappeared, he released my neck, leaving me to collapse, barely catching myself as I stumbled to the floor.

"Fuck no, you're going to be awake for this and if you scream, I swear to God I'll kill you and that fucking nigga you chose over me! Now get the fuck up, bitch!"

I was mortified. I wanted to cry. I wanted to scream, but I couldn't. I was in shock. Every emotion bottled inside of me lay dormant ready to erupt but the door was shut.

"Quinton, please!" I begged as he lifted his colossal, ex-football playing hand into the air, causing me to curl into a fetal position. "Quinton, please don't!" I said before his hand threatened to connect to my face.

"I fucking love you, Stacey!" Quinton's words caused me to lift my eyes from the ground as I peered into his.

"Quinton…I didn't know. I thought we were just having fun," I said sincerely as my eyes darted around the restroom for anything that might be able to help me escape this man.

"Don't do that! Don't! Do! That!" Quinton said as he placed both hands on top of his head and paced around in a circle, in a way that could only be described as deranged, unhinged, psychotic. How hadn't I seen this? How had I missed this side of him that was now so unmistakably present?

"You knew, Stacey! You fucking knew! And I *tried*! I did everything I was supposed to do! I did!" he said as he continued to pace. "Fuck, fuck, fuck!"

I hadn't removed myself from the ground as he ran toward and cowered over me. "Do you know I would have given you the fucking world!? Do you know that?" he yelled, spit flying from his mouth as tears filled his eyes.

My lack of emotion seemed to trigger Quinton just as harshly as my mishandling of his heart, as he picked me up and tossed my body across the floor. I landed punishingly against the ground as Quinton punched the marble wall, causing a crack to flow through the thick material, as blood began to trickle down his fist.

"See what you made me do!? I didn't want to do that to you, Stacey! I fucking love you! And you're going to love me back!" Quinton grabbed his head with both hands and leaned his body against the cracked wall staring at the ceiling. "You gotta love me back. I know! I know what will fix this! We need to fuck! When we fuck, you'll remember how much you miss me!" Quinton said in a villainous tone that caused me to snap my head in his direction.

I had reached my emotional levy, the thought of him penetrating me against my will caused tears to flow from my eyes as I panicked looking for my clutch. Quinton nonchalantly strolled towards me and when I spotted the purse I instinctively scrambled on my hands and knees clawing at it, snatching it just as Quinton grabbed me by the ankles. He gave me a hostile yank with enough force to pull my entire body to him within seconds. I fumbled with the opening of my clutch and managed to grab the small caliber pistol Anthony had insisted I carry every time I left the house. Just as Quinton prepared to grab me by the back of my hair, I flipped over, landing on my back with the gun drawn.

"Stop!" I managed to shriek as my wobbly hands held the gun positioned at Quinton's chest.

"Ohhhh, so you're going to shoot me now?" he said calmly, as if his life were not in the palm of my hands and at this moment, I was sure that he was mentally unstable.

I managed to raise myself from the ground with one hand, my other hand still gripping the gun, but with more authority. I was willing to kill if it meant getting back to my man and the life I was destined to live with him. Quinton smirked as he took a step forward testing my ability to take a life. When the gun discharged, Quinton's knees buckled as his hands flew to his ear. He grasped the side of his face in disbelief as glowing-red blood began to slide down the side of his face. When I realized I had only grazed his ear, which ignited his fury, I began to take small steps towards the restroom door.

"You bitch!" he growled, as he charged at me full speed.

I heard commotion outside of the restroom door. Seconds later the door flew open violently as Tank and Bear entered, followed by Anthony. When Anthony closed the door behind him, he locked it. It was no surprise that he had the key to unlock the door from the outside since he most likely owned the building.

I didn't move. I kept my gun pointed at Quinton, almost in a daze. I could vaguely hear a voice calling my name but was unable to comprehend what was happening. It wasn't until Anthony approached and lowered the gun to the ground that I felt myself step back into reality as I blinked away tears and stared at him.

"What did I tell you about those tears, Love?" Anthony said gently as he swiped away the fallen droplets from my cheeks, causing me to square my shoulders and dry my eyes with the back of my hand. "That's my girl. I'm proud of you Amor, you did well. Are you okay?" His eyes slowly scanned my form, inspecting my body for harm.

I shook my head vigorously, unable to speak any words.

Quinton's body language changed. He was no longer in a position of supremacy. As lethal as Quinton thought he was, he was no match for either of the twins, not even one on one. He'd be lucky to only experience an ass whooping from the twins because Anthony was the shooter. If it were left up to him, a bullet to the head would be the end, but the large crowd of people was the only thing keeping Anthony from putting an end to this shitshow.

"Quinton, right?" Anthony said as he casually strolled towards him, his eyes flaming with fury at the audacity of this motherfucker to enter into his personal space with intentions of hurting his future queen.

"Yeah, I recognize you. The day you attacked my queen, I saw you from a distance, but now that I've got eyes on your punk ass, I know it was you," Anthony said as he stood with both hands in his pocket.

I knew this demeanor; I had seen it before in Mexico and in my apartment with Savior. The more reserved Anthony DeLeon became, the more deadly he was. Quinton didn't speak. He stood there, fists balled, as if he were preparing for a fight.

"You look like the type of hoe ass nigga to attack a woman," Anthony stated as he removed a hand from his pocket to flick his nose with his thumb. Tank and Bear stood on either side of Quinton; menacing scowls plastered on each of their faces.

Anthony unbuttoned his custom suit jacket and removed it before setting it on the white marble countertop, exposing both guns he wore in his shoulder holster.

"Baby," I called out, my voice sounding more like a warning in lieu of trying to get his attention.

He shifted his gaze to me momentarily.

"Baby, noise, no guns," I said, causing Anthony to remove his hand from his holstered weapon.

My small caliber gun could barely be heard outside of the restroom, but if Anthony were to shoot either of his forty-five caliber pistols, the shots would surely be heard by all the guests attending the party. I was right, and he knew it. Hell he even knew better, but something about me made him lose his fucking sense of judgement, apparently. Anthony extended a hand to me and motioned for me to join his side. I intertwined fingers with him, staring up at his handsome, reassuring face. He spoke and his words caused me to blink multiple times, as if my eyes had anything to do with my hearing.

"Make the call, Love," Anthony said again, peering in Quinton's direction.

I knew what was being asked of me, but was unsure if I was capable of completing the request. Suddenly, I was pulled from my body and into a place that was unfamiliar, yet memorable because I had just been there when I pulled the trigger wounding Quinton. I had been in this unfamiliar place when I refused to put my pistol down before Anthony took it from me, the place that let me know I could kill if I had to.

"Put him on his knees," I requested of Tank and Bear.

Quinton struggled, fighting the two Goliaths but found himself down on his knees from heavy blows to the head as the twins took turns pummeling his face. I slowly approached Quinton to speak but the words leaving my mouth didn't seem like my own as I asked, "Will you stop this foolishness? Will you leave me alone to live my life?"

I looked at Quinton's, silently hoping he answered yes. When he raised his eyes from the ground revealing a sinister smile he responded, "Fuck you bitch! If I can't have you, no one can!"

I closed my eyes, sucked in a deep breath and exhaled, "snap his fucking neck", as I turned on my heels to face Anthony.

The loud crack of Quinton's neck, coupled with the sound of the thud of his body on the floor caused me to shudder as I walked back to Anthony, never turning back. I turned to the mirror, fluffed my curls, and applied more lipstick from my clutch before grabbing Anthony's hand.

"Tank, Bear, clean him up and carry him out. The guests will think he's drunk. I never want to hear a word about this again." I looked at Anthony and flashed him a loving smile before saying, "The wedding will be in three months, I don't want to wait," and we made our exit from the restroom, hand in hand.

EPILOGUE:

It had been eight weeks since my thirtieth birthday party and everyone including Anthony had respected my wishes by not mentioning Quinton's untimely departure. I didn't have time to lose sleep over my decision, I was planning a wedding with over two hundred and fifty guests, and could spare no amount of brain power to give two fucks about a man that would have effortlessly taken my life the moment the opportunity presented itself. I made a boss decision and wasn't looking back. Fuck Quinton and anyone trying to take me away from my forever love.

"Alexandra, please call Sandra and check to see where she is on the final centerpieces. Oh! And remember to inform her of the change from traditional red roses to black magic roses. I'm unwilling to compromise on the color, make sure she knows that," I demanded.

Anthony had insisted on providing me with an assistant and a wedding planner, which consisted of a team of five wedding correspondents to ensure everything wedding related moved smoothly. The truth was, Anthony immediately noticed how stressed I had been with planning our wedding in three months and I had become a fucking bridezilla. He strolled past me and smacked my ass, which seemed to be something he couldn't resist. It was as if my ass and his hand were opposing magnets. I stood at the edge of the bed flipping through my wedding planning book as I grinned.

"You better stop before you start something you're not ready to finish!" I warned, flashing Anthony a seductive smile, causing him to cup his dick and balls as he bit his bottom lip.

"Damn, Love! You don't know what you do to me," he teased.

The house was full of people and Anthony knew we couldn't have sex right now because what would the caterer, the cake lady, my assistant Alexandra, and my mother think if we disappeared for thirty minutes? Because he was going to use every single minute to dig into me, but my freaky ass would have found a way to make it happen if he kept messing with me. My sex drive was at an all-time high, and ever since the unmentionable situation at the club, it was as if I was releasing my frustration out on Anthony's dick. He wasn't complaining, but one night of rest couldn't hurt either of us.

"*Anthony!*" I yelled from the master bedroom suite in an attempt to get his attention. "Baby, did you check on your tux?" I asked, certain he hadn't.

"Yes, Love. You know you don't technically have anything to worry about, right? That was the point in hiring a team of six people so that you don't have to stress this much," he reminded me.

I dropped my shoulders, revealing a puppy dog face. "I know, but what if they mess something up?" I asked sincerely.

"Shit, with the amount of money we're paying them, they better not mess shit up! Ain't that right Alexandra?" Anthony said loudly, directing his attention towards my personal assistant, catching her off guard.

"Yes sir, Mr. DeLeon," Alexandra answered without having a clue as to what he was talking about.

I giggled. "Stop messing with her, you know she'll agree with anything you say." I slapped his chest playfully for teasing my assistant. "You know what could relieve some of my stress?" I said, lowering my eyes from Anthony's eyes down to his dick as I leaned into him and slid my hands into his shorts.

"But what about your mom? She's in the great room with the vendors and I know she'll be looking for you soon! Fuck." Anthony's loud moan caused Alexandra to glance over in our direction and upon seeing my hand in Anthony's shorts, she turned her back and put her earbuds in.

I increased the speed of my hand as I gently tugged at Anthony's dick. "So are you telling me no, Mr. DeLeon?" I asked with a raised brow.

"Fuck it!' Anthony said as he lifted me and carried me into our bathroom, closing the doors behind him. "And don't do that running shit since you wanna be all bold and fuck with all these people in the house."

"Worry less about me running and you try not to moan like a bitch when you slide into this pussy!" I said, knowing it would trigger him and ignite the beast I needed.

"I got your bitch," he said as he walked towards me, moving with intention, causing me to backpedal into the two-story closet.

"*Where are you going*? You talking a lot of shit to be backing away." Anthony gripped my wrist and turned me around aggressively, pinning my arm behind my back as he pulled my yoga pants down with the other hand. "Let's see if you can back up that shit you were just talking." he said as he walked me over to the double wide mirror he had built into the wall. "Bend over."

With a smile on my face, I enthusiastically did as I was told. Anthony took a step back, admiring the view as he smirked. He could see my wetness as he approached me from behind, placing both hands onto my ass as he guided himself into me.

"*Shit*," he moaned loudly.

I smiled as I whispered, "Checkmate."

"So fucking wet," he said as he stroked me long, deep, and hard.

"Mmmmhmmm," was all I managed to say because if I opened my mouth any more I was sure everyone would hear me getting my back blown out.

It didn't take long for Anthony to find a steady stroke and when he did, he reached around to fondle my nipple rings, which caused my knees to shake as my body began to erupt internally.

"Mmmmhmmm, talking all that shit and you're about to cum, it hasn't even been five minutes!" Anthony teased, stroking mercilessly, enjoying watching my ass bounce against his dick.

"Ohhhh, baby, right there!"

I didn't have the wherewithal to meet him at his level of petty because I was indeed about to cum. I let out a satisfying moan and when Anthony felt my pussy contract on his dick and splashes of wetness began to shoot from my pussy, he couldn't hold back either.

"Fuck," he erupted as he wrapped his arm around my waist, leaning onto my back as his body jerked uncontrollably as he busted inside of me.

I turned around to face Anthony and gently kissed his lips.

"Thank you baby, I needed that," I said, leaning into his body, wrapping my arms around his firm midsection.

"Shit, apparently, so did I, since neither one of us even lasted ten minutes!" he chuckled. "You know when you squirt I can't control myself."

"Uh-oh!" I said as I cupped my hands between my legs to catch Anthony's seed as I penguin waddled out of the closet to the bathroom toilet.

He hadn't pulled out of me during sex since the night I accepted his proposal. I was on the pill and hadn't missed a day – well, except for the night of my thirtieth birthday party and one other time – but I wasn't worried. I was diligent about taking my pill on time every day since those two days I had forgotten.

As I sat on the toilet, I scrolled through social media when my phone dinged with a text message. It was a picture of Rachel and Tank. His big ass was actually smiling in the picture all nuzzled up under Rachel's neck taking a selfie.

"Babe! Come look at this!" I smiled as I shoved my phone in Anthony's direction.

"Is that nigga smiling?"

I giggled. "Yep! Rare sighting, right!?"

Anthony leaned in to kiss me. "I have to go handle some business, we have a shipment coming in from Sinaloa, I need to meet with my cousins to discuss details. I'll call you when I make it and when I'm on my way back."

My forehead wrinkled in discontent. I hated that Anthony still employed his disloyal ass cousins, regardless of how long ago it was when they tried to kill him, it had still happened, but I was unwilling to battle with Anthony over his decision. He was adamant in regards to family over everything, even when family didn't choose him. However, when I became Mrs. DeLeon in four weeks, my plan to get rid of them would begin. Anthony meant too much to me to allow anyone in his space that meant him harm, no matter how old the beef was. Afterall, he was giving me more responsibilities now and one unspoken responsibility was for me to see the things he couldn't. I planned to be my man's second set of eyes with every situation.

I was exhausted after a full day of wedding planning and with Anthony out handling business, it was the perfect opportunity for me to get a quick nap in. However, my nap was short lived when I was awakened by a nightmare, and when I wiped away the sweat from my forehead, I realized I was also crying.

"What the hell is going on?" I whispered as I held my hands up in front of my face to reveal that they were shaking profusely.

The dream had me unhinged. I stood from the bed and began pacing in an attempt to calm my nerves. Anthony was stranded, alone, at the mercy of his cousins. They planned this; they knew he would be caught off guard. Anthony could have begged for his life, but he refused, which inevitably resulted in multiple shots to the head. I immediately picked up my phone to call Anthony. No answer. He always answered. *Always*. I threw my phone onto the bed in frustration as I gripped a handful of curls and began pacing again.

"*Jesus, please*," I whispered as I began to feel weak with nausea setting in.

At the sound of my phone ringing, I sprang onto the bed, fumbling through the sheets to answer and breathed a sigh of relief when I heard his reassuring voice on the other end of the phone.

"Baby, are you okay?" I asked, my voice trembling.

"Yeah, I'm good I didn't let you know I made it because Alexandra texted and told me you were taking a nap. I didn't want to disturb you, but I'm headed home now," he informed me.

"Okay babe, I love you. See you soon," I said as I hung up my cell phone.

I placed a hand over my chest in relief. Even though I knew it wasn't real, I began crying as I recalled the dream. I saw a maze of deaths within one dream which was confusing because I had never remembered any of my dreams this vividly. I had also dreamed that I had just given birth to a baby – a son – and as soon as I handed the baby to Anthony, masked gunmen entered into the delivery room, gunning him and our newborn baby down.

It all seemed so real, so much so that my vagina ached as if I had just given birth. Realistically, it was most likely the aftermath of our closet escapades, even then, it still contributed to the very realistic outlook of the dream. I ran to the bathroom and rummaged through a cabinet retrieving an unopened box of pregnancy tests Rachel had playfully gifted me weeks prior when I told her about Anthony not pulling out the night of my birthday. I ripped through the box as I read through the instructions. I kicked off my panties and sat on the toilet with my legs gapped apart.

"Jesus please be negative, please be negative, please be negative," I said, head tilted towards the ceiling before I looked down, allowing my stream of urine to flow onto the early detection pregnancy test.

I replaced the cap onto the tip of the stick and set it on the floor as I paced for what seemed like two hours, but in actuality was only about two minutes. I closed my eyes and said another quick prayer before popping them open to stare at the stick. The stick flashed right before my eyes.

Pregnant.

To be continued...

Made in the USA
Monee, IL
08 March 2025

13681529R00157